CHRISTMAS BELLS AND WEDDING VOWS

A MARRIAGE OF CONVENIENCE ANTHOLOGY

JODY HEDLUND LACY WILLIAMS MISTY M. BELLER

Christmas Bells and Wedding Vows: A Marriage of Convenience Anthology

Jody Hedlund, Lacy Williams, Misty M. Beller

Cover design by Evelyne Labelle at Carpe Librum Book Design: www.carpelibrumbookdesign.com

ISBN-13 Trade Paperback: 978-1-954810-66-2

ISBN-13 Large Print Paperback: 978-1-954810-67-9

ISBN-13 Casebound Hardback: 978-1-954810-68-6

CLAIMING THE COWGIRL

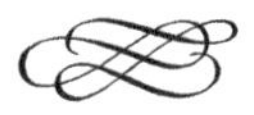

JODY HEDLUND

Claiming the Cowgirl

Northern Lights Press

www.jodyhedlund.com

Scripture quotations are taken from the King James Version of the Bible.

CHAPTER 1

FAIRPLAY, COLORADO
DECEMBER 1878

She had to stop procrastinating and force herself to pick a new husband.

Serena Taylor tucked her list of potential husbands into the pocket of her day dress. She'd crossed out all but four of the men who lived in the Fairplay area. But maybe just four was narrowing her choice too much?

The bitter December wind coming off the mountains swirled around her, and she hugged Tate closer to protect his plump cheeks from the chill. Burrowing against her chest, he sucked his thumb, content to ride on her hip for as long as she could carry him—which were shorter periods now that he was two and growing bigger every day.

"Only one more visit," she whispered against his forehead before brushing a kiss to his silky light brown hair that was a shade fairer than hers. "Then we'll head home."

Home? She hadn't had a home since running away two months ago from Stony Creek Ranch near Pueblo. Even then, the large spread hadn't felt like home in the few years she'd lived there with Palmer and his parents. It had felt even less so after her husband's death this past summer. In fact, life there had become oppressive—so much so that she'd decided to move back to Oklahoma and live with her family.

She hadn't anticipated that her father-in-law would not only agree that she move away but require her to relinquish her rights to Tate and let him raise her child. When she'd protested, Mr. Halifax's solicitor had presented her with a legal document claiming that a single woman was an unfit mother, mentally unstable, financially irresponsible, and unable to raise a child.

Mr. Halifax was a hard man who always got what he wanted one way or another. So, with only as much of her belongings as would fit into a carpetbag, Serena had ridden away in the middle of the night, afraid that if she stayed even one more day, she'd never see Tate again.

She hadn't known where to go, just that she couldn't return to Oklahoma since it would be the first place Mr. Halifax would look for her. So, she'd traveled to the South Park area until she'd reached Fairplay, and her money had run out.

At least the Courtney Boardinghouse had been a safe haven for the past weeks she'd lived there, working to earn her room and board.

But as she'd learned early in life, all good things had to come to an end eventually. And she couldn't stay at the boardinghouse indefinitely. Not if she hoped to keep Tate. No, she had to stop putting off the one thing that could alleviate all her worries about losing him to Palmer's parents. She had to get remarried. And the sooner, the better.

Serena straightened her petite frame and squared her shoulders, then started down the boardwalk of Fairplay's business district, heading to her final destination and the fourth candidate on her list—Mr. Dankworth, the owner of the mercantile at the end of Main Street. He was a widower with several small children and seemed like a good father.

A good father. That was her number one qualification for a husband. She didn't care how he treated her. As long as he cared about Tate, that's all that mattered.

Well, of course, she also wanted him to be a God-fearing, upright, and law-abiding man. He had to be able to provide financially for her and Tate so that Mr. Halifax would have no reason to question whether Tate's every need was being met.

Her father-in-law was powerful and wealthy, with enough connections that he would learn of her whereabouts eventually —if he hadn't already. And although the mountain passes were now covered in snow and made traveling difficult, Mr. Halifax wouldn't let that stop him from tracking her to the high country.

Hopefully, once she was legally remarried, her father-in-law's accusations would no longer have any merit. At least then her new husband could help her keep custody of Tate.

In the late afternoon, Fairplay's streets weren't yet busy with miners and mill employees who would soon finish work and head to their boardinghouses and the saloons. Even so, the rattle of passing wagons and the clatter of horses mingled with the calls and greetings of the townspeople—mostly men—milling about.

At least she hadn't faced a shortage of marriageable options. In this mountainous area miles from the big cities, men outnumbered women by far. Although Fairplay was a thriving town and had some families, as a single, widowed woman she'd attracted plenty of male attention.

Of course, she needed the right man and couldn't just settle for anyone, which was why she'd been so carefully whittling her list down over recent weeks. The men on her list obviously hadn't realized the so-called chance encounters were interviews, but with each trip into town, she'd purposefully orchestrated time with the candidates so she could get to know them better and see how they interacted with Tate.

Now, with only four remaining on the list, she'd done the same today. She'd coordinated the meetings with each and had only Mr. Dankworth left.

When she finished visiting him, would she finally be able to make her choice?

With her boots tapping firmly against the wooden plank boardwalk, she neared the two-story false storefront with the name *Dankworth's* painted in bold letters above the wooden awning.

Her arms had begun to ache from carrying Tate, but once she reached the interior, she'd set him down as she browsed the wares she couldn't afford and wouldn't be purchasing. Hopefully, Mr. Dankworth would come out from behind his counter and talk to her as he had the past several times she'd stopped in. His oldest daughter, who appeared to be about eight years old, took care of her siblings and had been kind to Tate. Would Mr. Dankworth's children welcome a new brother into their family?

At the door, she paused and straightened her hat—a Gainsborough with round crown and a brim turned up on one side. Navy blue and trimmed with flowers, it was starting to grow shabby, just like the rest of the few garments she'd brought along.

Lifting her chin in resolve, she opened the door to the scent of leather and tobacco as well as the welcoming warmth emanating from the potbellied stove at the center of the store, a coal bin and spittoon beside it.

Floor-to-ceiling shelves lined most walls and were crammed with every conceivable item—canned foods, spices, crockery, fabric, sewing notions, and medicines. The countertops ran the length of one side, and they were piled with ready-made clothing, blankets, hats, and more. Horse whips and farming tools hung from the ceiling.

Several other customers were in the store: an older man near the back examining harnesses, a fellow sitting in a chair near the stove and reading a newspaper, and another man at the counter—a tall, dark-haired man she immediately recognized.

Weston Oakley. He had lean facial features with a squared jawline, a prominent chin with a noticeable cleft, and a nose with a slight dorsal bump. His coat stretched tightly across his broad shoulders and thickly-muscled arms. And his torso and legs radiated equal strength, although his wool trousers hung more loosely and were tucked into worn leather boots.

"My family doesn't think I'm capable of getting married," Weston was saying. "And if I don't round up a wife by Christmas, they'll never leave me alone."

The very handsome Weston Oakley had recently belonged to Felicity Courtney. Perhaps *belonged* wasn't the right word, but the two had been nearly engaged. The rumor was that Weston had even built a house for her.

However, Felicity had broken Weston's heart when she'd married someone else and moved away.

Serena liked Felicity. After all, Felicity had been the one running the boardinghouse and had taken her in during her time of need.

But Serena wished Felicity hadn't hurt Weston so terribly. She hadn't been fair to the kind, hard-working man. Although Serena had contemplated making him number five on her list of potential husbands, she'd witnessed firsthand the heartache he'd experienced from Felicity's rejection, and she'd seen the misery in his expression ever since.

She'd concluded that he wasn't ready to form another relationship so soon after losing Felicity. But what if she was wrong?

As the door closed behind her and she stepped farther into the store, every eye shifted her way, including Mr. Dankworth's and Weston's.

"Good afternoon, Mrs. Taylor." Mr. Dankworth stood suddenly straighter, adjusting his bow tie and collar before slicking back his thinning brown hair. On the shorter side of average, Mr. Dankworth wore an apron over his suit, which seemed overly large on his trim frame.

"Ma'am." Though Weston nodded at her politely, his blue-black eyes flitted over her and dismissed her all in one motion—just as usual.

Also just as usual, his gaze came to rest on Tate.

The boy lifted his head from her shoulder and slid his thumb out of his mouth. Now he was staring at Weston with his wide green eyes—the color another trait she and Tate shared.

"Hey there, little fella." Weston offered Tate a tender smile.

"Ball?" Tate asked timidly.

Serena lowered Tate to the ground. He promptly latched on to her skirt, clinging to her as he always did whenever they were around other people. She had to stifle the urge to flex her arms and stretch the ache out of her back.

"Sorry." Weston stuffed his hands in his pockets. "I don't have a ball today."

The last time she and Tate had encountered Weston was several days ago at church. When Tate had gotten restless during the service, Weston, from the pew behind them, had handed Tate a marble to play with.

She'd been grateful for Weston's consideration, especially when he'd insisted afterward that Tate could keep the marble, since he'd apparently picked it up off the street and had no use for it.

Weston pulled a hand out of his pocket and held out a stick of light-pink candy. "I've got this candy . . . if your ma says it's okay for you to eat."

At the sight of the offering, Tate's beautiful eyes rounded even more. He shifted his questioning gaze up to her. "Candy, Mama?"

How could she say no when his face was filled with such innocence and sweetness? He'd had so few pleasures during his short life—had more frightening experiences than anything. Besides, with the little she earned working at the boarding-house, she didn't have much to spare for simple gifts.

She brushed his hair out of his eyes. "Alright."

Tate released his grip on her skirt and took a tentative step toward Weston. Then, in a burst, he raced the last of the distance. As he took the stick, Weston ruffled Tate's hair.

"What do you say to the nice man?" Serena prompted.

Tate was already running back to her side, his eyes containing an equal measure of both fright and excitement. As he latched on to her skirt again, she tucked a finger under his chin and leveled stern eyes upon him. "Tell Mr. Oakley *thank you*."

"Thank you." Tate's voice was so soft she doubted anyone heard him.

But Weston nodded, then gathered up a parcel from the counter, tipped the brim of his black Stetson toward Mr. Dankworth, and crossed to the door, his boots clunking against the wooden floorboards. As he passed by, he ruffled Tate's hair again. "Enjoy the candy, little fella."

Then, with a polite touch of the brim of his hat in farewell to her, he exited the mercantile.

She couldn't keep from watching him through the glass panes on the front door as he crossed the street and seemed to head toward the bank. His stride was long and determined, and he carried himself with strength and purpose, as though the whole world yet needed his conquering.

After his declaration to Mr. Dankworth about needing a wife by Christmas, did she dare turn him into her fifth matrimonial candidate?

He always interacted so thoughtfully with Tate, and Tate

seemed to be drawn to him the most, even aside from the gifts of the marble and candy.

Yes, Weston Oakley would most definitely qualify to be on her list. The question was, would he consider marrying her after his recent heartache? He hardly seemed to realize she existed—probably wouldn't regard her at all if not for Tate.

"What can I do for you today, Mrs. Taylor?" Still behind the counter, Mr. Dankworth had donned a wide and welcoming smile, appreciation lighting up his face as it normally did whenever he looked at her.

Like the other three candidates, he was always eager for her visits, going out of his way to talk with her and pay her compliments. He hadn't yet proposed as the others had, but she predicted it wouldn't be long before he did.

She could have her choice of the four.

But shouldn't she at least test Weston and determine if he was a possibility too?

For a long moment her mind spun, doing what it did so well—scheming and plotting to make circumstances work to her advantage. As an idea began to evolve, she nodded at Mr. Dankworth and turned to the door. "I guess I won't be needing anything today after all. But I do thank you for the offer."

With Tate clinging to her skirt and sucking on his candy, she exited the mercantile. She had to hurry if she had any hope of facilitating a *chance* meeting with Weston before darkness fell.

Hopefully, this time he would take more notice of her and perhaps even consider her a prospect for the wife he needed by Christmas.

CHAPTER 2

"Cold, Mama." Tate wrapped his arms around Serena's leg.

The winter wind buffeted them as they stood on the road north of Fairplay. Miles of grassland, hemmed in by mountain ranges, spread out all around them, forming a valley in Colorado's high country, perfect for the many ranches that made the South Park basin home.

Serena squinted to see down the well-worn wagon path and crossed her fingers for a glimpse of Weston Oakley. But in the fifteen minutes or more they'd been waiting, there hadn't been a single sign of him.

She didn't know if there was another route to his ranch in addition to the winding road that ran along the South Platte River, but it was possible he'd ridden home another way.

"Up." Tate tugged at her skirt with sticky fingers, his candy finally gone. Even with a cap on his head and a warm woolen coat, his nose was rosy from the cold and matched his cheeks. And the December air was growing colder as daylight dissipated.

She didn't want Tate to suffer and would have to set aside

her plans for the evening and perhaps try again tomorrow. With a sigh, she stuck two fingers into her mouth to whistle and call back Belle.

But before she could make the sharp sound, a plume of dust whipped by wind rose in the distance. A team pulling a wagon was headed her way. Was a customer riding out to one of Weston's mills to collect lumber or grain? Or was the man himself finally coming?

Just in case it was him, she let her shoulders slump and began to amble along while carrying Tate.

The rumble of the wagon grew more distinct until it wasn't far behind her. She stopped, turned, and waited for the approach. At the sight of Weston's black Stetson, broad shoulders, and thick arms, relief warmed her limbs and gave her renewed energy for her scheme.

When he was almost upon her, he tugged on his reins. "Whoa."

As he halted the team and wagon beside her, she wrapped her arms more firmly around Tate and let herself visibly shudder.

"Mrs. Taylor?" His tone was tight with worry, and he scanned the fields beyond her as though waiting for a wild creature to rush out and attack them. "What are you doing out here this time of the evening?"

She whispered a silent plea for forgiveness for deceiving this good man, but sometimes desperate times required desperate measures. "My horse got away from me, and I headed after her, hoping I could catch her." It was technically the truth, even if she had purposefully let Belle wander off.

He glanced both ways on the wagon path as though he might spot her. "She came north, you think?"

"Yes, I believe so." She nodded down the path ahead that led to his home. "I thought I caught a glimpse of her a few minutes ago. She can't be too far away now."

He searched the barren landscape again. Although the river wasn't visible from the wagon path, the tall cottonwoods and shrubs that lined the waterway stood a short distance away. Beyond them to the west, the foothills began their gentle rise, leading to the majestic peaks crowned with gold and royal blue as the sun faded behind the mountains.

Though the high summits were already snow-covered, South Park's almost-ten-thousand-foot elevation didn't have a covering of snow—at least, not one that stayed beyond a day or two. As the cold wind slapped her again, she didn't have to fake her next shudder.

In the next instant, Weston was hopping off the wagon bench to the ground. "Reckon you better let me take you home, ma'am."

"Oh, I couldn't trouble you." She made sure to emphasize her Southern accent, since it often worked in her favor.

He took a step toward her. "I don't mind none."

She paused as though to consider his offer. Then she shook her head. "I'm sure Belle isn't far."

"She's probably halfway back to the boardinghouse by now."

So, he did know where she lived. What else did he know about her? "I'm fairly certain she's just around the corner ahead." Serena started walking but made it only three steps before his footsteps crunched against the ground and he stopped her with a touch to her arm.

"No sense in walking." He drew back, his forehead furrowed. "I'm headed up the road and can give you a ride."

She hesitated. "Are you certain I won't be a bother?"

"Not a bit."

She offered him a tenuous smile. "Then thank you. Tate's tired, and he's not as easy to carry as he once was."

"Reckon it won't be long before he learns to ride." Weston led the way to the wagon.

She wanted to protest that her son was too young, but she'd

been riding herself when she was but a girl of three. "He already loves horses, don't you, Tate?"

The little boy nodded, having lifted his head to watch Weston's every move. Now, as the handsome man took hold of her elbow and guided her up to the wagon bench, she could feel Weston's scrutiny upon them too.

As she positioned herself with Tate on her lap, she visibly shuddered again.

The movement seemed to spur Weston into action, and he stalked around the wagon to the other side. "Looks like you've been out too long."

"Yes, I'm afraid we're both frozen through." She held her breath. Would he take the hint or not?

"You're welcome to ride on to my house to warm up. It's just a few shakes of a horse tail down the road."

She held back a smile. He'd taken the hint well. "I really don't want to impose. If I find my horse, I'll be fine—"

"I insist." He hopped up and positioned himself next to her. "If you're worried about me, I guarantee I ain't a shady fella. I promise you'll be safe. I've got a housekeeper . . ."

It was her turn to touch his arm, and the brief contact brought his words to a halt. "I'm not worried, Mr. Oakley."

"You're not?" He shifted on the bench, and she could feel his gaze taking her in, perhaps really seeing her for the first time.

This was going well. Just the way she'd hoped. "I haven't been in Fairplay long, but I've learned enough about you to know that you're trustworthy."

"That right?"

"Yes." She fidgeted with wrapping Tate closer, pretending not to notice Weston's continued scrutiny. Felicity Courtney wouldn't have given Weston a second glance if he hadn't been trustworthy. But now didn't seem the right time to bring up Felicity's name. Not when his hurt over her rejection was still so fresh.

He started his team on their way and then cleared his throat, obviously intending to carry on more conversation.

Good. That's exactly what she wanted.

"What brought you to Fairplay?" he asked.

She'd practiced her answer to those kinds of probing questions before she'd arrived in the high country, knowing she needed to have a story for her sudden appearance as a single woman with a toddler in tow.

So far, she'd tried to stick as close to the truth as possible—that her husband had passed away, she was a widow, and she was hoping to find work. At some point, she would have to reveal the trouble with her father-in-law trying to take Tate from her, but for now, such news was best left unspoken. "I grew up on a ranch and thought this might be the perfect place to start over, since the area has so many ranches."

Weston didn't respond for a beat. The wagon rumbled comfortably down the path, the wilted brown grass cushioning the ride. With the sun sinking even further behind the range and with darkness settling, the air held an almost peaceful aura, like the lull before a storm.

Had her response not been convincing enough? Could he see through her answer? "What about you, Mr. Oakley? What brought you to Fairplay?" The best way to avoid more questions was to take the attention off herself and place it squarely on someone else.

"My family has a ranch up in the Breckenridge area." He held the reins loosely in his gloved hands—hands that were clearly accustomed to hard work. "But I got the itch to strike out on my own eight years ago and came on down here to Fairplay to start my own ranch."

Tate snuggled into her side, now sucking his thumb after having pulled his mittens off. He watched Weston with a fascination that mi[illegible]rs.

"What made you decide to build your lumber and grain mills too?"

Even though Weston had a powerful build and held himself with a rugged confidence, he also seemed comfortable riding and talking with her, as though he made an everyday practice of riding and talking with women. "I like new ventures. Keeps me busy."

Would he like the new venture of gaining a wife and son? More importantly, would he be a truly viable candidate for becoming Tate's father?

She bent and pressed a kiss to Tate's forehead. From the corner of her eye, she could see Weston watching her.

"How long you been a—" He paused. "How long's the boy been without his pa?"

From the tentativeness in his tone, he was likely trying to determine if she was still grieving. Perhaps some widows were reluctant to speak about their former spouses, but she wasn't. She was ashamed to admit she'd never grieved for Palmer—had felt relief more than anything when she'd received news of his death.

"I'm sorry." Weston rushed to speak. "Ain't none of my business."

"It's alright. My husband died in a brawl six months ago." He'd been shot in the head by his mistress's husband, but Serena kept that fact to herself, not wanting to speak ill of Palmer in front of Tate. The boy didn't need to know about his daddy's problems. It was already going to be hard enough to someday explain why she'd left Palmer's home and family, let alone how he'd died.

"Reckon that wasn't an easy way to lose him." Weston still spoke hesitantly.

"Nothing about my previous husband was particularly easy." She may as well hint that she was ready to move on. Then if he took an interest in her, he didn't have to worry about her harboring feelings for another man.

As the wagon rounded the bend, the mills came into view. Two tall wooden buildings along the river's edge gleamed now in the last glow of the sunset. Stacks of cut lumber surrounded the one closest to them. Gray sacks—likely filled with grain—were stacked on the loading dock of the other mill.

The spacious, cleared yard in front of both buildings was silent and deserted, the workers having gone home for the evening. Now that crops had been harvested, Weston's business was likely slower throughout the winter.

"Don't see a horse anywhere." Weston surveyed the leafless brush along the riverbanks. "Do you?"

She pretended to search too, but she knew well enough that one whistle was all it would take to call Belle from wherever she'd wandered. Belle had been her favorite horse for years, and she'd needed something of her own when she'd moved so far from her childhood home and family.

She shook her head. "I don't see her either."

Tate lifted his head. "Hungry, Mama."

She never went anywhere without snacks and extra clothing for Tate and had brought snacks for him just in case—an apple, a roll, even a pickle. She shifted the bag from her shoulder—the one she'd tucked into the saddlebags but taken out before she'd slapped Belle's hindquarters and sent her on her way.

"My housekeeper will have some vittles ready." Weston spoke before she could find the drawstring on the bag. "You're welcome to have a meal."

"You're already doing enough, Mr. Oakley. I couldn't impose any further."

"You're not imposing. Maude'll be more than happy to have someone else to dote on besides an old scallywag like me."

"I don't know . . ." This *chance* encounter with Weston was going better than she could have predicted. Regardless, she didn't want to lead him on or encourage him unnecessarily. He wasn't yet on her list, although she had every intention of penning his name there the moment she was in her room at the boardinghouse. In fact, she had to admit he was already climbing high on the list, might even already be at the top.

"Maude makes the best biscuits this side of the Divide." Weston reached over and gently bumped Tate's arm with his fist. "You can't leave without trying them, right, little fella?"

Tate nodded vigorously. "Me try."

"Guess it's settled." Weston guided the team down a long lane that ended at a two-story colonial-style house painted a pale yellow, with a wrap-around porch and front windows brightly lit from within. "You'll stay for supper."

"Thank you. That's very kind of you." Truthfully, Weston Oakley was probably on a list all of his own. But she still had to be careful about moving too fast and making quick judgments. One bad marriage had been enough. Even though she didn't have high expectations for the next husband, at least she had the right to choose and didn't have to go along with what her daddy wanted.

Hopefully, this time she'd end up with a better man.

CHAPTER 3

How long had he been dreaming of having a woman sit at the table with him and share a meal?

Weston pushed his empty plate away and reclined in the dining room chair across from Serena Taylor and her boy. He reckoned he'd been wanting it longer than an old-timer waiting to find a mother lode.

"So, now that Charity and Hudson have located a nurse to care for Mr. Keller," she was saying about the invalid at the boardinghouse, "they no longer need my assistance in that manner."

He'd hardly been able to pay attention to their conversation throughout the meal. Not only because Maude had been in and out of the dining room a dozen times, her smile wider than a transatlantic railroad, but also because Tate had needed Serena's attention—everything from cutting up his food into bite-sized pieces to prompting him to use manners.

But the biggest distraction hadn't been Maude or Tate. It had been his own runaway thoughts. About Serena.

Of course he'd noticed her around town over the past weeks since she'd arrived in Fairplay. What man wouldn't notice her?

She was too pretty to miss. Her face was dainty, delicately framed with slender lines along her jaw that led to a long, graceful neck and a generous swell of curves that her tight bodice highlighted much too well.

Her hair was plaited in a single braid—not quite the same pale shade as Tate's but a pretty mingling, as if it couldn't quite decide whether to be blond or brown. Her eyes, though, were most definitely green—the green of a forest of lush pine trees.

As fine-looking as she was, he was surprised another man hadn't already gotten his loop around her. It had been plain as day that Mr. Dankworth had caught Cupid's cramp over her. No doubt the mercantile owner—and a dozen other men—were biding their time for her to be ready for marriage again.

From the few things she'd mentioned about her late husband during the wagon ride to his house, maybe she was already willing to tie another knot.

She wiped Tate's mouth with a napkin. "Of course, Charity is the sweetest woman I've ever met, and she told me I can live at the boardinghouse as long as I want."

"That's mighty nice of her." Had he said the right thing? Or did he sound like a blathering idiot?

"Yes, the Courtney sisters are very nice women—kind, helpful, lovely. I don't know where I'd be if not for Felicity . . ." Her voice trailed off, and she focused intently on Tate's plate, scraping a fork along the edge as if she intended to get every last crumb off even though there was nothing left.

Was she embarrassed to talk about Felicity after what had happened to him? Did Serena think he was pining after the beautiful redhead?

Reckoned if he was honest, he was still sore about Felicity falling for another man so quickly after he'd been trying to court her for months. He could admit, he'd even had the house built with the hope that she'd finally accept one of his proposals.

Worse, he'd been so certain Felicity would marry him that

he'd told his entire family on his last visit home a couple of months ago that he'd have a wife by Christmas. They'd scoffed at his words. They all knew his history, that he'd been searching for a wife for years and hadn't had any luck—not even with the matrimonial catalogs or newspaper advertisements.

Of course, he'd had to insist that this time things were different. And he'd vowed to show them that this Christmas he'd finally have a wife by his side when he arrived at the ranch for the holiday.

With Christmas only three weeks away, he was gonna be riding home with his tail tucked between his legs. His family would tease him to no end. But what he dreaded most was the pity. Even if they tried to hold it back, he'd see it, just like he had in the past—those long, meaningful glances that said they were thinking about Electra, his first love, the woman he'd almost married.

No one ever said her name. Even after eight years, just hearing her name or thinking about her still brought swift pain to his chest.

He wasn't sure how he could face his family's pity one more time. He'd half a mind to skip the Christmas festivities just to avoid the questions . . . and another serious jawing from his pa, which was bound to be more of the same advice to let go of his past and move forward into the future.

Holy high heavens. He'd built a house for a wife. What more could he do to prove he was moving forward into the future?

His pa's words from the last visit echoed in his head. *When you find the right woman, just make yourself get married this time. Don't come up with any more excuses why you can't.*

"I apologize." Serena was rising from her chair across the table and picking up Tate. "I didn't mean to bring up Felicity. I know it can't be easy . . ."

He stood quickly. What should he say? That the sting wasn't hurting quite as much anymore? That he was doing better? That he was even beginning to realize Felicity might not have been the right woman for him after all?

Serena hefted Tate to her hip and pushed in their chairs. Then she paused, staring at the candles Maude had lit and placed at the center of the otherwise undecorated table. In fact, the entire house was undecorated, with only the most basic of furniture in some of the rooms. Many rooms were still unfurnished.

"Thank you again for coming to our rescue, Mr. Oakley—"

"Weston."

Her gaze shot up to his, her eyes wide and questioning. Was she surprised he was giving her permission to use his given name so soon?

He was surprising himself. "There's no need to apologize for talking about Felicity. I think she married the man she was meant to be with."

Serena nodded, as though agreeing. "Regardless, I know it couldn't have been easy."

"It's my fault for letting my Cupid's cramp get the best of me."

"Cupid's cramp?" Her lips curved into the beginning of a smile.

"Reckon it's a common ailment around these parts for most men."

"Maybe for women too." Her words came out soft and were accompanied by a flush to her cheeks. She buried her nose in Tate's hair as if to hide from her confession.

But it was out there. For the taking. And he didn't quite know what to do with it.

"Well, I'll be going." She started to round the table. "I've got quite a walk ahead of me."

"Whoa now." He stepped into her path. "I won't be letting you walk anywhere tonight, Mrs. Taylor—"

"Serena." She stared at the undone top button of his flannel shirt, clearly embarrassed by her own boldness at permitting him to use her given name.

"Serena." He let the name roll off his tongue. It was pretty.

She didn't make a move to leave. And strangely, he wasn't ready for her to go.

"Weston?" Maude's voice came from directly behind him in the hallway, nearly making him jump.

The native woman had a knack for creeping up on him without notice. He reckoned she must've learned to walk as silently as a cougar during her youth, when she'd hunted with her Ute tribe all throughout the high country.

He shifted and gave his housekeeper his attention—or at least as much as he could, because half of it was still on Serena.

Maude clasped Ranger's collar, holding the black-spotted pointer back from lunging forward in his excitement at being around a rare visitor in the house. "You let the pretty lady and her boy stay here while you go look for her horse." Maude's leathery face was creased with age and her top front teeth were long gone. But her hair hung in two black braids, hardly touched by gray, and her body was still straight and lithe.

She had been a part of his family for years. In fact, he'd been the one to stumble upon her in a mountain cave near their home shortly after they'd moved to Breckenridge after the end of the War of Rebellion.

At first he'd believed Maude had been left for dead by her tribe. But at the faint signs of life within her frail body, he'd taken her home to his ma, who'd nursed her back to health. Maude had stayed with the family ever since. And when he'd said he was moving to Fairplay, she'd informed him she was coming with him.

That was the thing about Maude. She hardly ever asked and almost always told him what to do. Most of the time he didn't mind. He'd gotten used to her bossiness. But when it came to women, he'd always been quick to remind her that he didn't need or want her help.

Tonight was no exception. "The wagon's still hitched. I'll take Mrs. Taylor on home now before it gets too cold, and I'll search for her horse tomorrow."

"You go look now." Maude pinched the back of Ranger's neck and motioned for him to sit, which he promptly did, his tongue lolling out one side of his mouth. "Wolves still roam the plains and are hungry."

"Oh no." Serena's gentle features tightened. "I didn't realize Belle would be in danger, or I would have taken more care with her."

"The horse'll be just fine." Weston shot a warning look at Maude—hopefully one she could read—cautioning her against saying anything more. "With the cooler temperatures, we might have a few wild critters who haven't gone to the lower elevations, but it ain't nothin' to worry about."

Serena's worry clouded her green eyes in spite of his assurance. "I can't let anything happen to her."

"Reckon she's back at the boardinghouse by now, but how about if I take a ride around and see if I spot her?"

"I'll go with you." She started to put Tate down, but the boy tightened his hold around her neck.

Maude was right. He'd be better off having Serena wait. Even without the little fella, she'd slow down his search, and he'd be able to cover more ground without her. "If I can't find your mare on my land, then I'll take you on back to the boardinghouse, and we can search on the way there."

She nodded reluctantly.

Within minutes he was outside on his way to the barn in the frigid night, bundled in his coat and hat and gloves. He saddled and mounted his gelding, then veered toward the river with Ranger trotting alongside him. As he took a last glance at the house, something strange warmed his insides at the thought of Serena and Tate waiting there for his return.

He didn't know all that much about the widow and her little boy, but he couldn't deny that after spending the past couple hours with her, he wanted to find out more. She was interesting and kind and soft-spoken. And she was also a good mother—he'd noticed that the very first time he'd watched her interact with her boy around town and at church.

But as much as she might intrigue him, he wasn't sure if he was ready to get calico fever again. He'd been hurt one too many times, and his heart couldn't take any more breaking.

CHAPTER 4

Was Weston Oakley the solution to all her problems and the key to keeping Tate?

Serena held Tate in her arms, his eyes closed in slumber and his thumb halfway out of his mouth. She brushed his hair off his forehead and then leaned her head back against the cushioned chair beside the fireplace in Weston's parlor.

Though the room was devoid of furniture and decorations except a simple settee and matching chair, the warmth, quiet, and peace of the house had settled around her, making her drowsy. Maude had kindly brought her a blanket for extra warmth, and Serena was sorely tempted to close her own eyes and let sleep claim her.

But what would Weston say if he returned and found her slumbering? She didn't want him to think she was an incompetent mother—the accusation her father-in-law had leveled at her when he'd told her she could no longer raise Tate as her own.

Deep inside, she knew she wasn't incompetent. She'd been a loving mother since the moment Tate had been born. But her father-in-law had catalogued her every misstep with Tate—

everything from how many rashes Tate had suffered to how many nights he'd been up crying. All the allegations had shaken her already rocky confidence—the confidence that had slowly eroded while she'd been married to Palmer.

Even now she couldn't keep from wondering what she'd done wrong as a new wife, why he hadn't been happy and satisfied with her. If she'd tried harder to be what he'd needed, maybe he wouldn't have had a reason to seek out other women.

At the creak of the front door opening and footsteps entering, she sat up. Was Weston returning? There was no clock upon the fireplace mantel to indicate the passing of time, but she guessed not more than half an hour had passed since Weston had ridden out to search for her horse.

She started to stand.

"Howdy, Maude," came an unfamiliar male voice.

Serena sat back down and held herself motionless. She shouldn't be in a single man's home like this. Even with his housekeeper present, it was improper for a woman—even a widow—to fraternize so privately. If people discovered she'd been at his house alone after dark, she'd risk ruining her reputation.

With a tarnished reputation, would any of the men on her suitable-husband list still want her?

"Maverick." Maude's voice held a note of affection. "You surprised me."

"Of course I did," the man replied, humor tinging his voice.

From the shuffling and muffling of Maude's reply, Serena guessed the newcomer was giving the old housekeeper an embrace.

"You stay here for the night," Maude said a moment later.

"Nope, just passing through on my way back home."

"Too late for travel. Dark. Bandits. Wild animals. You must stay."

Maverick gave a soft guffaw. "You know I'll be just fine."

"Then you eat before you go."

"How long before Weston returns?"

Serena wasn't sure how the newcomer knew Weston was gone. Perhaps because Ranger wasn't there to bark a greeting?

"Weston is looking for his wife's horse."

"Wife?" Maverick's question rang with surprise.

It echoed the surprise jabbing at Serena, making her sit up straighter.

Did Maude believe that because Weston had brought her into his home, she was his wife? Or maybe Weston had said something that made Maude think they'd gotten married?

"Wife and son," Maude persisted.

"Really?" Maverick's tone filled with skepticism. "When did this happy occasion occur?"

"Today."

"I won't believe it until I see it."

"She is here now."

"Now?" Maverick's voice dropped to a whisper.

A beat of silence passed. Was Maude nodding her head?

"Well, I'll be hanged." Maverick's whisper was still loud enough for Serena to hear. "Never thought I'd see the day. None of us did."

What did that mean? In the mercantile earlier, Weston had mentioned something about his family not believing he was capable of getting married. Did this have something to do with that? And was Maverick family?

"Last news I heard," Maverick whispered, "the Courtney sister he was pining over got married to someone else."

"I don't know nothing about that." Maude's gravelly attempt at whispering fell short. "This here lady, she's real nice."

Why had Maude decided that Serena was nice? Had the housekeeper eavesdropped during the supper conversation?

Before Serena could determine what to do, a dark-haired

man with the same lean facial features, squared jawline, and prominent chin as Weston filled the doorway of the parlor.

Yes, she had no doubt whatsoever that this visitor was Weston's family, possibly a brother. The resemblance was too striking to be otherwise. Not only was he as handsome and muscular, but his eyes held the same intensity.

He was slightly shorter than Weston, and his eyes were a lighter shade of blue. Those eyes were fixed upon her, widening with every passing second that he took her and Tate in.

Serena needed to clarify that she wasn't married to Weston to both the housekeeper and this man. But Maude was nowhere in sight.

What could Serena possibly say that wouldn't make things go from bad to worse? Already Maverick assumed she was married to Weston. If she denied it, would he assume that she and Weston were having illicit relations?

Lunacy of lunacies. What should she do?

At the very least, she needed to stand and greet the newcomer. That was the polite thing, and she was, after all, still a born and bred Southern woman with manners. She started to scoot to the edge of her chair and push herself up.

But Maverick shook his head and placed a finger over his lips with a meaningful look at Tate—one that said he had no wish to wake her son and that she didn't need to rise on account of him.

Once again, she stayed in the chair, but this time she sat stiffly, her mind racing to find the right explanation that would rectify the situation.

"Nice to meet you, ma'am," Maverick whispered as he studied her again. "My congratulations on being the woman to finally rope Wes into marriage."

She had to say something. "I apologize, but—"

"Shoot, look at me forgetting proper introductions." Maverick's lips turned up into an easy grin. "I'm Maverick, one of

Weston's younger brothers. Obviously much more charming and handsome."

The front door opened again, and this time, the scamper of a dog was followed by Weston's heavy steps.

Maverick backed out of the doorway and into the hallway.

"Thought that was your horse tied up out there," Weston said, his voice filled with welcome.

"Yep. Passing through the area. Was checking into a new stud for one of the broodmares." Several backslaps told her the two brothers were embracing. At Ranger's whining, Serena guessed the dog wanted his share of attention too.

"Maverick met Serena." Maude's claim rose above the clamor.

"Never thought I'd see the day." Maverick had abandoned his whispering, and his tone contained mirth. "But looks like we were all wrong."

"What's new about that?" Weston's quip was good-natured.

"With as many failed attempts, what'd you expect?"

"Failed attempts?"

"The Courtney gal. Was she the fifth or sixth gal you proposed to?"

Serena's pulse was beginning to tick faster. Weston was probably growing more confused with every passing comment. Should she go out into the hallway and intervene so that Weston didn't mistakenly assume she was to blame for the mix-up?

She made it to her feet this time, Tate still blissfully unaware of the turmoil brewing around him.

"Reckon you ain't much better." Though Weston's tone still was light, it held an edge this time. "How long you been courting Hazel? Five or six years?"

"Whoa now." Maverick's tone turned hard. "We ain't courting and never will. We're just friends."

Weston snorted. Then silence descended in the hallway. And tension. In fact, the tension was so thick Serena could feel it.

"You come eat now." Maude's command cut through the silence. "Weston will go check on his wife."

Serena pulled in a breath. Then she waited for Weston's anger to flare to life. Surely it would now.

CHAPTER 5

Wife? What in the blazes was Maude talking about?

Before he could get the question out, Maude grabbed his arm and propelled him toward the parlor door. "Go now. You talk with Serena first while I feed Maverick."

"Sure, Wes." Maverick's wide grin was back in place. "Go *talk* with your wife."

"Hold on now." Protest rose swiftly inside Weston. But Maude was already shoving him into the parlor, and Serena stood beside a chair near the hearth, Tate asleep in her arms.

Her eyes were wide, almost frightened, and she took a step back.

Obviously she'd heard the part about being his wife. There was no other explanation for her reaction. Not when she'd been so open and friendly with him earlier.

He came to a halt just inside the door and waited as Maverick and Maude moved down the hallway toward the kitchen with Ranger trailing them, his paws thumping against the wood floor. When the kitchen door clicked closed and Maverick's and Maude's voices became muted, Weston took off his Stetson and cleared his throat. "Guess you heard Maude tell my brother you're my wife?"

"Yes. I'm not sure what happened to lead her to believe we're married. I guarantee I didn't say anything." From the distress drawing lines into her delicate forehead and at the corners of her eyes, he knew her answer was sincere, that she wasn't responsible for whatever misunderstanding had taken place during his absence.

If anyone was to blame, it was likely Maude. Even though the old native had learned to speak good English over the years, she didn't always comprehend everything, and they'd had their share of miscommunication.

This miscommunication was a big one, though.

Maverick believed Serena was his wife, and when he returned to the ranch, he'd tell everyone.

Weston twisted his hat. On the one hand, the pressure from family would finally go away. On the other hand, when he showed up at Christmas without the expected wife, he'd only be humiliated more than ever.

Unless . . .

Serena's eyes took on a wariness, as if she could see the wheels in his head rolling faster, picking up momentum.

What if he actually took her to his family's home? Since everyone would already believe they were married, maybe he could convince Serena to spend Christmas with him.

And what? Pretend to be his wife for a few days?

He gave a curt, frustrated shake of his head. He wouldn't be able to deceive his family. And he'd never ask Serena to join him in such deception. Not that she'd even consider it. She seemed like an honest and upright woman.

"I apologize," she whispered. "This is all my fault for being here. I shouldn't have come."

"It's not your fault."

"It really is." She cast her sights down to Tate, her cheeks flushed. "I was interested in meeting you—I mean, I liked how you treated Tate. You're good with him."

She'd been interested in meeting him? Weston's thoughts halted their tumultuous rumbling, and an eerie quiet settled in to replace the noise. "Tate's a real cute little fella."

"He is." She brushed her fingers across his forehead and smoothed back strands of his pale hair. As she moved her hand back to his arm, her fingers trembled. "And truthfully, I'd like him to have a father again."

A father?

The tension he hadn't known was building in his chest suddenly eased, as if someone had loosened a noose that was tightening around him. She wasn't necessarily looking to get a husband. Nope, she wanted a pa for her boy. That was a noble goal, wasn't it? To provide a home and stable life for the little fella?

Maybe they could have a mutually beneficial relationship. By marrying her, he'd get himself out of this embarrassing situation with his family and finally make them happy. And by marrying him, she'd be able to give her son a pa and home.

"Listen," Weston started, but then stopped. What in the blazes was he thinking? He couldn't really be considering going through with such a rash plan, could he? He hardly knew Serena. And she certainly wouldn't agree to it since she hardly knew him.

Yet he was already more acquainted with her than some of the women he'd met through the matrimonial catalogs and newspaper ads. He was also acquainted with her better than some of the random women his sisters and mother had tried to foist upon him. If he'd considered marrying strangers before, why not now?

"Please forgive me. I shouldn't have said anything." She rounded the chair and started toward the door. "If you'll be so kind as to loan me a horse, I'll depart now so that you can spend time with your brother without my interference."

And explain to Maverick that he wasn't really married.

As she passed by, he took hold of her upper arm. "Wait."

Less than a foot from him, she halted but kept her gaze on Tate's sleeping face.

A strange sense of turmoil swirled inside him. It was one he'd experienced with all the women he'd courted, including Felicity. He couldn't explain the feeling, hadn't ever wanted to analyze it. And this time he didn't want to think about it either. He just wanted to shove it away where it couldn't bother him.

He let himself study Tate's face now too. Weston had always wanted children. He wasn't building a successful empire of businesses just for himself. He especially wanted a son who could work with him and who he could pass his holdings along to someday.

"Maybe I can be Tate's pa." He forced the words out before he could think of all the reasons why he shouldn't become the boy's pa.

Serena's gaze rose to his. Her eyes were filled with a dozen questions. Did she doubt his motivation? Think it was too soon?

"As you can see," he continued, "my family is all fired up about me taking a wife. They've been yammering on about it for a while."

"But do you want to take a wife? Especially this soon after having been hurt by Felicity?"

Maybe if his family weren't bothering him so blamed much, he'd wait longer and give himself more time to get over the sting of losing Felicity. But what if marrying Serena helped him put the hurt behind him?

If he didn't marry Serena? He'd eventually have to go through all the hard work of finding another woman and getting to know her. And he was plain tired of the endless cycle of meeting, courting, and rejection.

He could feel the muscles in her arm tensing beneath his touch, so he released her. "I reckon I'm as ready as I'll ever be."

"Are you sure?" Her tone was hesitant, almost as though his hesitancy was making her feel the same.

He'd thought he'd been sure with Felicity, but clearly he'd been wrong. How could a man ever be totally certain? "My pesky family doesn't think I'll ever get married. And I'm aiming to make them eat crow."

"But you don't know me—"

"I know enough for now. And we'll get to know each other better once we're married."

She resituated Tate in her arms, cradling his head against her shoulder. "When would you plan on having the wedding?"

His mind rapidly calculated all the options and then landed on the best one. "Tonight."

Her brow wrinkled again above her nose.

He wasn't convincing her well enough. In fact, she was probably starting to think he was a madman, and at any second she'd run from the house and tell him she never wanted to speak to him again.

He glanced through the doorway into the hall. The voices from the kitchen were still muted, which meant Maverick remained occupied with Maude. "I'd prefer not to lie to my brother or my family. Reckon if we get hitched tonight, then when Maverick trots on home and tells everyone I'm married, that'll be the gospel truth."

She was silent a moment, studying him. "That makes sense. But what if you change your mind in the morning?"

"What if you do?"

She grazed Tate's cheek. Her eyes always contained so much love whenever she looked at the little fella. "I won't change my mind. I need this for Tate."

"And I won't change my mind. I need this for my family."

She wavered again, her expression solemn.

His muscles tensed. "Is there another fella you've set your heart on?"

"No. But Mr. Oakley—Weston?" Her voice dropped to a whisper. "You should know if I do this, it'll be for Tate's well-being. Not for my own. I've been married once already, and I'm not expecting love."

What was she saying? That she had no interest in developing a relationship with him? That she didn't want to have a real marriage? That she was opposed to sharing the marriage bed?

Fact was, he was a single man who'd been waiting a long time for the marriage bed. And Lord in heaven above knew that if he had a wife, he wasn't planning to remain celibate. At least, not for long. Someday soon he'd also be ready to have children.

On the other hand, he'd told her they needed to take some time to get to know each other. Would a few weeks be enough? Maybe by Christmas?

He stuffed his hands into his pockets. "Listen." He cleared his throat. "I'm alright with taking things"—his voice cracked—"you know . . . real slow to start with."

Blast. Having this kind of conversation was incredibly awkward. The growing flush in her pale cheeks told him it was awkward for her too.

But it needed to be said so that she knew his expectations.

"Let's wait for—until after Christmas to share—uh, intimacies," he continued. "That oughta give us a heap of time to stop being strangers."

She nodded. "That's very kind of you."

Somehow her words didn't sit quite right with him, but now wasn't the time to analyze them.

"Then a wedding tonight?" he asked softly.

"Alright," she replied just as quietly. "A wedding tonight."

CHAPTER 6

She was almost married again.

Serena stood stiffly beside Weston in the parlor as the pastor, Father Zieber, read the closing remarks from his prayer book. "Those whom God hath joined together, let no man put asunder."

The minister smiled wearily.

Poor fellow. The hour was late—much later than she'd anticipated when she'd agreed to marry Weston tonight.

But Maverick had stayed for a short while after his meal, talking with Weston and catching him up on family news. Even though Serena had joined them in the kitchen, Tate had been awake and hungry, and she'd been busy with him.

She'd heard enough to know that Weston's family had a ranch north of Fairplay, that it was smaller than those in the South Park basin, but that his family had apparently done well enough to make a living from it. From what she gathered, Weston's family was large, and he had more younger brothers and twin sisters.

After Maverick left, Weston had ridden to town to fetch the reverend. Then he'd made a detour to the boardinghouse to let everyone know about the wedding and that she and Tate would no longer be living there. Someone had helped pack her belongings—which hadn't been much, still only one bag. And he'd also located her horse wandering outside the boardinghouse barn.

By the time Weston had returned, the reverend was also just arriving.

Now Maude, standing by the parlor door, was one of their witnesses. And Weston had gone to the cabin out behind the barn and brought with him one of his ranch hands—a middle-aged cowboy with a pock-marked face and one droopy eye, who went by the name Dusty.

Attired in a flannel shirt and wool trousers that reeked of cow flesh, Dusty had positioned himself next to Weston and wore a proud grin, almost as if he were the father of the groom.

Tate leaned against Serena, his hands tangled in her skirt, his grip tight. All of the new people and the new place would be difficult for him as usual. But she prayed that since he liked Weston, he would adjust quickly. He was already fascinated with Ranger. And thankfully the big dog didn't seem to mind Tate's attention, was even now sitting beside Tate almost as though he were a wedding guest too.

Father Zieber continued to read from the order of service in his prayer book. "For as much as Weston and Serena have consented together in holy wedlock and have witnessed the same before God and this company, and have given and pledged their troth either to the other, and have declared the same by giving and receiving a ring . . ." The reverend cocked a brow at Weston.

"Nope." Weston rubbed at the back of his neck as if attempting to ease the tension there. "Don't have a ring yet."

"Do you have anything we can use?"

Weston glanced around the parlor, as if somehow a ring might magically appear. "I'll get a ring tomorrow in town, first thing."

"See that you do." Father Zieber returned his gaze to the prayer book and read silently—likely skipping over the rest of the ring part—then he continued. "I pronounce that they be man and wife together. In the name of the Father, of the Son, and of the Holy Ghost. Amen."

"Amen." Dusty's call rang out cheerfully.

Maude, with her arms crossed, nodded. "Good. Finally."

Weston didn't move, seemed frozen in place. Was he already regretting his decision?

Serena's stomach tightened, her own nerves taunting her. She guessed he was probably feeling the same as she was—wondering if the decision was the right one and praying they hadn't just made a huge mistake.

"Congratulations." Father Zieber snapped the prayer book closed. "I wish you many happy years together."

Dusty clamped a hand against Weston's back. "Oh, don't you worry, Reverend. Weston's gonna be real happy with his new wife. She's a looker. And you know what they say about widows, since they got some experience in—"

"Now, Dusty." The reverend cut in, his voice rising and ending on a squeak. "We're in polite company here." He gave a pointed nod at Serena, then Tate.

Dusty's grin fell away, and he bobbed his head at Serena. "Sorry, ma'am. Not used to havin' a fine lady such as yourself around and needing to watch what I say. Will try harder, that's for sure."

She offered a smile. "I grew up on a ranch, so I'm not quite as delicate as I appear."

Dusty's smile rose once more, brighter than before. "In that case, I'll be lookin' forward to seeing lots more little ones running around the ranch real soon."

Weston tugged at the bow tie he'd hastily donned before the ceremony, rolling his neck as if he were being strangled.

Serena was uncertain how to respond to such a comment.

Saying *thank you* or *me too* seemed slightly inappropriate. But truthfully, she did want to have more children, had hoped Palmer wanted more too. However, since her late husband had been an only child, he'd seemed all too content with just Tate. He'd stopped visiting her bedroom soon after her announcement that she was pregnant, and he hadn't returned after Tate was born.

Even so, she could admit that Weston's plan to get to know each other first seemed to be the wisest course of action. Maybe if they learned more about each other and were able to form a companionable relationship, he might not run off and find pleasure in the arms of another woman the first chance he had.

Whatever the case, she had to be a better wife this time. Yes, she'd married Weston so Tate would have a pa and so that her father-in-law wouldn't be able to take Tate away from her. But what if Weston decided he didn't like her? What if, during the next few weeks until Christmas, he changed his mind—maybe gave her a divorce or an annulment? If he did that, her situation would only look worse. And her father-in-law would have more reasons to accuse her of being an unfit mother.

Father Zieber didn't linger long after the wedding, even though Weston invited him to join them for coffee and dessert. Dusty didn't stay either, winking at Weston on his way out and telling him to have a real good night.

Weston had all but wrangled his bow tie off the moment everyone was gone. Tossing the offending item to the settee, he plunged a hand into his hair, his muscles taut, his jaw clenched tight.

Beside her, Tate continued to cling to her skirt, now staring at Weston with wide eyes. Ranger was still sitting at the boy's side, and the two were nearly the same height. The dog was watching Weston with the same curiosity as the boy, his floppy ears cocking first one way then another, and his eyes shifting with every move Weston made.

Weston blew out a breath. "Reckon I can show you around the house so you can unpack and settle in."

She didn't have much to unpack. Surely he could see that. Regardless, she followed him out of the parlor and tromped behind him up the stairs to the second floor with Tate on her hip and Ranger on her heels.

"The first bedroom is small." Holding up his lantern, Weston pushed open the door to reveal an empty room that was only big enough for a twin bed and perhaps a chest of drawers. "Do you think Tate might like it?"

She stepped in and slowly circled the room. She wasn't a good seamstress, but she could at least make curtains and find a few decorations. It wouldn't be like the spacious nursery at Stony Creek Ranch in Pueblo that had been filled with toys and books, but she could make it cozy and inviting for Tate, couldn't she? "What do you think, Tate? Would you like your own room?"

He lifted his head from her shoulder and peered down at Ranger. "Doggie's room too?"

"No, the doggie already has a bed . . ." She looked to Weston for help. Where did Ranger sleep?

Weston waited in the doorway. "I don't mind if Ranger sleeps in Tate's room."

"Me sleep with Rangie." Tate leaned down low and held out his hand toward the dog.

Ranger lifted his snout, sniffed the boy's fingers, then began to lick them, likely tasting something left there from a meal or snack.

With the dog's tongue tickling him, Tate released a giggle.

At the rare sound, Serena's chest squeezed. When was the last time she'd heard Tate giggle? She couldn't recall. There had been so much tension during their last months at Stony Creek Ranch. Then recently, she'd been so preoccupied with surviving that she'd had little time for small pleasures.

As another of his giggles echoed in the barren room, Serena couldn't hold back a smile.

Weston was watching the interaction between the boy and dog, and a smile quirked at the corners of his lips, softening the strain in his features. "Ranger likes you, Tate."

"I love doggie."

The grip on Serena's chest pinched harder, and heat formed at the backs of her eyes. This place, Weston, the dog—all of it would be good for Tate. Even if the new living arrangement would be strange and challenging for her, it wouldn't matter—not if Tate could finally flourish.

As Weston moved back into the hallway, she trailed after him. He nodded at the closed door across from Tate's room. "Maude sleeps in there."

Weston took several long strides to reach the end of the hallway and a final door. He opened it to a more spacious bedroom.

She approached slowly, not wanting to overstep the boundaries by entering his bedroom, but he motioned her inside as if he thought nothing of her being there.

If it didn't bother him having her in so private a place, then maybe she needed to put aside her own embarrassment.

She sidled past him until she was standing in the middle of the room. It was as sparsely furnished as the rest of the house. A wide bed with a glossy, dark headboard took up one wall and was positioned underneath a large picture window. The cover was neatly pulled up and tucked under the mattress. A tall chest of drawers stood against the opposite wall, and a simple bedside table and chair were the only other furniture. A large stove for heat was positioned in a corner, the wood bin beside it full.

"This is my—our room." Weston had leaned against the doorframe and ducked his head, focusing on Ranger, who was sitting in front of him. "You can unpack your clothing and personal items into the empty drawers, which is most of them. And there's also a closet for you to hang gowns and such."

Gowns? The night she'd run away, she'd only packed the most basic of clothing—her most serviceable dresses and skirts along with her sturdiest shoes. But after wearing the same clothing day after day, she was starting to look shabby. And so was Tate.

However, the condition of their clothing had been—and still was—the least of her concerns.

"Thank you, Weston. You're very kind."

Tate wiggled against her to be let down. She settled him on his two feet, and he bounded over to Ranger and wrapped both arms around the dog.

"Careful now, Tate," she cautioned. "The doggie might not want to be hugged."

The moment she spoke the word *hugged*, Ranger swiped his tongue across Tate's face in a big kiss.

Tate laughed and bent in and kissed the dog's head.

Above the heads of both, Serena caught Weston's gaze. He was smiling again, and she realized that she was too, and that they were sharing the sweetness of this moment together. She'd always longed to share such moments with Palmer, but he'd rarely spent time with Tate, and then only a few minutes at the longest. She guessed Palmer likely would have invested more as Tate got older, would have helped him learn to ride or hunt or fish. But he'd considered the baby stage to be her responsibility.

Weston might too. But at this moment, she liked being able to enjoy Tate's antics with someone else.

Besides, Weston had such a nice smile. It wasn't flashy or overly winsome. Instead, it was simple and straightforward, bringing out the cleft in his chin. It made him more good-looking—if that were possible. Maybe it was the contrast of his smile to the rugged scruff on his face. Or the contrast of his straight white teeth to his tanned skin.

Whatever the case, he was a handsome man. There was no sense in denying that fact.

As though hearing her thoughts and disapproving of them, his smile disappeared. "I'm sorry I only have the one bed for now."

"Me and Mama share bed." Tate's statement came out matter-of-factly. He clearly didn't realize the awkwardness of the predicament, and he released Ranger and ran to the bed as fast as his little legs could carry him.

At the edge, he hefted himself up over the wooden frame, swinging his legs up until he was on the mattress. He scrambled farther onto bed before shifting around and smiling at her. "Look, Mama. Me sleep." He flopped down.

She shook her head and crossed toward him. "No, Tate. This is your new daddy's bed."

As she reached the bed, Tate crawled backward out of her reach. Then he looked at Weston. "Daddy?"

Weston didn't respond. Instead, his eyes widened as if he wasn't sure what to think about being called *Daddy*.

She hadn't discussed with Weston how he wanted to handle Tate. They hadn't really had the time. Did he want Tate to call him *Daddy* or *Pa*? Or would he rather the boy address him as Mr. Oakley?

And the bigger problem was, if this was Weston's only bed, where would she and Tate sleep?

CHAPTER 7

Tate had called him *Daddy*.

Daddy. He'd become a pa.

Weston wasn't sure if that thought should make him happy or scare him. At the moment, he felt a little bit of both.

What did Tate think of having a new pa? From the boy's wide-eyed look, Weston guessed he was trying to figure it all out too.

Serena held out her hands to Tate. "Come to Mama. This isn't your bed."

Tate slowly began to inch toward her. He didn't seem like a willful child, but he definitely didn't want to get off the bed.

Maybe Weston would have to ride to town tomorrow and start tracking down a bed for the boy. Doing so would take some time. In the meantime, with the winterlike temperatures at night, Weston wouldn't even consider rolling out a pallet for Tate on the floor. And he doubted Serena would want the boy to sleep on the settee downstairs.

Of course, Weston could throw down a pallet for himself and give up his bed for the two of them. But that would end up being cold for him too. Besides, it was his house and his bed, and she was his wife. They had every right to sleep near each other.

After all, Serena may as well get used to sharing a room with him, and even the bed, because he was a married man now. Married.

A shimmy of anxiety plied at him. He really was married. Wasn't dreaming.

"I know I said we'd wait and get to know each other . . ." His voice cracked, and he cleared it loudly. "But I reckon it won't hurt nothin' to share the same bed."

Serena kept her focus on Tate. "I understand."

"We can still wait—" He paused and tried to think of chaste words that wouldn't offend Serena or be inappropriate for Tate — "to start having more children."

Tate—and Ranger—were both staring at him again. Weston wasn't a blushing man, not in the least. But he couldn't remember ever having had a more awkward conversation in his life—one that would have made him blush if it were possible.

Serena's cheeks, on the other hand, were turning a shade pinker. "Whatever you want, I'll be fine."

"I promise I won't do nothin' to make you uncomfortable." He wasn't a brute with women. The honest truth was, he'd never forced himself on any woman in the past, and he didn't intend to start now with a wife.

"I'll be fine. Truly." She still didn't look his way.

What was she trying to tell him? That she'd done her duty to her previous husband and would do it with him too?

But was that what he wanted? For her to do her duty? What about a mutually loving and satisfying marriage? Was that possible? Or was that only a dream that few married couples achieved?

"Daddy sleep with me and Mama?" Tate's little voice took on a hopeful note.

Weston shoved away from the doorframe and began to cross

to the bed. As he reached the end, he stood next to Serena. "I'm your pa."

"Pa?"

"Yep. And you can sleep right there, little fella."

Tate nodded. "I be good."

"Of course you'll be good." Weston leaned in and tweaked Tate's nose. "You can sleep in our bed, but only until I get you a bed of your own."

"For me and Rangie?" He held out his hand toward the dog.

Ranger rose from where he'd lain down in the center of the room and sauntered over to the child, his backside wiggling with each shake of his tail. While Tate inched closer to the edge of the bed, Ranger lifted his big black nose and nudged the little boy.

As Serena smiled again at the interaction between the dog and child, the sliver of worry pricking Weston eased just a little. Even if he'd been hasty in making the decision to marry her, and even if he was a little anxious about it, her smiles had a way of soothing him, making him think that he'd done the right thing after all.

"It's late." He turned away from the bed and headed to the stove to add more fuel. "I'll leave you to get ready for bed."

"Thank you." Serena's gratefulness was clear enough. Had she gotten tired of living in the boardinghouse? Or had she really just wanted a pa for Tate? Whatever her motives for accepting the marriage arrangement, he prayed he hadn't made a mistake.

Weston busied himself for the next hour checking on one of the steers with foot rot and another suffering from bloating. When he returned through the back door, Maude wasn't around, and the upstairs was quiet. He turned off his lantern and made his way up the stairway in the dark. He tried to keep his tread soundless, the way Maude was able to do, not wanting to wake up his new family, especially not Tate.

He didn't know much about children, but he reckoned the night would go better if the little fella stayed sound asleep.

Weston slowed even further as he padded down the hallway and entered his room. His pulse stuttered at the realization that never again would he sleep alone. Never again would he be a bachelor. Never again would he come home to an empty house.

Faint moonlight cascaded in through the window above the bed, and it highlighted the two sleeping forms under the thick layers of covers. They were crowded against the edge of the bed as far as they could possibly go without falling off. Both were facing away from his side, with Serena in the spot closest to him and Tate curled up against her.

He couldn't see either of their faces well in the darkness, but from their silence and the even rhythm of their breathing, he could tell he hadn't disturbed them yet.

He shed his coat, but as he slipped out of his suspenders and let his trousers puddle on the floor, he paused. Maybe he shouldn't get entirely undressed the way he normally did. Maybe he oughta sleep in his clothes instead? He didn't want to scare either Serena or Tate if they woke up to find him in only his undergarments.

On the other hand, they were his family now. They'd have to get used to him being less than proper at times.

As he finished shedding the last of his clothing down to his underdrawers and a light cotton shirt, he flipped back the covers and slipped into the bed.

He situated himself on his pillow, then held his breath, waiting to see if Serena and Tate remained asleep.

At the continued silence from their side of the bed, he closed his eyes and let himself relax. What was his family gonna say when they heard Maverick's news? He almost smiled thinking about their surprise.

"Weston?" came a soft whisper beside him.

His eyes flew open. As he shifted his gaze to Serena, he

found that she was lying on her back and had turned her head so that she was looking directly at him. Her blond-brown hair was loose and free of the constraints of her braid, and her features somehow seemed softer.

He didn't answer her, but he met her gaze. In the darkness, he couldn't see the green of her eyes, but he could feel her scrutiny.

"You've been so kind to Tate," she whispered. "I can't thank you enough."

No one should have to thank a person for being kind to their child. Maybe she and Tate hadn't experienced enough kindness. Maybe that's why they'd come to Fairplay. "You don't have to worry. I'll treat Tate like he's my own."

Her eyes seemed to glisten. Were those tears? "You're a good man."

"I'm just doing what any other man would."

She was quiet for a moment, as though perhaps she was holding back her disagreement. What had her husband been like? She'd said that nothing about him had been particularly easy. Maybe he hadn't been kind to either her or Tate.

"I'll try to be a good wife in return," she whispered.

He shook his head. He didn't want her thinking she had to repay him for anything.

"And I'll try not to bother you—"

"Whoa now." His voice rose, and he quickly dropped it back to a whisper. "You're my wife, and you won't be a bother."

"It's just that this happened so fast, and I don't want you to have regrets."

"I ain't planning on having regrets."

"You're sure?"

He nodded, even though there was still a deep, dark, undefinable place inside that was nagging him. "I have a lot to learn about being a pa and a husband. But I'm a quick learner, and hopefully I won't make too many mistakes."

"It's okay if you do."

"And it's okay if you make mistakes too."

He could see enough of her face to know that he'd made her smile. And for some unexplainable reason, he liked that he'd been able to do that.

She shifted her head and fell silent.

He turned to stare at the ceiling, which was better than staring at her outline. Not that her outline gave him lustful thoughts or anything. But he couldn't keep from thinking on the fact that he had a woman in his bed. A very beautiful woman.

Even so, she was a stranger to him. They'd only met just hours ago—not counting the brief times they'd seen each other around town. There was so much he didn't know about her—so much he probably should've asked before getting married.

But it was too late for that. Come what may, this woman was a part of his life. And now all he could do was make the best of this unexpected marriage.

CHAPTER 8

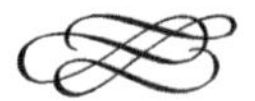

"Quiet, Tate." Serena pressed her finger to the little boy's lips as he perched on the bench beside her at the kitchen table. "Your pa is still asleep."

She'd decided to use Weston's term for himself. It wasn't one she'd ever used to address her daddy, but she wanted to do everything she could to make sure Weston loved Tate.

The boy paused in rolling his marble around an obstacle course on the table that she'd made from a few twigs she'd gathered on their way back from the privy. "Pa sleeping?"

"We don't want to awaken him, do we?" The lone lantern at the center of the table cut through the darkness of the predawn hour.

Tate shook his head, his eyes solemn.

"So let's play just as quietly as possible."

Maude was still asleep, too, and Serena didn't want Tate's playing to awaken the housekeeper either.

Tate had always been a light sleeper and early riser. At the boardinghouse she'd simply kept him in their room until she heard noises in the kitchen.

But with Weston asleep in the same bed, she'd hurried Tate from the room at his first waking sound. Thankfully, Weston hadn't stirred, hadn't reached for her, hadn't even accidentally brushed against her. In fact, he'd slept heavily. She should know since she'd hardly dozed throughout the long night.

The truth was—and she'd been too embarrassed to admit it to Weston—her previous husband had never shared a bed with her. After their wedding, Palmer had kept his own room. His infrequent visits in the early months of their marriage hadn't ever lasted long. He'd done what was expected of a husband and then left.

Her marriage to Palmer certainly hadn't been what she'd hoped for. But her daddy had made the arrangements with Mr. Halifax, a longtime friend of his, after Mr. Halifax had written to him about needing a wife for Palmer.

As the second youngest daughter out of ten children, Serena had understood that Daddy was tired of having to make matches for his children and was still grieving over Mother's death. Without Mother's voice of wisdom to guide him, her daddy had sent her west to Pueblo and the Halifax family close to three years ago, when she'd just turned nineteen.

Of course, the Halifaxes were a fine and respected family. They'd offered her a lifestyle similar to what she'd known with her wealthy family. But it had become clear almost from the start that Mrs. Halifax was unhappy with her husband and spent large portions of her day locked away in her bedroom with her laudanum.

At first, Serena had been too naïve to understand Mrs. Halifax's disappointments. But when she'd learned of Palmer's mistress one Sunday at church, she'd finally begun to understand that the Halifax men weren't faithful to their marital vows.

She'd tried to speak of the matter to Palmer, but he'd

silenced her with a slap on her cheek. The hit had been hard enough to send the message that she didn't dare talk about the issue again.

Even if her marriage to Palmer had been less than ideal, she'd poured everything she had into being a mother to Tate. She'd loved the little boy as dearly as her own mother had loved her and all her siblings.

But her efforts hadn't been enough, at least for Mr. Halifax. She supposed his grief over losing his Palmer had been difficult to bear. Her decision to take Tate and return to Oklahoma had only added to his sense of loss.

Whatever the reasons, Mr. Halifax had decided that Tate belonged to him more than her, and he'd even told her that she ought to willingly hand Tate over to him to raise now that Palmer was gone, since she was young enough to get remarried and have other children.

But she wasn't ready to give up her son—not to Mr. Halifax, not to anyone.

Tate held out one of the sticks toward Ranger as he rested under the table at their feet. The dog had spent the night sleeping by the bedside and had followed them downstairs when they'd arisen.

Ranger sniffed the stick, then lowered his head back to his outstretched paws.

"Rangie play?" Tate whispered.

"Ranger is still tired." Just like her. She stifled a yawn behind her hand.

"You awake early." Maude's voice came from the doorway.

Serena startled at the housekeeper's unexpected appearance.

The older woman brushed past them to the stove. She was attired in a plain calico skirt and simple matching blouse, but she wore leather moccasins and also a simple beaded necklace.

"I didn't sleep well." Serena pushed up from the bench at the table, wanting to assist Maude in any way she could with the morning chores. While Serena had grown up having servants and had relied on them while living with the Halifaxes, she'd learned a great deal while working at the boardinghouse.

Maude grabbed a handful of kindling. "Weston keep you too busy?"

"Busy?" The moment Serena spoke the word, Maude's implication became all too clear. "Goodness gracious. No." A flush rapidly spread through her. "Not at all."

Maude stood then, abandoning adding fuel to the fire that Serena had already stoked. The old woman narrowed her eyes at Serena, then Tate. "Boy needs his own bed."

At heavy footsteps overhead—Weston's—more mortification pulsed through Serena. She had to put an end to this conversation with Maude before Weston came into the kitchen. She absolutely didn't want him to discover she'd been discussing their bedtime activities—or lack thereof—with his housekeeper.

"Would you like some help getting breakfast ready?" She started toward the large cupboard against the opposite wall. "I can make coffee."

Maude waved a hand impatiently. "No. I do the cooking. You go now. Make Weston happy. That is all."

Make Weston happy?

Serena took a step back from the cupboard. It seemed like such a simple command. But she'd learned from her relationship with Palmer that making her husband happy was one of the hardest jobs.

What could she do to make Weston happy? She didn't know him well enough yet to have learned the things he liked or disliked. Maybe she needed to start a new list with ideas.

She patted her pocket and felt the crinkle of her previous list—the one with the potential husbands. She no longer needed it. But even though she'd accomplished her mission and had a husband, would she be able to keep him?

As Weston's footsteps thudded on the stairway, Ranger

crawled out from underneath the table and started to wag his tail. Serena smoothed down her blouse and then her skirt. As she put her hand to her hair, she realized she hadn't yet plaited it.

She ran her fingers through it like a comb. But before she could start a braid, Weston's long stride resounded in the hallway, and in the next instant he filled the doorway. His dark hair was mussed, his shirt unbuttoned, and his stubble thick. He took in first Tate at the table, then Maude adding fuel to the stove, before his gaze landed upon her.

The blue-black of his eyes was filled with questions, almost as if he'd been worried that her absence in the bedroom meant she'd run off during the night. As the taut lines in his face smoothed out, tension also seemed to ease from his shoulders. "You're up early."

His statement was nearly identical to Maude's from a few moments ago. But this time, Serena wouldn't make the same mistake about referencing her sleepless night. "Tate is always up early, and I didn't want him to wake you."

"Don't worry about me." His trousers were low on his hips, one of his suspenders dangling down his leg. As he stretched his arms over his head, his undershirt rose, revealing a span of his stomach—a hard, muscular span tapering into a V that disappeared beneath his trousers.

She'd never witnessed a man so casually attired. Her mother had always been strict regarding the rules of propriety. The Halifaxes had been proper in their conduct and attire as well. Even when Palmer had come to her bed, he'd been covered in his nightclothes and hadn't bared himself in front of her.

This sight now of Weston—she didn't know what to think.

As he lowered his arms and finished a yawn, he stopped short at the sight of her staring at him.

She closed her mouth—which she hadn't realized was open

—and spun to face Tate, who was now getting up from his bench.

He clutched the marble in his hand and held it up toward Weston. "Ball, Pa."

She could feel Weston's gaze still upon her and prayed her cheeks weren't turning pink. Maude, in the process of mixing something in a bowl on the opposite side of the table, also halted to stare back and forth between her and Weston.

Serena rapidly began to braid her hair, wishing she'd thought to do it before Weston had awakened.

"Yep." Weston patted Tate on the head at the same time that he thumped Ranger affectionately. "Looks like you've got your ball."

"Mama build roads." Tate returned to the maze of sticks on the table.

Weston approached, still scratching Ranger, the dog thrusting his nose up and giving Weston little choice but to pay him attention.

Tate began to roll the ball through the *roads*. "See."

Weston bent over and followed Tate's movements. "Your ma made the roads?"

Tate nodded.

Weston's profile was rugged, brawn and muscle in every conceivable place. His presence in the kitchen seemed to take up half the room. What was it about him that was so overpowering?

"Looks like your ma is creative." He slid a sideways glance her way, as though he'd felt her staring at him. His dark eyes had a liquid quality—one that was strangely magnetic.

She tore her attention from him and focused instead on Tate, running her fingers through his hair, which hadn't been combed yet either. "I wasn't able to bring any of his toys, so I've had to be creative."

Weston watched Tate for another minute, asking him questions and showing interest in his playing. When he stood, he stretched his arms again and arched his back. That spot of stomach showed once more.

When he patted a hand there, she tore her gaze away only to find him gauging her reaction.

Had he seen her ogling him? This time, she could feel the heat moving into her cheeks. How embarrassing. He was going to think she was a loose woman with the way she was behaving.

She pretended to be preoccupied with finishing her braid, but even the act of braiding seemed too intimate to do in front of Weston, and her fingers fumbled to finish and tie the ribbon.

Maude remained busy in front of the stove, and the scent of both coffee and something cooking began to fill the air. Even as the housekeeper flipped whatever was sizzling in her pan, she was halfway turned, still watching them as if they were putting on a stage production purely for her pleasure.

Weston lowered himself into a chair at the head of the table.

Maude poured a cup of coffee and slapped it down on the table in front of Weston, the thick sludge-like mixture sloshing over the edge. Then she motioned to Serena and pointed at the spot beside Weston. "Sit."

Serena dropped down and sat unmoving. Tate climbed up on the bench beside her and imitated her motionless posture.

A moment later, Maude plopped another mug of coffee onto the table, this one in front of Serena.

"Thank you," she murmured.

Maude grunted as she moved away.

Weston tapped his thumb against his cup. "How about if we ride into town this morning and do a little shopping?"

She wasn't about to admit to her dire financial situation—that even with what she'd been earning while working at the boardinghouse, she hadn't been able to save much.

Nevertheless, if Weston wanted her to come along to town with him, how could she say no?

"Very well." She hadn't anticipated spending time with him today, had assumed his work would demand his time.

But she wouldn't mind the opportunity to get to know him a little better. In fact, she wouldn't mind it at all.

CHAPTER 9

"Take as much time as you need to shop." Weston veered the team onto a side street on the outskirts of Fairplay.

Tate was wedged between him and Serena on the wagon bench and was holding a portion of the reins Weston had given to him. The little fella had been pretending to guide the team the whole way to town. It was the cutest thing Weston had ever seen.

Even now, Tate was clicking his tongue at the horses the way Weston had.

Weston bit back a smile. Tate was something else.

"I won't need much time," Serena was saying as she held on to her pretty straw hat to keep the breeze from blowing it loose.

"Go and get whatever you need."

"I don't need anything." Serena's statement was quiet, almost embarrassed.

He quirked a brow at her. "What about Tate? Reckon he could use a few new toys."

Tate's green eyes, so much like Serena's, peered up at him. "Toys?"

Serena was shaking her head at the boy in warning.

Weston turned his attention back to the street and the horses and tugged on the reins. "Don't think I've met a better roadbuilder than your ma. But you might find some other toys you like too."

"Me like."

Though the sunshine was warm, the wind gusting from the north brought the reminder that winter was creeping up on them mighty fast.

Serena pulled Tate's cap lower over his ears. "You'll have to be content with what we have for now. Mama is saving for Christmas."

"Your pa is paying for everything today."

"No. Your pa is not paying, because we do not accept charity."

He should've figured that was the issue—that Serena didn't want to be in debt to him for anything. "Your pa is buying Christmas presents today for you and your ma. You can't turn away gifts, can you?"

Tate's eyes widened at the back-and-forth.

Serena shook her head, her lips pursed as she silently tried to communicate with him that she was seeing right through his effort to get Tate on his side.

Did she really think he wasn't gonna be generous and provide for her and Tate? If so, she was about to learn how stubborn he could be when he put his mind to it.

He lifted a hand in greeting to a fellow loitering outside the tenement where many of his mill workers lived. The three-story building contained a dozen apartments. They were dilapidated and hardly livable, but they were cheap.

Lately, every time he visited, he had half a notion to construct his own set of nicer tenements and make them available to his employees. But he already had several other construction projects in various stages and didn't have enough manpower to start more.

As he brought the team to a halt in front of the building, he shifted on the bench so that he was facing Serena squarely. "Listen." He spoke so softly it almost came out a whisper. "You're my wife now, and I'm aiming to take care of you."

"I appreciate that." Her voice was soft too. "But I meant what I said. I don't need anything."

He lifted a brow to challenge her statement.

"Well, maybe a few things. But we're getting by." The bright morning sunshine illuminated her face, turning her skin into soft cream and her eyes into a warm green.

It was clear she didn't know exactly how rich he was. That wasn't a surprise, since he was private with his financial affairs and not many people realized the wealth he was earning from all his ventures in Fairplay and the surrounding towns.

In fact, he could buy her every last item being sold in Fairplay and he wouldn't come close to spending even a fraction of what he'd saved.

"I want to do this for you and Tate," he whispered.

"But—"

"I've been waiting a real long time to take a wife shopping. Let me do it. Alright?"

She seemed to swallow her ready response and instead studied his face.

He liked when she studied him. He'd caught her doing it a few times earlier and hoped it meant she appreciated what she saw.

At the call of his name from an upstairs window, he waved at Mrs. Shaw hanging half out.

Serena followed his gaze, and a tiny frown formed in her forehead.

He hopped down from the wagon and started toward the

front door of the building. "I'm checking on one of my injured workers. Won't be but a minute."

He didn't wait for her response as he ducked past the rickety door into the dank, cold interior lit only by the half-moon window above the door. He took the steps two at a time to the second floor, then he strode down the hallway to the back apartment, where his head saw operator lived with his wife and two young children. The man had nearly lost his arm a couple weeks back when he'd been trying to save one of the other workers from injury. Thankfully, Fairplay had two experienced doctors who had worked together to save Bob's arm.

As Weston knocked and waited, Serena entered below holding Tate on her hip, her eyes widening as though she'd never been in a tenement before.

Her gaze snagged on him, and she started toward the stairs, apparently having every intention of coming with him. As Mrs. Shaw opened the door, he waited for Serena to reach the landing and join him, made the introductions, then stepped inside the dingy apartment.

He spent a few minutes jawing with Bob about how he was feeling. Same as the last visit, Bob declared he was ready to be back at work in the mill. Weston insisted he recover first, that he'd continue to be compensated for the lost wages.

All the while he spoke with Bob, Serena conversed with Mrs. Shaw and her two children, Tate clinging to her skirt and sucking his thumb.

They stayed longer than he'd anticipated, but once they were back on the wagon bench and heading down Main Street, Serena was full of questions about his employees and their families.

After he parked the wagon near the mercantile and they started toward the store, she paused on the boardwalk, her cheeks flushed and her eyes more alive than he'd seen them yet.

"Do you really want to buy me gifts?"

"Yep. Sure do."

"What will you allow me to get?"

"Anything." At that moment, with how pretty she looked, he'd buy her the world if he could.

"Anything at all?"

"Sweetheart, you can have whatever your heart desires." He liked the idea of being able to spoil her and make her feel mighty special.

A smile worked at the corners of her lips, and he suddenly wanted that smile to be aimed right at him every time.

"Then here's what I'd like." She took a deep breath and lifted her shoulders, as if gaining the courage she needed to state her wish. "Instead of buying anything for myself, could I use the money to purchase Christmas presents for the families who work for you?"

Presents for the families who worked for him? He opened his mouth but couldn't find a suitable response.

She continued before he could gather his thoughts. "I could give them each a gift basket, including some necessary items, maybe baked goods, perhaps even a few toys for their children."

He'd offered her anything. Told her she could get whatever her heart desired. Most women he knew would have enjoyed purchasing new items for themselves and for the barren house.

But Serena? What kind of woman was she to want nothing for herself and instead ask if she could give her portion to strangers?

"I realize this would be a big task." She spoke earnestly, clutching Tate's hand as the little boy tried to pull her forward. "But my mother did this on occasion for some of the poor families who lived near our ranch. I helped her fill the baskets and deliver them."

It'd be a mighty nice thing to do for all the mill workers and their families. But it'd also be a heap of work, and he didn't want to burden her with all that.

Her eyes shone with expectation.

He couldn't say no and disappoint her. "Let me think on it."

"Thank you, Weston." Her smile spread, bringing a beauty to her features that caught him off guard. In the sunshine, with her lips curved upward and the worry lines gone from her face, she was more than pretty. She was stunning.

He opened the mercantile store door, and she moved inside ahead of him with Tate. Had it been only yesterday that Weston had been jawing with Mr. Dankworth when she'd stepped into the store with the little fella?

"Mrs. Taylor," the store owner called from behind the counter, offering Serena the same smitten smile that he'd given her yesterday. "I didn't expect to see you again today, but what a pleasure." He rounded the counter and shuffled past several barrels, smoothing back his thin hair.

Weston closed the door and stepped directly behind Serena, a strange possessiveness taking hold of him. With the late hour of their wedding last night, the news of their nuptials obviously hadn't spread. He needed Mr. Dankworth and every other single fella in town to know Serena belonged to him now, so that no one got any ideas about stealing her away.

Not that anyone would try it. But with all that had happened so recently with Felicity, he reckoned he was a mite jumpy.

"Mr. Dankworth," Serena said hesitantly, probably wondering how to tell the store owner she was no longer available.

Weston knew exactly how to help her. He closed the last few inches that separated them by pressing his chest into her back and sliding his arms around her waist, embracing her from behind.

At his touch, she drew in a sharp breath but thankfully didn't pull away.

Weston leaned his head down so that his cheek nearly brushed against hers. Was he taking this too far? He hoped he wasn't. He didn't want to scare her away. But at the same time, he needed to show everyone that he had his loop around her. "Serena and me, we got married last night."

Mr. Dankworth halted, as did the other few customers throughout the store, and all eyes turned upon him and Serena and Tate. Mr. Dankworth's expression held more surprise than any of the others.

Weston liked the fella and wasn't fixin' to make him feel bad, but single women in the high country were as rare as a sober man in a saloon. Fair or not, Weston had been the one to win her, although he wasn't exactly sure how.

Her body was soft against his, not even the least stiff, which hopefully meant she wasn't opposed to him putting his hands on her now and again. Course, he wasn't intending to make a regular practice of it yet. Nope, he'd promised her he'd wait for all the touching and kissing and the likes until Christmas, and he was a man of his word.

But today, at this moment, he had to make a statement. "Told Serena she could buy everything in the store if she wants to." Would dangling the possibility of spending a heap of money at the mercantile help smooth over any ruffled feathers?

Mr. Dankworth stared a moment longer, his smile turning forced. "That's very nice of you, Mr. Oakley. Let me know if I can be of assistance." He sidled back around the counter, his shoulders slumping.

Weston shifted his hold on Serena, suddenly conscious that he'd spread his hands over her waist above her cloak. Even though layers of garments separated his hands from her stomach, he could feel the length of her torso almost all the way to her ribs. She was thin, but she had amazing curves and a womanly figure that were hard not to notice.

Even her backside against him was difficult to ignore. And the scent of her hair and skin. It was a combination of maple, cinnamon, and sugar. He was tempted to dip closer again and take another breath.

But he was making an idiot of himself by standing in the doorway continuing to embrace her. So he dropped his arms away and took a step back. "Ready to shop?"

She glanced around at all the wares, and a small flicker of longing crossed her features before she hid it as she dropped her attention to Tate and fiddled with his hat. "I'd like to wait until you decide on my doing the gift baskets."

Her aspiration was noble, and he liked that she was so thoughtful and giving and selfless. All the more reason to shower her with gifts. But he was gonna have to do so without her realizing he was giving them to her.

"I've already decided." Really, there wasn't anything to decide.

"You have?"

"Yep. You go on and do them."

"Really?" Her beautiful eyes fixed upon him with genuine gratefulness.

"Only if, in the meantime, you help me start picking out stuff for the house."

"I can do that." She looked around again, this time more eagerly.

He held back a smile. He'd waited a long time for a wife, and he was gonna take full advantage of his ability to spoil her. Every way he could. And maybe, just maybe, this time he'd find true love.

CHAPTER 10

Serena loved watching Weston teach Tate to ride a horse.

From her perch on the corral fence, she had the perfect place to observe the two—Tate on a gentle old gelding named Sam, and Weston walking alongside, encouraging and instructing him.

"Attaboy." Weston repositioned Tate's hands on the reins. "Now turn Sam my way."

Tate tugged against the reins, his face scrunched with concentration. Old Sam shifted his direction, and Tate broke into a proud grin. "Look, Ma."

Over the past week and a half of living with Weston, Tate had started calling her *Ma* instead of *Mama,* since that's mostly how Weston referred to her. Even though she missed the old name, she could admit she was relieved at just how much Tate adored Weston—enough that he was imitating everything the man did and said.

"I like how you're holding the reins so well." She smiled back at the boy, relishing the late-afternoon sunshine on her face.

Even though the day was cold and her breath formed white puffs in the air, the sun made being outside bearable.

Across the corral, Dusty and another ranch hand had sauntered over and now leaned against the split rails to watch the riding lesson. The men who worked the ranch and mills had been accepting of her as Weston's wife and so far treated her respectfully. She could see that they also respected Weston, which didn't surprise her considering how generous and kind he was to them. That had been clear enough during their visit to the Shaws that first day she'd ridden into town with him.

She'd been slightly embarrassed that day at the mercantile when she finally realized that every time she'd suggested something for the house, Weston had immediately added it to his tab —rugs, curtains, vases, candle holders, doilies, framed pictures, decorative pillows, globe lanterns, and more. He hadn't stopped to question any of her suggestions—not even the furniture.

They'd come home with the wagon piled high with all that Weston had purchased not only from Dankworth's but also from Hyndman Bro's and Simpkins.

In addition to assembling the gift baskets for the mill employees, her days had been busy arranging all the new purchases for the house. Slowly she'd begun to transform the place—including Tate's bedroom, which now contained a dresser and night table. Weston was having the bed made by a local carpenter, and for the time being Tate still slept with her in Weston's bed.

In some ways, she was relieved to have the little boy there to distract them. Not that she didn't trust Weston to keep his word about waiting until Christmas to consummate. But somehow, just the act of sharing the bedroom and bed heightened her awareness of him, and she could admit the arrangement was strangely appealing.

Was it because he was so attractive?

Today he was wearing his black Stetson and heavy leather-rimmed trousers with a matching leather coat. The spurs on his scuffed boots jangled with every purposeful step he took. His work-hewn body had the tough look of rawhide but also a rugged swagger of confidence.

Most of the time when she was with him, she just wanted to stare at him. And most of the time she resisted the urge. But right now while he was in his element in the corral with a horse, she couldn't keep from admiring the fine picture he made. Fine, fine picture.

As though hearing her thoughts, Weston shot a glance her way.

She rapidly shifted her attention to Tate with a new Stetson perched on his head—a black one that matched Weston's. He also had new trousers and a thick wool coat. Weston had insisted on buying it all for Tate during the same shopping expedition when they'd picked out the items for the house.

Tate had been thrilled to match his new pa. As if the clothing hadn't been enough, Weston had also purchased almost every toy being sold in the Fairplay stores. Tate had come home with toy horses, play guns, balls of every shape and size, an entire bag of marbles, picture books, a top—more than he'd had in his nursery at Stony Creek Ranch.

When she'd taken Tate over to the boardinghouse a few days ago to say goodbye to everyone and to thank the Courtney sisters for allowing her to stay there, Tate had been excited to share as much as he could about his new home and toys and clothes. She'd only had to think about the solemn and scared little boy he'd been when she'd arrived to know that she'd done the right thing in escaping from the stresses of living with Palmer's parents.

"You're doing great, Tate," she called.

He flashed his adorable smile again. "Me great."

"Yes, you're catching on fast." Although she could have taught Tate everything he needed to know about horses and riding, she wanted him to have the time with his new pa. Weston was busy most days from before dawn until after dusk. But once he walked into the house after dark, he spent the rest of the evening with them, having supper together and then talking and playing with Tate until the boy's bedtime, which was when she went to bed too.

She supposed at some point she would need to get accustomed to being with Weston alone. But, as with the bed situation, having Tate constantly with her brought a sense of security. His presence kept at bay any awkward moments with Weston.

For now she was content to allow their marriage to grow slowly. And it was growing. Even with Tate's presence, she and Weston had engaged in many conversations. He'd talked more about his family living in Breckenridge, how hard his pa had worked to build the ranch, the difficulties of their early years living in the mountains, and his parents adopting two of his brothers, Ryder and Tanner, after their pa had died. He'd also told her about his start in Fairplay and all that he'd accomplished.

He'd asked her about her family, and it had been easy to tell him about her parents and siblings and the sprawling cattle ranch she'd grown up on. She'd been surprised at how well he'd listened when she'd talked about how, at seventeen, she'd watched her mother die slowly from pneumonia.

Thankfully he hadn't pressured her to share about her marriage to Palmer, but a part of her worried that perhaps she needed to be more honest with Weston about all that had transpired with her father-in-law after Palmer's death. She wasn't necessarily deceiving Weston. She just hadn't explained her entire situation.

Now that she was married again, hopefully none of it mattered anymore. She prayed that she could finally put that chapter of her life behind her and forget all about her father-in-law's threats.

"How about if we take a little ride?" Weston halted with Tate a few feet from where she sat. His question was directed at her, and his eyes filled with expectation.

She gauged the sun's position above the western range and guessed sunset was at least an hour away.

"I've got something to show you both." Weston's tone had a mysterious and yet excited note to it.

"Me ride." Tate wrapped the reins more securely around his hand.

Weston chuckled. "Not today, little fella. But if your ma says it's okay, you can sit with me and help me with my horse."

Tate's eyes widened. "Ma?"

"Of course."

Weston gave a hand signal to his ranch hands. They grinned at him before ambling toward the barn. As Weston instructed Tate on how to dismount, she climbed down and tugged her cloak around her body, thankful for the heavy garment and the hood.

A moment later, Dusty reappeared leading Belle and Weston's gelding. With both horses already saddled, it was clear Weston had been planning the outing, and she couldn't keep from being just a little thrilled at his efforts.

In no time they were riding across the narrow bridge that spanned the South Platte River. Weston led the way into the foothills for a short while, reining in as they reached the edge of a thicket of blue spruce.

"Here we are." Weston swung his leg over his saddle and slid down effortlessly, surveying the pines.

The hills cast long dark shadows over the trees and brought

the chill of the cloudless evening. But the sunlight was still cascading over the distant snow-covered peaks.

Weston hefted Tate down, and Serena dismounted at the same time. Then Weston flipped open his saddle bag and removed an axe. As he slung it over his shoulder, he nodded to the evergreens, their boughs thick and the air laden with their scent. "Since we have less than two weeks until Christmas, reckon we need to get us a Christmas tree."

Tate peered at the nearest tree, one that had only half its branches. "Kiss-mas tree?"

"Yep."

Since Tate was only two, he likely didn't remember Christmas the previous year. Even though Mrs. Halifax hadn't thought to decorate for Christmas, Serena had done the best she could to add some festivity to the home. But finding and cutting a tree had been out of the realm of her abilities.

Serena reached for Tate's gloved hand, clasping it in hers. "A Christmas tree is a special tree that we bring into our home at Christmas time. We'll decorate it with all kinds of ornaments—strings of popcorn, buttons, and dried fruit. Then we'll also make ornaments from paper and candy."

"Me decorate Kiss-mas tree?"

"Oh yes. You and me and your pa." She glanced to Weston, hoping she wasn't overstepping herself by including him in the decorating.

He nodded. "As soon as you and your ma have the decorations ready, then we'll do it together."

Tate hopped up and down, his face alight with excitement.

For a short while they meandered through the trees, searching for the right one. She soon found herself laughing with Weston over Tate's antics, as he seemed drawn to the most deformed and disfigured of trees, especially those missing pine needles. Or he picked out impossibly tall trees or those too small to decorate.

Finally, they managed to find the right tree. Weston made short work of chopping it, then he tied it to the saddle behind him, and they reached home just as the sun was beginning to set. As Weston carried the tree inside, Tate held on to a branch, hefting and hauling the same way Weston did.

A small piece of Serena's heart ached at the picture of her son imitating the strong cowboy. It was almost as if she was grieving for all that she'd never had with Palmer. Even if Palmer hadn't died in the brawl, she couldn't picture him suggesting going to get a Christmas tree, much less bringing it inside and setting it up. He'd never been interested in the doings at home, had always spent his free time in town or visiting with friends. Weston, on the other hand, genuinely seemed to relish every moment of their time together.

After Weston nailed two boards to the bottom of the tree to form a stand, he positioned it in the corner of the parlor.

"It's beautiful." She'd shed her cloak and had helped Tate from his. The warmth from the fireplace was beginning to thaw her fingers and toes, but her nose and cheeks still tingled from the ride. Now she held Tate's hand to keep him from interfering with Weston's efforts.

Thankfully, Tate had waited patiently for Weston to complete the base, and he watched with rounded eyes, taking in the spruce tree that looked absolutely perfect even without any trimmings.

Weston stepped back until he was standing beside her. He was close enough that his arm brushed against hers. His coat was discarded with theirs, and he'd rolled up his sleeves, revealing the muscular tendons and prominent veins that ran up and down his arms.

He was a strong man. Not only physically, but he exuded an inward strength as well—one that wasn't overpowering or demanding or arrogant but steady and dependable and humble.

She could feel him giving her a sidelong glance, so she

shifted enough to meet his gaze. "Thank you for this and for everything."

"You're welcome." His eyes were especially dark, almost like midnight. Intense and probing. Was he searching her? If so, what did he want to see?

She shifted her attention back to the tree, suddenly breathless.

His hand brushed hers.

She didn't move. Was it accidental?

His fingers touched hers again, this time his pinky caressing the length of her pinky.

Her heart picked up its pace. That was most definitely not an accident. So what did it mean?

As he made another trail, he hooked his pinky through hers. Then he simply stood there, his pinky linked with hers as they stared straight ahead at the tree.

She could hardly focus. All she could think about was this slight connection she was having with him. It was sweet and tentative, almost as though he wasn't quite sure what he really wanted yet from their marriage.

She'd been trying not to think about the fact that he hadn't yet given her a ring—even though he'd told Father Zieber he would get one for her right away. But at this hesitant touch, she could sense that perhaps he was fighting fears of his own.

Was it possible they could both fight their battles together? And come out stronger as a result?

Before she could decide how to approach the question, he slipped his hand away from hers, breaking their contact. He pivoted away, swiped up his coat from the back of the chair where he'd draped it, then stalked across the room.

"I need to finish some chores. I'll be back for dinner." Without another glance back, he exited the parlor. A moment later, the front door closed behind him.

She exhaled a shaky breath. She'd never been in love before

—never even had feelings for a man, not even Palmer. So whatever this was she was beginning to feel for Weston was new, strange, even a little frightening.

Maybe it was for the best if she squelched it now while she still could, before it got too big. Although she feared that maybe she was already too late.

CHAPTER 11

"It's just around the next bend." Weston glanced behind him to make sure Serena was still on his trail.

Serena and Tate were draped in a bearskin robe atop Belle and plodded steadily along only a few paces away, the snow having given way to damp leaves and soil now that they were in the open Blue River Valley.

He breathed out a puff of relief that the trip hadn't been as difficult as he'd anticipated. Serena's faithful horse had handled the snow-covered trail and Hoosier Pass just as well as she'd predicted. Even though the distance between his home and his family's ranch was only twenty-two miles, the hard trek over the pass added extra time. On a good day he could cover the distance in three hours. They'd made the journey in a little over four.

"You're a good rider," he said over his shoulder.

"You sound surprised."

"Reckon I shouldn't be, not with you having grown up on a ranch."

"I can ride better than a lot of men."

"Blamed right."

His offhand compliment earned a half smile from her.

He slowed his mount and fell into step beside her. Engulfed in the thick dark fur, she looked like a pale fairy princess. Even though she had a rosy nose and cheeks, she'd assured him every time he'd asked that she was fine. Tate seemed warm enough too and had fallen asleep in spite of the jarring ride.

Weston let himself feast upon Ten Mile Range to the west with its snowy slopes and white peaks and miles upon miles of mountains running from north to south. The sight was as majestic as it had always been from the moment he'd first stepped into the area.

The higher elevation was a rugged and often difficult environment, even more so than Fairplay, and had helped shape him into the man he was. He was thankful for that. Yet he was glad he'd made his own way. As much as he loved his family, his ambitions had always soared beyond his pa's. He'd always been more driven, his plans bigger, his goals higher.

There hadn't been enough in Breckenridge to keep him there eight years ago. Not after losing Electra. But over recent years, as the settlement had grown and more people had moved to the area, he'd begun to see the potential for buying land and developing it.

He was even considering the option of building another mill since the Blue River flowed through the valley. While he was visiting his family for the next few days over Christmas, he wouldn't pass up the opportunity to investigate land options.

For now though, he needed to prepare Serena for meeting his big and overbearing family.

With Christmas only two days away, it was hard to believe he'd been married for about three weeks. Parts of the three weeks had gone faster than a greenie flying from a greased saddle. He'd helped decorate the Christmas tree so that it had been real pretty. When Serena had finished putting together the gift baskets, he'd joined her in delivering them, much to the surprise and delight of each of his employees.

Course, he'd kept up the riding lessons with Tate as often as he could—a couple times a week. And he'd gone shopping with Serena again, this time so that he could get her help buying for his family. Now his saddlebags were full with all that he'd purchased.

Yep. He and Serena had fallen into a real nice routine together. She was easy to talk to and be with, and so was Tate. Their presence in the home—and all her work at fixing it up—had been everything he'd ever dreamed of having in a wife and child.

But . . . parts of the three weeks had gone slower than a cow crawling through a cactus patch. Especially those parts where he'd been in the same bed with her. Like every night.

It'd been a good thing she kept the same bedtime routine as Tate and was already asleep whenever he lay down so that he wasn't tempted to reach for her. It was a good thing he was a heavy sleeper so that he didn't accidentally pull her into his arms while he slept. And it was a good thing she got up every morning before he did and was well out of the room before he could drag her back down when she was all sleepy-eyed and flushed.

Somehow he'd managed to make it through the nights. And maybe it was for the best Tate's bed wouldn't be finished until the day after Christmas. Because having the little fella sleeping only inches away had also squelched the temptation to draw Serena close.

He could admit he was still afraid things were too good to be true. It'd been that way with every woman he'd courted. He'd thought he was making progress, thought he was winning her over, thought things would work out, but in the end everything always fell apart.

Whatever the case, the getting-to-know-each-other phase

with Serena was fast coming to an end. Was it time to finally put his fears to rest and stop holding himself back?

He stuck his gloved hand into his coat pocket, and his fingers connected with the square box containing the ring he'd purchased the day after their hasty wedding. He hadn't given it to her yet. He'd been waiting for the right moment, but one hadn't come along—at least, not one that had felt right.

"This sure is different than Oklahoma." Her voice held a note of awe as she surveyed the mountains on both sides of the river valley.

"And different than Pueblo?" he asked.

She hesitated. Except for the brief comments she'd made on their wedding day, she hadn't spoken again about her first husband. She hadn't even talked about Pueblo and the ranch there. The honest truth was, he wanted to hear what her experiences had been like. Had her husband loved her? Had he loved Tate?

Weston couldn't imagine anyone not loving either of them.

Loving. His grip tightened on his reins. It was too soon to be falling in love with Serena. Wasn't it? He'd figured with their marriage being one of convenience—a mutually beneficial arrangement for both of them—that it might take a while for them to learn to love each other.

But the fact was, she was an amazing woman. He couldn't remember ever meeting another woman as giving, generous, and considerate. And she was an excellent ma to Tate, always loving but firm when needed.

Even Maude liked Serena—and that was a feat, since Maude didn't like too many people.

He drew in a breath of the thin but crisp high-altitude air and watched as the first sight of the ranch came into view: the split-rail fencing that ran the length of the wide-open grassland. At the center of the long stretch of fence, smooth log beams formed an entrance surrounding the wide metal gate. The top log was emblazoned with black metal letters that spelled out the name: *High Country Ranch*.

A dirt road wound back for at least a quarter of a mile before reaching the main house, which was situated at the base of a slope.

"There." He pointed to the wisp of smoke rising from a large log house, barely visible among the pines that surrounded it and provided a buffer against the snow and cold.

Serena straightened and followed his gaze to the house then looked north to the barns and corrals near several other smaller cabins for the hired men.

During this time of year, the main herd of cattle grazed in the enclosed fields around the ranch. But during the summer and autumn months, the cattle had free range to wander into the gulches and higher grassy pastures.

Mostly, though, his family bred horses. With the influx of settlers since Colorado had become a state, the need for horses had swelled. His pa and younger brothers were making a decent profit as they attempted to keep up with the demand.

Weston nodded toward the south field closest to them and the dozens of horses grazing there—the bays, chestnuts, blacks, grays, and roans. "My pa has invested more in horses over recent years."

She studied the herd. "Looks as though he has Morgans and mustangs?"

"A few Percherons and Clydesdales too."

"Some Appaloosas?" She nodded toward the group of spotted horses grazing together.

"Nope. Actually, those are a new breed my pa's been developing—one he's calling Colorado Oakley."

"They look tall and tough."

"Yep, they're bred to be steer savvy and hard workers."

They were approaching the gate, and he slowed his mount. As soon as his family converged, he likely wouldn't get any more time alone with Serena until they started back to Fairplay in a few days. He could admit he'd enjoyed the extended time with her over the past hours of traveling, and he wasn't ready for it to end.

"Reckon I oughta warn you about my family." He reined in at the ranch entrance.

She halted beside him. "That sounds ominous."

He peered down the dirt road but didn't see anyone. His pa and brothers and the other ranch hands were probably hard at work on one project or another at a remote part of the property or busy in the barns. The work on a ranch was never-ending, which was why he'd kept his spread in Fairplay small, so that he had the flexibility to pursue other ventures.

"No doubt about it, I love my family." He slid down from his mount. "But they're loud and busy. And they let you know what they think, whether you want them to or not."

"As they did with you about a wife?"

He slipped open the gate latch. "Yep. They've been nagging me worse than horseflies."

"I'm honestly surprised you didn't have a wife yet with as kind and good-looking—" She halted and then gave her head a curt shake as if admonishing herself. "I mean kind and generous."

As he swung the gate wide, he couldn't keep a grin from kicking up his lips. "So you think I'm good-looking?"

"Of course you are." She dipped her head, avoiding his gaze. Were her cheeks getting rosier? "It's a plain fact, and I'd be lying if I told you otherwise."

"Well, you're mighty fine yourself." She was more than *fine*. Even more than *mighty fine*. Especially sitting atop her black mare, wrapped in the bearskin, with the white peaks forming a backdrop behind her.

She kept her focus on Tate, whose long lashes rested against his cheeks.

What would it hurt to tell Serena some of how he was feeling about her? He might as well give her the compliment he'd been wanting to since they started out of Fairplay. "The honest truth is, you're so beautiful that I'd rather look at you than anything else."

Okay, so maybe that was too much sharing. He could have tamped down his ardor just a pinch instead of blathering like a besotted boy.

"That can't be the truth," she responded softly, peering out over the landscape again. "Nothing can compare to this."

"You can." There he was, doing it again. Making a fool of himself.

Though she didn't smile, her eyes filled with gratitude. "Thank you, Weston. You've been kinder to me and Tate than we deserve."

"This ain't about kindness, sweetheart. This is about the truth." Maybe his tongue was looser after the hours he'd just spent with her. Or maybe it was just getting harder to ignore his growing attraction. Whatever the case, his words were getting away from him today.

Thankfully, Tate chose that moment to open his eyes and sit up. As Weston climbed back on his horse and they started down the lane, he couldn't keep from stealing more glances at her, unable to stop himself from admiring her.

As they passed through the woodland of towering lodgepole pine, the house came into view, festive with boughs and wreaths decorating doors and windows. Before they could dismount, the front door swung open, and his ma stepped out onto the spacious raised porch.

Wiping her hands on her apron, she beamed as though she'd won a fortune in gold. Her face retained a youthfulness that belied the all-gray bun piled loosely on her head—gray that had come early. He didn't remember exactly when her hair had stopped being blond-red, but he suspected the change had happened when Pa had been fighting in the war and life had been especially stressful.

"Weston Charles Oakley," she called even as her gaze settled upon Serena and Tate. "I heard you were married, but I told Mav I wouldn't believe it until I saw it."

"Yep, Ma. I'm married." Thank the good Lord for that. He wasn't sure he could've survived one more visit with all the pestering.

Before Ma could get another word out, Clementine and Clarabelle were stepping onto the porch, drying their hands on their aprons too. As slender as Ma, the two were nineteen and nearly identical in their looks, having wavy blond hair with hints of red, bright green eyes, and naturally pretty features.

"I still don't believe it." Clementine flashed her sassy smile. "I predict Wes bribed the woman to pose as his wife."

"Clementine." Ma leveled a stern frown upon the girl.

"What?" Clementine pretended false innocence. "I'm simply repeating what Pa said."

Weston didn't dare meet Serena's eyes and chance giving away the truth—that they were almost correct. The marriage had been a bribe of sorts.

"You're being rude." Clarabelle, the quieter and more reserved of the twins, could still match Clementine with the amount of trouble she could cause. But thankfully, today she seemed inclined to be polite. She gave Serena a welcoming smile. "We're so glad you're here. Thank you for finally getting Wes to commit when no other woman could."

Weston sighed. One thing was for certain with his family: he never knew exactly what to expect.

CHAPTER 12

Serena awakened to a strange sense of contentment. She blinked in the early morning light and tried to gain her bearings in the loft where she, Tate, and Weston had been sleeping at his family's home

The memories came rushing back of the past two days at High Country Ranch with Weston's family. He'd been right to warn her. His family was loud and busy and always getting involved in each other's lives.

But after the initial introductions, the Oakleys had easily accepted her and Tate, welcoming them in as if they belonged. In fact, Weston's mother, Hannah, had gushed over Tate so much that the little boy had taken to her faster than he ever had to anyone else.

"He's my first grandchild," Hannah had declared with one of her warm smiles. "Of course I'm gonna spoil him."

Tate had not only become enamored with his new grandma but with his aunts too. Although it had taken him longer to trust Clementine and Clarabelle, by last evening he'd been sitting on their laps, letting them hug and kiss him and read him stories by the firelight.

The time with Weston's family had gone by quickly, mostly filled with cooking and eating and talking. But they'd also taken a sleigh ride around the ranch, gone sledding on nearby foothills, and attended a Christmas Eve service last evening at the church in Breckenridge.

She'd enjoyed spending time with Weston's family, including not only Maverick but Weston's other adopted brothers—Ryder and Tanner. Weston's pa was quieter and more reflective than the others, but he exuded a strength and wisdom that everyone respected.

Serena turned in the bed and reached for Tate to draw him closer. Feeling the empty spot beside her, wakefulness rushed in, and her pulse picked up speed. Where was he? Had he wandered off somewhere?

At his giggle coming from the living quarters right beneath the loft area, her heart rate slowed. Of course he was safe. Hannah had probably tiptoed up to the loft and carried him down just as she had yesterday morning when she'd heard him stirring. Except yesterday Serena had already been awake and trying to keep Tate from talking and waking Weston.

Clearly, without Tate in bed wiggling around, poking her eyes, or patting her cheek, she'd been able to sleep later this morning. How long had it been since she'd had that luxury?

She stretched languidly, but her bare foot brushed against another foot. Weston's. She held herself motionless.

His breathing remained even and heavy, as it always was when he was sleeping.

They'd had accidental contact under the covers over the past month, but thank goodness, the brief touches had never woken him.

She started to inch her foot away from his, but before she could move, he rolled from his back to his side, draping his arm across her waist.

She froze. What was he doing?

Once again she listened to his breathing. It remained unchanged. She turned her head enough that she could see his face. From the glow of a lantern and the fireplace down in the front room, enough light filtered up that she could see his features.

The layer of scruff on his jaw was darker and thicker than usual. His hair was endearingly messy, strands begging her to run her fingers through them and brush them back. And his normally taut muscles were relaxed, as if all the worries of his life had disappeared for just a few hours.

She rotated a little more, the chill of the loft skimming her nose and cheeks, but underneath the layer of thick blankets, her body was plenty warm, especially with Weston's heat against her.

She'd never thought she'd get accustomed to sharing a bed with a man, had assumed it would be as awkward and unpleasant as Palmer's visits had always been. But after the first few nights of worrying next to Weston, she'd realized she had nothing to fear from him. In fact, the sharing of their bed had become strangely companionable. His strength and power beside her was actually comforting.

Did she dare admit she liked this man who was now her husband?

His arm lay heavily over her, but it didn't feel suffocating or disagreeable. In fact, his touch was even somewhat exciting.

His hold was warm and solid . . . and caring. Weston cared about her. And that's what made him different from Palmer. Her first husband had never cared about her, hadn't even taken the time to get to know her. They'd been strangers when they married, and they'd remained strangers until he died.

But Weston . . . Since the first day, he'd shown her in large and small ways that he valued her and Tate—the shopping trips, the horse-riding lessons, the Christmas tree expedition. Even while here at his family's home, he'd made sure she was included, had everything she needed, and was enjoying herself. Sure, he'd gone off with his pa and brothers often to talk and work. But even when he was gone, she'd known he'd be there for her if she needed anything at all.

She let herself take in his broad chest, his undershirt stretching taut from shoulder to shoulder. She hadn't been exaggerating that day when she'd called him good-looking. Maybe she hadn't meant to tell him, but it had been the truth.

You're so beautiful that I'd rather look at you than anything else.

His reverent words had played over in her mind dozens of times since he'd spoken them before their arrival at the ranch. Even now the compliment swelled within, adding warmth to her body.

"Merry Christmas." His gravelly whisper startled her.

Her gaze flew to his face to find that his eyes were half open. And oh, goodness gracious, with his head on his pillow, he looked even more appealing than he did when he was all rugged cowboy.

"Merry Christmas," she whispered back. She had a little gift for him, something she'd managed to purchase with the meager earnings she had left from working at the boardinghouse. Should she give it to him now in private? It wasn't much, but hopefully he'd realize it expressed her gratitude to him for all he'd done for her.

His eyes opened a fraction wider, taking in the empty spot next to her. "Where's Tate?"

"Your mother must have come for him." She paused and listened. Tate's voice still mingled with Hannah's in the room below.

Weston seemed to also listen for a moment too before his lips curved into a gentle smile. "She's in heaven to finally have a grandbaby to love." He shifted his arm that was across her, then startled as he took in his position.

"Darn it all," he whispered as he started to lift his arm away. "Didn't mean to—"

Her hand darted out before she could think through her actions, and she captured his hand and brought it back down on her waist.

He grew entirely motionless, didn't even seem to be breathing.

Instead of immediately releasing him, she held on for an extra second. Then before she could make herself let go, she shifted his hand so that it was flat on her stomach.

Slowly he fanned his fingers out, spanning most of her abdomen and covering part of her ribs.

The heat of his touch seared through her nightgown so that she almost felt as if there were nothing between them. With her hand still upon his, she couldn't move, couldn't breathe, couldn't think of anything but the intimacy of his hold.

He seemed to start breathing again, but raggedly.

She waited, her muscles tensing for what he might do next. Would he do something else? Now that she'd given him permission to touch her?

Did she want him to caress her elsewhere? Was she really ready for that next step in their relationship?

He shifted his head on his pillow, his uneven breathing now closer to her ear.

She closed her eyes, bracing herself, unsure of what was happening but wanting more, maybe even *needing* more from him.

The warmth of his exhalations filled her ear, echoing so that suddenly her whole body seemed to awaken to him and the realization that his long, hard body was nearly brushing against her.

The awareness of him left her almost breathless, and she waited again—for what, she didn't know. Him to press a kiss on her ear? Into her hair? Maybe lean his body against hers more fully?

He didn't move for an agonizing few seconds, then he dropped his head lower so that his breathing now caressed her neck.

Would he kiss her? Oh yes, she wanted him to. She couldn't deny it.

Her fingers, still over the top of his hand on her stomach, tightened with need.

In turn, his hand beneath hers widened, his muscles growing taut. In the next moment, his lips touched her neck.

She couldn't hold back a soft gasp—one of both pleasure and surprise. She supposed it had been loud enough that anyone listening in the room below might have heard her. But with Weston's lips upon her neck, she couldn't find the decorum to care.

His mouth was tantalizing—so much so that she nearly arched up, need rising within her. Need she didn't understand but that she wanted to explore with him.

He laid first one kiss and then another on her neck, making a trail toward her collarbone, following her pulse. With each kiss, she gasped again, then again. Each barely audible, but distinct enough to draw Weston closer so that, before she realized it, he was flush against her side.

As his mouth finally closed over her collar bone, she arched into his hand on her stomach. She couldn't hold back a murmur of pleasure and might have even released a strangled cry, but then Tate called out from the steps. "Ma? Pa? Me open presents?"

The call sliced through Serena's haze of wanting. She scrambled up and away from Weston, attempting to put as much distance between them as possible before Tate arrived, no doubt with Hannah on his heels.

Sure enough, a second later Tate's blond head appeared on

the steps, with Hannah right behind, keeping a steady hand on his back to prevent him from toppling down the stairs.

Hannah's smile was smug as she helped heft the boy up the last steps. "He heard your hanky-panky and came to investigate, even though I tried to distract him to give you a little more time."

Tate climbed to his feet and then came running toward the bed as fast as his little legs would allow. "Me presents?" His face was filled with such expectation, and his eyes were rounded with wonder.

"He's ready for Christmas." Hannah stared at Serena and Weston and made no effort to hide her curiosity. "Too excited to wait for his ma and pa to—"

"Okay, Ma," Weston cut in. He reclined against his pillow, one arm propped behind his head, looking as calm as if he were talking about the weather. But oh so handsome, his biceps straining, his body stretched out, his legs crossed casually.

Tate crawled up onto the bed and plopped down between her and Weston.

"You ready, little fella?" Weston tousled Tate's hair.

Tate nodded vigorously. "Me ready."

Serena couldn't get her voice or thoughts to work like they normally did. Instead, she made the mistake of looking at Weston's mouth. At those lips that were just seconds ago taking their sweet time kissing her neck—lips that she wanted upon her neck again.

Could she find an excuse to send Tate back down with Hannah? Maybe Hannah could feed him his breakfast?

Hannah's smile moved into her eyes and crinkled the corners. "I just love seeing you two acting like newlyweds, and I'm sorry you couldn't have more time alone this morning."

"It's alright." Weston's tone took on a note of embarrassment.

"Sheesh, it's Christmas morning," someone called from

downstairs. Was it Maverick? "You can finish up later when we're not all waiting for you."

Oh no. Serena's heartbeat crashed to a halt.

"Let them at least have a last good morning kiss," came another call—a woman's voice. Clementine?

Had the entire family been awake when Weston started kissing her? Maybe the hour was later than she'd realized. Or maybe they'd all heard Tate and had awoken early to be with him.

Whatever the case, the family was congregated downstairs.

Serena could feel the heat of mortification moving into her cheeks.

"That's a good idea," Hannah was saying to Weston. "Give your wife another kiss and then come on down."

"Nope, we're fine." Weston's response was quick.

"Go on and give her a kiss, Wes." This call came from his pa. "We can wait a minute."

"Or five." Another voice dripped with humor. Was that Ryder? Or Tanner?

Goodness gracious. The whole family *was* downstairs waiting. And Weston had been entirely right about them all interfering in each other's affairs. In fact, they took interference to a new level.

Serena pressed her cold hands to her cheeks.

"You're not getting out of it, Wes." Hannah chuckled. "Give Serena a final kiss. I could tell she wanted more."

Could this moment get any more embarrassing? Serena sank back into the mattress.

Before she could grab her pillow and bury her burning face into it, Weston bent closer. He hovered above her, his eyes apologetic.

Tate, who had moved near their feet, was staring between her and Weston as if waiting.

Since it appeared that she and Weston were destined to kiss

again in the bed this morning, she'd have to keep it short and sweet with Tate looking on.

"They kiss yet?" The question rose to the loft.

Weston leaned in even farther, his chest brushing hers. Somehow, just that tiny contact took her back to a few moments ago when he was kissing her neck. The delicious heat returned but this time in a rolling wave that rippled through her.

He brought his hand up to her face, his fingers soft as he grazed her skin and then cupped her cheek. He focused entirely on her mouth, as if it were the prize and he wanted it more than he wanted anything else.

Her breath hitched, her chest rising against his and feeling the weight of him pressing in. She had the undeniable urge to wrap her arms around him and hold him close and never let go. But before she could manage to slip her hands around to his back, his mouth descended upon hers.

She wasn't sure what she'd been expecting. Perhaps the hard and unrelenting tension that had resulted when kissing Palmer. Never tender. Never passionate. It had almost been angry.

But with Weston, his mouth covered hers tenderly, as though he didn't want to push her too far, as though he intended to keep the kiss light and short, as though he was afraid he'd crush her.

But she wasn't crushable. She'd had to prove that many times over the past years—with her mother's death, with Palmer's unfaithfulness, with her father-in-law's accusations. She was a strong woman. And she wanted a strong kiss.

Without caring who was watching and listening and waiting, she reached for Weston's neck just as he began to back away. She wrapped her hands behind him and held him in place. In the same moment, she tilted up and chased after his lips.

He paused, clearly uncertain and unprepared for her initiating more.

She glided her fingers through the hair at the back of his neck and at the same time stroked his lips, asking him, urging him for more.

He hesitated just a moment longer, then dove back into her with a soft groan. This time he didn't hold back. Instead, the pressure was certain and hungry, as if she'd offered him a delectable dessert and he planned to have every morsel.

She wanted to have every single taste of him too. He was delicious—more delicious than anything she'd ever tried before.

His kiss turned hard and deep, each needy surge faster than the last, as if he was trying to get as much as he could before the feast was taken away. For a reason she didn't understand, his need only seemed to make her hungrier for more.

Little hands upon her legs tugged at her. Tate.

Tate was watching them kiss. Oh, lunacy of lunacies.

She broke away from Weston and scrambled off the bed. She stood as much as the slanted ceiling would allow, her breath coming in bursts, her chest heaving, her body trembling.

With her hands against her cheeks, she didn't dare look at Weston. She was too embarrassed to meet Hannah's gaze. Instead, she reached for wide-eyed Tate and hefted him onto her hip.

"Are you ready for Christmas?" Her voice came out shaky.

He nodded.

"Me too." She'd married Weston to keep Tate safe, hadn't thought about herself or what she wanted from a marriage or really even in life. But here with Weston and his big, endearing family, she wanted everything she'd thought she'd lost and would never have again—love, happiness, and the promise of a future.

Hannah had already started back down the stairs. And the murmur of voices from below told her that the rest of the family had been satisfied with their kiss and were moving on to other things.

But Weston? He'd draped his eyes with the crook of his arm and lay silent, unmoving in the bed. What was he thinking?

A moment later, he rolled over and climbed off the other side of the bed. As he stood, he swiped up his trousers from the floor and rapidly stuffed first one leg, then the other in them. With his back facing her, she couldn't see his expression or measure his reaction to all that had just transpired.

As he reached for his shirt, he started toward the stairs, slipping an arm into one sleeve as he walked. His back was rigid and his jawline taut, almost as if he was upset.

He paused on the top step as he drew up his suspenders. "Take your time. I'll meet you downstairs." He spoke quietly, almost tersely, and then continued without waiting for her response.

Had she done something wrong? Maybe she'd been too forward with the kiss. She opened her mouth to apologize but then stopped herself. She'd offered him her love. And there was nothing wrong with that.

Her love. Was it possible she was already falling in love with Weston?

Her heart swelled, longing mixing with fear. Yes, it had been easy to fall for a man as wonderful as Weston. But what if he wasn't ready to love her in return? What if he decided she wasn't enough for him? Especially when he learned more about her past?

She should have been honest with him from the start about the true reason she'd married him—to avoid losing Tate to Palmer's family. And she should have confessed that she'd planned their chance meeting that day on the road to his house.

She had to tell him—she would tell him . . . Maybe on the long journey back to Fairplay tomorrow.

In the meantime, she'd keep trying to win his fondness. And she'd pray that this time, with this marriage, she could finally be enough.

CHAPTER 13

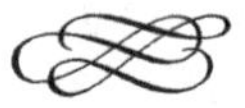

Serena couldn't remember ever having a Christmas celebration as festive as the one she was sharing with the Oakleys.

Even if the kisses with Weston had been an unexpected way to start the day, his family had teased them for only a minute or two before Tate's excitement over the opening of gifts had distracted everyone.

She lifted the coffee pot from the back burner and began to refill Weston's cup. The laughter and conversations in the front room wafted even to the far corners of the kitchen. The morning sunshine bathed the room, warming her. And the scents of cinnamon and sugar lingered in the air from the sweet rolls one of the twins had made and served while they'd been opening the gifts.

"I thought I saw you sneaking off." Hannah's cheerful voice came from behind Serena.

"Weston's coffee was low." Serena finished pouring the cup.

Hannah stood at the table and was sliding another sweet roll onto her plate from the few left in the pan. "He shouldn't be asking you to do that for him, dear. He's capable of refilling his own coffee."

"He didn't ask me." Serena set the cup on the table and reached for the small pitcher of cream. "I wanted to do it for him to be a good wife."

Hannah wiped her sticky fingers on the apron that covered the red calico dress she'd donned for the holiday. With flushed cheeks and sparkling eyes, the matron looked as though she'd never been happier. Likely, having all her children back in her home was the greatest Christmas present they could give to her.

"Now, now, dear heart." Hannah spoke matter-of-factly. "You already are a good wife."

"I'm trying—"

"In fact, not only should Weston be filling his own cup but he should also be the one tending to yours."

"It's alright." Serena poured a small amount of cream into Weston's mug, just the way he liked it—a fact she'd learned over the past weeks of watching him fix his coffee every morning. "I don't mind."

"That's the way Boone taught the boys—to look out for the needs of their women."

"I don't mind."

"No, no, no." Hannah began to bustle back to the kitchen door. "I'm getting Wes in here to do things right."

"Mrs. Oakley, please—"

"I insist you call me Hannah. Better yet, call me Ma."

Before Serena could stop the woman from making a fuss over the coffee, she disappeared into the front room.

"Wes!" Hannah's voice rang out. "Come here, son."

Serena pressed a hand against her forehead. She didn't want Weston to think she'd been complaining about him when all she'd been trying to do was be wifely and make sure he was happy.

The calls and conversation from the other room grew loud with teasing and instructions for Weston.

"Go on and kiss her again!" said one of the twins.

"Might as well take all the time you can get." The voice sounded like Maverick's.

Serena wanted to slink down and hide under the table, but as Weston was shoved into the kitchen, she held herself motionless.

He was grinning good-naturedly. Even so, mortification was rising swiftly within Serena, and she had no doubt her cheeks were coloring as a result.

At some point during the morning, Weston had groomed himself so that his hair was now neatly combed, and he'd donned a flannel shirt along with trousers held up by suspenders. He was as handsome as always, maybe even more so this morning—although she couldn't say exactly why. Maybe it was because he'd been smiling more often, especially during the gift exchange.

Now, as he came to a halt, he shot a glance her way, his expression filled with humor and a little embarrassment.

At least she wasn't the only one feeling the awkwardness of his family's matchmaking.

She held out the cup of coffee to him, the steam rising. "I just wanted to do something nice for you and didn't think I'd be stirring up trouble."

"Thank you kindly." He approached and took the mug. "But my ma is right, though. I should've been the one coming in and refilling your coffee."

She was just relieved the strain from their early morning kisses had dissipated and that Weston was back to interacting with her the way he normally did.

He took a sip, then gave her a grateful smile. "Next time, I'll be sure to take good care of you."

"You already are." And that was the truth. From the first day, when he'd driven her back to his home and searched for her horse, he'd done everything his ma and pa had taught him.

He set the cup of coffee down on the table, then stuffed his hand into his trouser pocket. He seemed to clutch at something there before pulling his hand loose. Then he stuck his hand in his other pocket and pulled out a small box tied with a red ribbon. "I was hoping I could get a minute alone with you to give you this."

He held out the box.

"This isn't necessary. Not after you've already given me so much." All month long, he'd constantly found ways to buy things for the house or for Tate or even for her.

He thrust the gift into her hands. "Of course it's necessary. It's Christmas morning."

She took it and fingered the satiny ribbon. She didn't want to keep comparing Weston to Palmer, but she couldn't stop herself. Weston was as opposite from Palmer as any man could get.

"Open it." Weston's voice rang with a note of eagerness, as though he truly cared about making her happy.

She tugged at the ribbon, and it unraveled and fell away. All the while, she could feel Weston's intense gaze upon her. What was he thinking about? Was he remembering their kiss from earlier? Was it vividly replaying in his head the way it was in hers? She wished she could study his face and decipher his thoughts, but she kept her attention on the gift.

With great care, she lifted the lid. There, on a bed of black velvet, was a gold necklace with a pearl at the center. It was gorgeous—and no doubt very costly.

"Weston." She breathed his name almost reverently. "You shouldn't have."

"I wanted you to have something nice."

"It's more than nice." This time she allowed herself to look up at him, finding him but inches away, his gaze upon her mouth, the dark blue swirling with hot sparks.

Was he thinking of kissing her again?

Her heart picked up speed. Did she want him to kiss her again? If it would be anything like the earlier kiss, then yes. She wanted it. Very much so.

Heat puddled low inside her belly—a delicious heat that made her want to press up against him and thank him with an embrace. Was this, then, what affection could be like between a man and a woman?

He was still staring at her mouth.

Should she tell him she would welcome another kiss? It was Christmas, after all, and their time of waiting had come to an end.

She couldn't be that bold, could she? But she also didn't want him to hesitate on account of her, especially if he was worried that she might not welcome him.

Surely there would be nothing wrong with giving him a hint that she wouldn't reject him if he did want to kiss more.

"Weston?" Her voice came out slightly breathless, and a flush moved into her cheeks at her brazen thoughts.

"Hmmm?" His voice came out a low rumble.

"I won't push you away—that is, if you want to—I won't be opposed . . ." The heat flamed into her skin. She was stumbling over her words worse than a drunk stumbling down a street.

Weston didn't move or respond.

Had she misread the situation? Maybe he didn't want to kiss her after all.

Finally, he cleared his throat and took a step back. "Listen . . ." He glanced toward the kitchen door as if he couldn't get out of the room fast enough.

She turned to face the stove. "I apologize—"

"No, don't. I should apologize."

"It's alright. I understand." But did she? What was going on between them when one moment he seemed interested and in the next he was pushing her away?

"Done kissing in there?" came one of his brothers' calls.

Serena busied herself pouring another cup of coffee—this one for herself, even though she wasn't particularly in the mood for more.

"I guess I should get back." Behind her, Weston's tone was hesitant.

She nodded and forced cheer into her answer. "Of course. I'll join you in just a moment after I get my coffee ready."

A moment later, his footsteps crossed the room and exited. Only then did she let her shoulders fall and a sigh escape from her lips.

Maybe she was letting her hopes get too high for her marriage to Weston. Did she need to keep her expectations more realistic?

After all, she couldn't forget that the good things in her life always seemed to come to an end. If she wasn't careful, she'd lose Weston. And she wasn't ready for that to happen.

CHAPTER 14

He was acting like a stubborn pack mule on an uphill climb, and he had been the entire ride back to Fairplay.

With the midday sun breaking through the clouds as Weston dismounted in front of his house, he could feel Serena's questioning gaze on him the same as it had been for most of the journey. No doubt she was full to the brim with questions—namely, why he was putting off their intimacy.

He wasn't sure himself. All he knew was that he'd about died and gone to heaven kissing her in bed yesterday. When he'd landed back on earth, it'd jarred him so that he hadn't been able to get out of the loft fast enough.

Then there'd been that interaction with her in the kitchen, when he'd given her the Christmas present. The strength of his desire for her had nearly swamped him, especially when she'd hinted that she'd be okay with him kissing her again. He was embarrassed to admit he'd had half a mind to drag her out to the barn and kiss her senseless. In fact, he'd been real close to it. He'd been almost desperate to taste her mouth again.

But a part of him hadn't quite been ready.

As she started to slip from the saddle, he reached for her waist, fitting his hands on both sides of her. Her hips were just as soft and curvy against his hands as he'd imagined. And yep, he'd been imagining a whole heap about her since holding and kissing her.

Even though he'd tried not to, his mind had wandered there anyway—every blamed second it could.

Shoot. No woman oughta feel as good as Serena did.

He set her and Tate on the ground and found his hands lingering on her a mite longer than they needed to. Tate wiggled against her, ready to be down after the hours of sitting and ready to greet Ranger who was circling around them with wagging tail. Tate's motion forced Weston to release Serena, but not before she glanced up at him again, her eyes uncertain and maybe even a little anxious, as though she knew something was bothering him but was afraid to ask.

"Me hungry," Tate declared as he toddled toward the front steps, Ranger right by his side.

The little fella had stayed awake this trip and had been talkative and full of questions nearly the entire way. It'd left little time for Weston to talk privately with Serena, which he clearly needed to do.

He probably should've found some time yesterday to have a conversation with her. But after exchanging gifts, they'd sung carols, played parlor games, feasted on an enormous Christmas dinner, and ended the day by reading the Scripture account of the birth of Christ.

By the time the house had finally been quiet, Serena had already gone to bed with Tate.

Now, as Tate began to climb the porch steps, Serena chased after him.

Weston wanted to follow after her, didn't want to confuse or hurt her by his stubbornness. But he had to take care of the horses and check on how things had gone during his absence.

Even so, he needed to say something eventually. He may as well say it sooner rather than later.

"Serena?"

She paused where she was holding Tate's hand as he attempted to climb another step. "Yes?"

"Reckon I need to do some jawing, if you've got the time." He forced himself to say the words, knowing he had to stop being a coward and face whatever was holding him back.

"Of course." Her eyes were solemn, and she set her lips into a straight line, as though she was already preparing herself for bad news.

He wasn't aiming to deliver bad news, was he? All he wanted to do was discuss what was happening between them. Maybe it was also time to tell her about Electra, his first love.

He waited for the stab in his heart that came at the thought of Electra. But strangely, he felt nothing—nothing but an angst to go after Serena right now and kiss her again. Serena was here in his life, more vibrant and alive than any of his memories of Electra from so long ago. Serena was the one who was his wife. Serena was the one he thought about day and night. Serena was the one he longed for more than he'd ever longed for anything else.

Not Electra. Not anymore.

And that was okay, wasn't it? After all this time since her passing, maybe he was finally moving the memories out of his heart and laying them to rest.

He patted his trouser pocket and the ring box. He'd wanted to give it to Serena yesterday on Christmas Day, but he'd held back and had instead given her the necklace.

She and Tate had given him a plaid wool scarf. He guessed she'd used the last of her earnings from the boardinghouse to be able to buy it for him, which made it even more meaningful.

The honest truth was, she was both beautiful and kind. There was no reason for him to hesitate in loving her. And he needed to allow himself—maybe even push himself—to move on.

He made quick work of unhooking their luggage from behind the saddles and emptying the saddle bags of everything his ma and sisters had sent home. He piled the goods on the porch outside the door, then led the two horses down the path behind the house toward the barns and corrals.

Dusty was in among the steers, clearing ice from the troughs. As Weston drew nearer with the horses, the cowhand straightened and pushed up his hat, revealing his roughened, scarred face.

Weston quickly surveyed his cattle, taking note of their condition, still as healthy and hearty as the day he'd left. "Much obliged to you for keeping an eye on the place while I was gone."

"Happy to do it." Dusty's normal smile didn't make an appearance. His expression was more serious than usual, making his droopy eye close up so that he looked like he was winking.

When Weston had passed by the mills and surveyed his place a few minutes ago, he hadn't noticed anything amiss. But that didn't mean nothin', since trouble had a way of creeping in without making a whole lot of racket.

He paused by the split-rail fence. "Something happen?"

Dusty lowered his axe and leaned against it. "Had an investigator come out this morning looking for your wife."

Whoa now. "What kind of investigator?"

"Said he was working for a man who goes by the name of Halifax."

Weston searched the corners of his mind for any recognition of the name. "Nope. Never heard of him."

"Apparently, Halifax is your missus's married name."

"It's Taylor."

Dusty shrugged. "Mr. Halifax says he's her father-in-law.

Claims your missus ran off with Tate, and that Tate belongs to him."

A cold shiver that had nothing to do with the winter wind prickled the back of Weston's neck.

Dusty glanced around, and seeing no one else, he continued, but not without dropping his voice a notch. "Said that the new missus is an unfit ma, and that before passing, his son said he wanted Tate raised by him."

The shiver slid down Weston's backbone, and he peered at the house, the cheery curtains in the windows all new since Serena had come into his life. Was there a lick of truth to the news the investigator had brought them?

Weston held out the reins of both horses to Dusty. The fellow set aside his axe, climbed the fence, and hopped down. "Reckon that fellow is stringing whizzers together worse than a politician."

"Yep. He's an old windbelly telling a yarn." But even as Weston agreed with Dusty, the certainty smacked him clear in the face. Serena had been hiding something from him all along—the real reason she'd come to Fairplay in the first place and why she'd agreed to marry him so quick-like.

Without another word he spun and stalked back to the house, his gut sloshing like it was full up with bad whiskey. It was time to get answers—maybe even past time.

As he reached the kitchen door and tromped inside, the sourness in his gut was lathered to a foam. He didn't pause to greet Maude, who was at the table slicing vegetables. He didn't pause to wipe his shoes or his hands the way Maude wanted him to. And he didn't wait for her scolding him as he crossed into the hallway. Instead, he listened for Serena—if that was even her real name.

Hearing voices and footsteps in the rooms overhead, he took the steps two at a time. As he entered into the hallway, he stopped short at the sight of her sitting on the floor with Tate in the bedroom, both still in their coats, Christmas presents from the family spread out around them. Thanks to Maverick, everyone had known about Tate and had been prepared with more gifts than one little boy needed.

Even so, it had warmed Weston's heart to see Tate so excited about the presents he'd opened on Christmas morning. Even now, Tate was touching each item with great pride—the little wooden trains, the harmonica, a knitted cap and mittens, and a ball and cup game.

At Weston's appearance in the doorway, Serena and Tate looked up at him. "Play with toys, Pa?" The eagerness in the boy's voice tugged at Weston. Did Serena's father-in-law really have more right to the boy than Serena?

Instead of answering Tate, Weston nodded curtly at Serena. "I need to talk to you. Now."

She rose right away, her brow furrowing. "What's wrong?"

He motioned to the hallway. Their conversation wouldn't necessarily be private from Tate, but at least they could speak without constant interruptions.

She stepped out, her face still flushed from the cold of the long ride. She untied the ribbon of her cloak as she turned to face him, strands of her hair having fallen, and now dangling around her face.

"Who's Mr. Halifax?" He kept his voice to a whisper, but it still came out as hard as a nail driving into a metal beam.

She blanched and took a tiny step back, clutching her cloak closed as if that could somehow protect her from his wrath.

"Don't lie to me anymore," he practically growled.

"I wasn't planning on it," she whispered. "I wanted to tell you, was going to tell you soon—"

"Who is he?"

"He's my late husband's father."

"And what's your real name? Is it Serena Taylor?"

"It's Anne Serena. And Taylor is my maiden name."

"So you're Anne Halifax?"

She jutted her chin. "I'm Serena Oakley."

He paced to the end of the hallway, swiped off his hat, and jammed his fingers into his hair. He should've known his marriage to Serena was too good to be true, should've known it would fall apart just like every other relationship he'd tried to have after Electra.

He stared up at the ceiling for several moments, then paced back to Serena.

Her eyes were round and full of remorse. "I'm sorry, Weston—"

"Does Halifax have the right to Tate?"

"No." The word came out hard. "Tate is mine. And I'll never let that man have him."

"He's saying your husband gave him Tate."

"Now that I'm married again, my father-in-law has no right to take my boy away."

Yep. This was why she'd been so ready to marry him. Because she'd wanted to find a way to protect herself and Tate from her father-in-law.

She'd used him, and that thought nettled him—although he had to quickly push aside the voice of reason that reminded him that he'd done the same thing, that he'd used her to appease his family.

Regardless, she'd lied to him about her identity, her reason for being in Fairplay, and why she wanted to be with him. Or maybe she hadn't exactly lied. Maybe she'd just left a whole lot of her story unspoken.

Either way, he had to get away from her and figure out what he was gonna do next.

"I'm going." He started toward the stairway.

She took a quick step after him. "Going where?"

"Reckon I'll ride into town and hear out Halifax and his side of things."

"He's a manipulative man," she called after him, no longer whispering.

"Manipulative? Really now?" He didn't bother whispering either. His question was loaded with insinuation. And it was unfair. But he was too angry to care. "I'll make up my own mind about that."

She didn't say anything more as he clomped down the steps and through the entry hallway. He shoved his way out the front door, and only then did he pause as he stood on the wraparound porch.

"Blast it all." He slammed his Stetson back on, pain riding his tail and shooting him full of bullets. He suddenly felt all out of air and energy, as if his lifeblood was draining from him. If he'd thought he'd been hurt by the other women who'd rejected him over the years, this pain couldn't even begin to compare. It was the worst yet, and he wasn't sure he'd be able to recover from it this time.

CHAPTER 15

Weston stalked into the dining room of Hotel Windsor and aimed for the corner table where the proprietor, Mr. Fehling, had directed him.

"Mr. Halifax?" he called, not caring about the stares he was drawing from the few other patrons lingering past the noon hour. The dozen or so round tables scattered about the dining room were still laden with plates and bowls mostly scraped clean, and the scent of beef stew lingered in the air along with the haze of cigar smoke.

Two men lounged at the corner table, and now one of them shifted to take in Weston as he wound his way toward them. With spectacles perched on his nose, the fellow watched with too much curiosity and calculation to be anything but an investigator.

How had the man tracked Serena to Fairplay? Currant Creek Pass leading into the South Park basin from the southern part of the state would have been snow-covered but not impossible to navigate. Even so, not many hiked up into the high country this time of the year.

Weston crossed the last of the distance and stopped at the table with a nod toward the investigator before homing in on the other man, who had to be Halifax. With brown hair sprinkled with gray, the fella had a hardened face, tanned from days spent in the sun and filled with leathery lines around his mouth that his long mustache didn't hide.

He held himself with a casual air, leaning back in his chair, puffing on his cigar and peering out the window to Fairplay's main thoroughfare, which was nearly deserted at midday.

Even though the fella was acting as though he hadn't noticed Weston's approach, Weston knew his tall, brawny body and imposing presence were difficult to ignore. Besides that, his anger had taken on a life of its own during the ride from the ranch to town. Now, that anger was stomping around inside him like a battalion about to attack.

Serena might have hidden her true identity for Tate's sake, and she might have failed to reveal her problems, but one thing was certain—Serena was a good mother. Weston had seen it from the first time he'd ever watched her interact with Tate. And if Halifax was saying otherwise, then he was lying.

Halifax blew out another cloud of smoke before dangling his cigar over the ash tray on the table and setting it into one of the grooves. "You must be Mr. Oakley," he finally said, his voice holding the swagger of a bull.

Weston didn't have the patience for fellas who thought too much of themselves, and he sure in high heavens wasn't about to let a dandy like Halifax come to Fairplay and push him—or Serena—around.

"Heard you're making claims on my son." Might as well lay out the cards and see if this man could play a straight game or if he'd bluff his way through it.

Halifax pushed back from the table, his chair scraping, both hands on his revolvers at his waist.

Weston tensed and let his hands rest upon his revolvers too.

The investigator quickly rose and backed away. No doubt he feared he'd end up in the middle of a duel. No doubt he was right. Weston didn't have to be around Halifax longer than a few seconds to realize the man wasn't right for Serena or Tate. He guessed the man's son—Serena's first husband—hadn't been right for her either.

Not that Weston was necessarily the right man instead. But if her previous husband had been anything like his father, then it was all too easy to see her marriage had been miserable.

"May as well head on back to Pueblo, Mr. Halifax." Weston spoke loudly enough that everyone in the room could hear him clearly. He wanted as many witnesses to this conversation and his claim on Serena as possible. "I married your daughter-in-law, and she's mine now."

The honest truth of his own words hit him hard. Serena was his. She belonged with him. And he wanted her.

That didn't mean they wouldn't have some things to work through. That didn't mean their marriage would be easy. And it certainly didn't mean they wouldn't have problems cropping up again. But Lord in heaven above, he loved her. And really, that's all that mattered.

Yep. He loved her. Even if he was mad at her for holding back all this about her past, he reckoned he could understand why she'd done it when she was facing a difficult man like Halifax.

"You can have the woman." Halifax held on to the handles of his revolvers. "I don't need her. But the boy is mine, and I intend to take him home with me."

"Tate belongs to Serena."

"Tate belongs to my son—"

"Belonged. Your son's dead and ain't got a claim on anyone now."

"He told me I could raise Tate."

"A mother has the right to raise her own child. And there's not a judge alive who would disagree with that."

"They will when they learn how unfit she is."

Weston scoffed. "Everyone in this town has seen with their own two eyes what a decent and kind woman Serena is. Won't be a single person who'll say otherwise."

"Weston's right." A fellow at one of the other tables spoke up. "Never met a nicer lady in all my days."

Mr. Fehling had stepped into the room, holding a coffee pot. "She gave Christmas baskets to each of the mill employees, even though she hardly knew them."

"That's right," said another. "And she took care of a sick old man out at the Courtney Boardinghouse and did a fine job."

"I saw her every week with her little boy in town," called someone else behind Weston. "And she was as sweet with him as could be."

Jericho Bliss, the Pinkerton agent who worked in the high country, hadn't said a word from his spot at another corner table, but he was watching Halifax intently.

Halifax's jaw twitched, as did his fingers. The man was lanky and wiry, full of muscle, and clearly a fighter, like most hard-working cowboys.

But Weston wasn't about to let the fella intimidate him. He braced his feet apart, willing to defend Serena's honor as well as her right to keep her son, even if he had to get hurt to do so. "Might as well admit defeat, Halifax. You heard only a handful of people praise Serena. You can bet the rest of the town'll say the same thing."

Halifax tipped up the brim of his hat. "She can have more children. Yours. But I'll never have anyone else."

Weston wanted to feel sorry for the fella, but he couldn't. Not after the way he'd threatened Serena, called her unfit, and had probably tried to take Tate away from her already.

Weston shrugged. "Someday when Tate's old enough to

make up his mind for himself, maybe he'll want to meet you. By then, if you work at it, you might be worthy enough to spend time with him."

"I'm not planning to wait that long."

Weston's backbone turned to steel, and he met the fella's gaze head on. "Stay away from Serena and Tate, do y'hear?" He couldn't keep the growl from his voice. "If you come anywhere near them, I'll make sure you regret it."

Without another word, he spun on his heels and started back toward the door. He wasn't sure what he'd do to Halifax if he showed up in Fairplay again. But one thing was certain. He planned to keep Serena and Tate safe, no matter what that took.

"Watch out!" Bliss, the Pinkerton agent, shouted and then a gun blast resounded behind Weston. He didn't stop to think. Instead he dropped behind the nearest table just as a bullet whizzed past him and crashed into the front window, shattering it.

Another shot came from the direction of Bliss, who was also down on the ground, taking cover behind a table but with his revolver out and pointed at Halifax.

The other men in the room were ducking, all except Halifax, who took aim at Weston again.

A blood stain was forming on the fella's shoulder, where he'd obviously taken a bullet from Bliss. Even though one arm was injured, Halifax squeezed the trigger of his second revolver.

Weston dove to the floor, narrowly missing another bullet.

Holy high heavens. Halifax wasn't messing around. No wonder Serena hadn't wanted to reveal her identity and chance having this man track her down.

Weston sucked in a quick breath, tossed a prayer heavenward, then rose and aimed, hoping he could hit and disarm Halifax before the man could hurt anyone else.

But Mr. Fehling had somehow managed to replace his coffee

pot with a rifle. The hotel proprietor didn't hesitate. He pointed the barrel directly at Halifax and shot.

As the bullet hit its target, Halifax met Weston's gaze, his eyes bearing sadness and regret. Then the momentum of the blast threw him backward against the table he'd vacated. He crashed into it, then fell to the floor.

Halifax clutched his chest where the second bullet had hit him, blood rapidly seeping through his garments and turning his hands slick with crimson.

Slowly Bliss stood, one revolver still trained on Halifax and the other on the investigator, who had both hands raised in a show of surrender.

Weston pushed up until he was standing. He brushed his hand over his body, expecting to feel blood or a wound, but there was nothing. He was alive and unharmed, and suddenly all he wanted to do was ride as fast as he could back home and make sure Serena and Tate were alright.

After exchanging a few words with the Pinkerton agent, he strode from the hotel and was mounted and galloping hard north, need pulsing through him with such intensity he could hardly breathe.

He loved her. The words pounded through his head in rhythm with the hoofbeats. But he'd been a fool and had almost pushed her away. His pa's words from when they'd parted earlier in the day resounded in his head: *Serena's a good one. Don't sabotage this relationship like you have all the others.*

Weston had nodded but had let the advice slide right out of his mind, like he had all the other words of wisdom his father had given him. But what if his pa was right? What if ever since Electra, he'd always been looking for ways to make relationships fail?

Maybe he'd been afraid to let himself love again for fear of losing. Or maybe he'd never believed he could love anyone the way he'd loved Electra.

Whatever the case, it was no coincidence that he'd failed at all his past relationships. Anytime something went wrong, he walked away.

Just like he was doing with Serena . . .

He'd been scared to give her his whole heart. Then, at the first problem that'd manifested itself, he'd done what he was good at—he'd pushed her away.

But the honest truth was that he loved her. That love had been building all month so that now it thrummed through him. The closer he got to home and to her, the stronger the need pulsed, so that he wasn't sure how he'd ignored it for so long.

Serena was everything he wanted and needed in a woman, and it was past time he told her that.

As he finally reached his land and raced down the lane past the mills, he didn't bother stopping to talk to any of his customers or employees. In fact, he didn't even wave a greeting. He headed directly for the house and hopped down before his horse came to a complete stop. He took the stairs two at a time, threw open the door, and started up the stairway.

"Serena?" he called.

The house was eerily quiet.

She was probably upset, and he wouldn't blame her if she didn't answer him.

"Serena, I'm sorry." His voice echoed loudly enough for her to hear, wherever in the house she might be.

As he reached the second floor, he stalked down the hallway, his boots clunking loudly. He glanced first in Tate's room and then in his and Serena's. She wasn't in either, and there was no sign of Tate.

Weston raced back to the stairway and stopped short at the sight of Maude at the bottom, her wizened brown face set into a scowl.

"Where's Serena?" He almost couldn't get the question out because he dreaded Maude's answer.

"What do you think?" Maude fisted her hands on her hips. "She and the boy left you."

CHAPTER 16

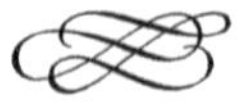

Serena dug her heels into Belle, urging the horse into a faster gallop. Only one thought charged through her —she had to get away from Mr. Halifax before he caught her and took Tate from her.

"No, Ma!" Tate's sobs reverberated against her. From his spot in front of her in the saddle, he wiggled as if he had every intention of sliding down. "Me go home."

A lump formed in her throat. It wasn't their home anymore. It couldn't be. As much as they cared about Weston and loved living there, she had to find a new place where she and Tate would be safe from the reaches of Mr. Halifax.

Besides, Weston didn't want her there. She'd had the feeling he was hesitant to love her. Now he was angry that she hadn't revealed the danger she and Tate were facing from Mr. Halifax. In the end, maybe Weston would be glad their marriage hadn't worked out.

"Please, Tate." Serena tried to hug the boy and comfort him as best she could. "We have to go away."

"Me want Pa!" His wail rose above the thundering of Belle's hooves, and it echoed in the grassland that spread out around them, dead and dry and deserted, not a creature in sight—not even the gophers.

"Pa can't go with us." Serena didn't know where they should run to next, but she found herself heading back up the road toward Hoosier Pass and Breckenridge—the same gradually inclining road she'd traversed a short while ago on the way back to Fairplay.

Weston's family had been so loving. Would they let her stay for a day or two until she could decide where to go and what to do next? Surely Mr. Halifax wouldn't track her there, would he?

"No, Ma. No." Tate's voice echoed with brokenness, slicing into Serena. She didn't want to hurt Tate by tearing him from Weston. Not after how quickly he'd grown attached to his new pa. Clearly Tate had sensed how genuinely Weston had cared about him. And that had helped Tate cling to her less and had even made him less afraid of new people.

After such progress, could she really take Tate away?

Even if Weston was angry with her for the deception, he was an honorable man and wouldn't cast her out. He'd also never collude with Mr. Halifax to take Tate away. Weston wouldn't be so cruel. It wasn't in his nature.

Besides, she'd done nothing wrong, and surely after thinking about it, Weston would realize that.

She'd done nothing wrong . . . except that she was running away like a coward . . . again.

Her hold on the reins loosened, and Belle immediately sensed the change in her intensity and slowed her gait.

Tate pushed away from her embrace. His cheeks were streaked with tears, and his nose was running. "Me love Pa."

She swallowed the swell of emotion that continued to clog her throat. "I love him too." She'd never loved a man before—at least, not the way she'd grown to care about Weston. And she didn't want to run away from him, didn't want to leave him, didn't want to lose him.

She wanted to spend her lifetime with him, learning to love him even more.

She tugged on the reins, bringing Belle to a halt.

Was it time to stop running away from her problems and instead stay and fight for her marriage? Maybe she needed to fight for her right to keep Tate too. She hadn't been a bad wife or a bad mother.

Yes, she'd need to apologize to Weston for deceiving him. She should have told him about her situation right from the start. But she was strong enough to stay. She was strong enough to fight. And she was strong enough to be a good wife to Weston.

In fact, maybe she'd been a good wife to Palmer too. After being with Weston and experiencing his kindness and consideration to both her and Tate, it was easier to see Palmer's insufficiencies. What if the problem hadn't been her? What if it had been him?

"Go home?" Tate peered up at her expectantly, as if sensing the resolve beginning to course through her.

If she ran away every time trouble came riding after her, she'd be teaching Tate to do the same. And she didn't want him to be a coward. She wanted him to learn to fight against adversity.

She veered Belle back around so that she was facing Fairplay. Yes, she'd let herself believe she wasn't enough for too long, and it was time to stop. She guessed that it wouldn't always be easy and that she'd still have many days when she doubted herself.

But today she could start by talking to Weston and telling him everything about Palmer and her time living with the Halifaxes.

"Let's go home." She kissed Tate's forehead, and he smiled through his tears.

She nudged Belle into a trot. As she rounded the riverbend and the open prairie spread out before her to the south, she caught sight of a lone figure on horseback riding hard in her direction. A man in a black Stetson, with broad, muscular shoulders that contained enough brawn to wrestle a bear.

Weston? What was he doing riding north? Was he coming after them?

Her heart gave an extra beat at the prospect. But she quickly forced herself to think realistically. He'd been angry with her. He deserved her apology. And he might need more time to learn to love her the same way that she loved him.

Either way, she needed to tell him she wasn't running away from him or their marriage and that she wanted to work through their issues.

"Serena!" His shout wafted across the barren plains.

At the sound of Weston's voice, Tate sat up straight, searching all around eagerly. At the sight of the horse and rider, he began shouting. "Pa! Pa! Me love Pa!"

Tears sprang into Serena's eyes. Weston was all too easy to love. It hadn't taken Tate long to love his new Pa. And it hadn't taken her long either.

"Me love Pa!" Tate shouted again.

Weston was rapidly closing the distance, his horse thundering powerfully.

Serena reined in, her fingers suddenly trembling. She prayed desperately that, at the very least, he'd listen to her, give her the chance to explain herself.

As he reached her, he jerked his horse to a halt. His jaw was clenched in tight lines. His brow was furrowed beneath the brim of his hat, and his blue-black were eyes filled with angst.

He slid down from his mount and came straight toward her, strength radiating from each hard step. "Serena—"

"Me love Pa." Tate held out his arms toward Weston.

Weston didn't hesitate for a second. He lifted Tate down from the saddle and into his arms, and the little boy went to him eagerly, wrapping his arms around Weston's neck.

Weston hugged him close, and Tate laid his head on Weston's shoulder, the stiffness dissipating from the little body as if he'd finally reached the place he wanted to be.

Tears sprang to Serena's eyes at the sight of her boy with such a man. This was one reason, among many, that she'd fallen in love with Weston: he was so tender and loving to Tate.

"I love you, too, little fella." Weston planted a kiss on Tate's head against the knitted cap covering his pale hair.

"Me go home." Even though Tate's words were muffled against Weston's coat, they reverberated through Serena.

She hadn't really had a home since leaving Oklahoma. But since the day she'd moved in with Weston, she'd felt as though she'd come home.

"I ain't letting you go." He hefted Tate closer, but his gaze locked now with hers. "You're mine now. And you belong with me."

Her heartbeat spurted forward. Was he talking to her now too?

"I'm sorry, Serena." His eyes held hers. "Or should I call you Anne?"

"Serena." The new name seemed fitting for the newer and stronger woman she wanted to become.

He nodded. "I should've never doubted you for a single second."

"I should have told you the truth right away, and I apologize."

"You had a real good reason for keeping quiet. And even if you didn't, I should've reacted differently, with a whole heap of patience."

"But I wasn't honest. Even that night when we got married, I purposefully set out to meet you on the road. I let Belle loose because I wanted a chance to see if I should add you to my possible-husband list."

He reached out a gloved hand and stroked Belle's muzzle. "Reckon I owe Belle a favor, then."

Serena's breath hitched. What did he mean? Wasn't he frustrated with her for more deceitfulness?

He glided his hand over Belle for another second before reaching for Serena's hand, still on the reins. He circled his hand around hers. "The honest truth is, I've been holding myself back from love for a long time. For the past eight years, to be exact—ever since my fiancée died."

His fiancée had died?

Weston met her gaze frankly. "She was out rounding up stray cattle when a winter storm struck. She got lost . . ."

How tragic. "I'm sorry, Weston."

"She never made it back to Breckenridge to her family's ranch. I didn't even know she'd gone missing until it was too late."

"I can't imagine how hard that must have been."

Weston nodded, swallowed hard, then took a deep breath. "I've been hanging on to her for too long. But since meeting you, somehow I've finally been able to let go. And you're the one I'm wanting to hold on to now."

The air inside her remained stuck. Could he really be saying what she thought he was?

"I was trying to fight my feelings for you, trying to protect myself from getting hurt. But it hurts more to think of you not in my life at all."

"But I don't want to bring you into the middle of all my problems with my father-in-law. He is a dangerous man—"

"*Was* a dangerous man." Weston's expression turned solemn. "When I rode into town, I told him to leave you and Tate alone. Reckon he didn't like me telling him what to do, so he started shooting at me."

"Shooting at you?" She scanned him, her chest tightening. "Did he hurt you?"

"I'm fine. Not even a scratch."

Weston had defended her and Tate to her father-in-law. She should have trusted him, should have known he'd see the truth of her situation.

"Turns out the other fellas came to my defense. And when I left town, Mr. Halifax was breathing his last."

She slumped in the saddle, relief weakening her. She knew she ought to feel some sadness for the man who was Tate's grandfather, but she was only glad that, finally, she'd no longer be in danger of losing Tate to him.

The afternoon sunshine was lending her some warmth, but she shivered anyway.

Weston tugged at her hand, and she dismounted so that she was standing in front of him. Tate was still clinging to him and probably wouldn't let him go anytime soon.

Weston didn't seem to mind. In fact, he was still holding Tate just as tightly. "What I'm trying to say is that I love you. I love you more than I ever thought it possible to love one woman."

A soft sob swelled and escaped before she could stop it. Quickly, she cupped her hand over her mouth to catch any more emotion. But even as she did, her eyes brimmed with tears.

The hardness was gone from his face, replaced by earnestness. "I want you to come back so that I can prove my love to you today and every day for the rest of my life."

This time a tear escaped.

His brow began to furrow. "Please, Serena. You don't have to feel the same. I promise that I'll do my best to love you enough for the both of us."

"You don't have to do that, because I already do love you."

At her declaration, the shadows in his eyes fell away.

She couldn't bear to be apart from him for a second longer. She stepped toward him and wrapped her arms around him.

Even though Tate's little body prevented her from hugging Weston completely, she sidled into the crook of his body.

For a long moment, he held her with one arm and Tate with the other. Finally, Tate began to wiggle, and Weston broke away from her to set the boy down on the road.

"Me ride with Pa?" Tate grabbed the dangling reins of Weston's horse.

"Yep. You can help me, little fella." Weston reached for Serena's hand. "But first, I want to give something to your ma."

Before Tate could question him, Weston lowered himself onto one knee before her. He pulled a small box from his pocket, then he lifted the lid and held it out to her. "I was a fool for not giving this to you earlier. Can you forgive me?"

The beautiful rose-gold band shimmered in the sunlight, revealing a pattern of twisted vines that surrounded an opal. It was exquisite, and she loved it because it was from him. "Of course I can forgive you. I just hope you can forgive me too."

"Done."

"Thank you." She tugged off her mitten and then gave him her hand.

Gently, he slipped the ring down her finger. "I'm claiming you, sweetheart. Now you're mine."

As he settled the ring into place, all the love that had been growing for this man swelled within her. She wished she had something to give him in return, something that would show him just how much she wanted to claim him too.

She could think of only one thing. She tugged at Weston, drawing him back to his feet. Then she pulled him toward her and captured his mouth with hers. She didn't have much to give, but she offered him a kiss that was filled with all her passion . . . and with the promise of all that was yet to come.

If you enjoyed Weston and Serena's story, I invite you to return to Fairplay, Colorado for more sweet romances with my **Colorado Cowgirl Series**:

Committing to the Cowgirl

After years away, Astrid Nilsson has returned home to Colorado, hoping to become Fairplay's second doctor and to find healing for her reoccurring consumption. Dr. Logan Steele is seeking to hire a male physician to take over his clinic after he goes back East. When Astrid, his childhood sweetheart, insists that she's the one for the job, he offers her a bargain she can't refuse: pretend to court him to appease his mother and he'll give her the doctor position on a trial basis.

Cherishing the Cowgirl

Charity Courtney is at her wit's end trying to save her boardinghouse from a bank foreclosure. Wealthy railroad magnet Hudson Vanderwater hears of Charity's plight. Although he comes across as cold and calloused, he is drawn to helping women in need because of a tragedy that destroyed his sister. He concocts a plan that will save Charity—he'll employ her and rent her boardinghouse for the month and in doing so alleviate her debt.

Convincing the Cowgirl

When unexpected visitors arrive at the Courtney Boardinghouse and claim the place belongs to them, Patience Courtney finds herself homeless and penniless. When wealthy rancher, Spencer Wolcott, proposes a marriage of convenience, Patience accepts the arrangement. In exchange for a new home, she agrees to become the mother to Spencer's precocious little girl so that he can manage his prosperous ranch.

Captivated by the Cowgirl

Now that her sisters are both married, Felicity Courtney manages the Courtney Boardinghouse alone. After nearly collapsing from exhaustion while caring for an invalid man and his wife who are staying at the boardinghouse, Felicity posts an advertisement for a hired hand. Philip Berg, a prince in disguise, is hiding in Fairplay while attempting to stay one step ahead of an assassin. When the spirited Felicity Courtney tacks up a notice that she is hiring help, he offers to do the job.

ABOUT THE AUTHOR

Jody Hedlund is the bestselling author of more than forty novels and is the winner of numerous awards. Jody lives in Michigan with her husband, busy family, and five spoiled cats. She writes sweet historical romances with plenty of sizzle.

A complete list of my novels can be found at jodyhedlund.com.

Would you like to know when my next book is available? You can sign up for my newsletter, become my friend on Goodreads, like me on Facebook, or follow me on Twitter.

The more reviews a book has, the more likely other readers are to find it. If you have a minute, please leave a rating or review. I appreciate all reviews, whether positive or negative.

DOCTOR'S SNOWFLAKE BRIDE

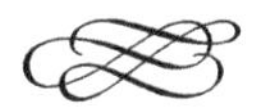

LACY WILLIAMS

Doctor's Snowflake Bride

lacywilliams.net

CHAPTER 1

Minnie Bannister heard the last hiss of brakes as the train slowly *chug, chug, chugged* its way out of the station, leaving her behind.

She felt as if she hadn't caught her breath since the conductor had passed through her passenger car calling for the stop—still faint and a little nauseated.

What if coming to Cooper's Hollow was a mistake?

She pushed aside the thought. She'd made this choice. Prayed over it. Besides, she'd severed all ties. Traveled several hundred miles to this tiny Wyoming town. It was even smaller than the last stop, Bear Creek.

This wasn't a mistake.

But it *was* cold.

She craned her neck, trying to see through the falling snow that seemed to be growing thicker by the moment.

It was December twenty-third. Almost Christmas. There had been a few people on the platform when she'd disembarked. That number had dwindled. Where was Mr. Black?

She didn't know what he looked like, other than the few details he'd written in his last letter.

Tall. Dark hair. Brown eyes.

A cold finger of wind slipped down the back of her worn woolen coat, and she shivered.

Mr. Black had agreed to meet her train. If he wasn't here, she would need to find a place to wait. Maybe the stationmaster would be able to help her.

She'd only taken two steps when a gust of wind seemed to split the falling snow like a curtain pulled back. A tall figure in a dark coat and hat appeared, and her stomach took a tumble.

Was that—?

He strode toward her, his steps sure.

It must be Mr. Black.

The sun had barely made itself known today, blocked by slate-gray clouds. It had to be sunset, because the sky seemed even more dim. A single lantern hung from the station roof, but it didn't offer much illumination in the blowing snow.

Mr. Black came to a stop before her. He'd spoken true in his letter. He was terribly tall. So much so that she had to stretch her neck to look up into his face.

She hadn't expected someone who advertised for a mail-order wife to be so handsome. He had a craggy look about him that fit what little of the distant mountains she'd seen today. His eyes were sharp and intelligent. And his gaze was inspecting her as if he felt the same catch in his breath that she did—as if he couldn't quite believe his eyes.

"You're here." She breathed the words more than spoke them.

"You're late." Somehow, his dry delivery made her smile. Perhaps because she sensed his annoyance was for show.

"My train was delayed out of Cheyenne."

Something shifted in his eyes at her simple statement. Or maybe she imagined it, the growing dusk and falling snow playing tricks on her eyesight.

He glanced behind her at the empty platform. "Where are your trunks?"

Her cheeks heated. She'd written that she did not have many physical possessions, but it was still painful to lift the carpetbag and force a smile. "I'm afraid this is all I have."

She'd written all about growing up in the orphanage, being turned out when she was fourteen, and working as a housemaid for the past six years. But she hadn't outright said that she'd barely earned enough to scrape by. Nothing of the nights she'd gone to bed with her belly rumbling in complaint because she hadn't had any supper.

She was determined to start this marriage off on the right foot, and dwelling on her poor prospects and meager belongings wasn't that foot.

"I can't believe how open it is." She gestured with her free hand, intending to encompass the wide sky she'd glimpsed earlier. It was a little silly to do so now, with the snow obscuring everything. "What I could see from the train was so beautiful."

His eyes narrowed slightly. "What about the isolation? I thought you were set against such a small town."

She felt a blip of unease. She'd never written any such thing. Had he misconstrued one of her missives?

She didn't want him to have any reservations. She'd lived in horrible tenement apartments. Once, in a tiny, suffocating closet in an attic eave. Anything would be an improvement over that. She was determined to make this work, to be happy with whatever came her way.

"I know you said your cabin was small, but I'm sure I won't mind. There must be chores that will keep me out of doors. And in the spring, perhaps I could plant a garden..."

His expression shifted from something bordering on pleasant to confusion, leaving his brow knitted.

Oh, dear.

"I'm not afraid of hard work," she went on. She knew she was rambling. Nerves always brought out the babbling brook of words, a reserve that never seemed to go away. She couldn't seem to stop. "And I can get to know the neighbors. Maybe join a quilting circle, if there is such a thing. Or maybe start one..." She trailed off because his expression had turned stormy.

"Are you joshing?"

She didn't know how to respond to his query, and the slight bite to his words had her shaking her head. Had she already irritated him? A shiver wracked her.

He noticed. And his frown grew. "I think there's been some kind of mistake."

Her stomach plummeted, landing somewhere near her toes.

He motioned toward the street behind him, flanked by clapboard buildings. "Come along, Miss Plum. Let's find someplace warm and—"

She'd started after him out of habit, but he turned back when she stopped walking.

"Who is Miss Plum?" Confusion swirled around her like the snowflakes that caught on her eyelashes.

He looked grim as he turned to face her again. "I am Doctor Jed Dawson. I was supposed to meet the new nurse in my employ. Miss Plum."

He wasn't Mr. Black after all. Embarrassment and a strange sense of disappointment flared through her.

"And I gather that you are not her."

She shook her head, ridiculous tears pooling in her eyes. She blinked them back furiously. It was an innocent mistake.

But one that meant Mr. Black wasn't here, after all. She glanced around the empty train platform. No one else remained.

The chill wind blasted her cheeks. "Mr. Black was supposed to meet me, but he must have been detained. Can you tell me how far it is to his homestead?"

"Mr. Black? Adam Black?"

Why did he sound so incredulous? She nodded.

"I expect," he cleared his throat, "that Adam is snowed in. He lives several hours outside of town."

Snowed in?

He must've read the surprise in her expression. "We've had an unprecedented amount of snow this year. Far more than the almanac predicted."

He motioned with his gloved hand to the nearest building, where a waist-high drift seemed like a tiny mountain. "We've had two weeks of snowstorms, and it hasn't moved off yet. What's your name?"

"Wilhelmina Bannister." She didn't know why she introduced herself that way. She used Minnie with everyone. "I'm here to marry Mr. Black."

The doctor seemed to choke on a cough. She couldn't read his expression, but the thundercloud of his brow didn't frighten her anymore. "Is there a stage or... a driver I might hire?"

She didn't have the funds for either. Mr. Black had sent her the train ticket. She couldn't have afforded one on her own.

He shook his head slowly, his eyes hooded and dark. "I doubt anyone is willing to risk their life to deliver you to—" another hitch in his voice "—Adam."

"Then what am I supposed to do?"

Mr. Black had written a little about the town. He'd never mentioned a hotel.

Doctor Dawson blew out a frustrated breath. "I don't have time for this."

She probably wasn't supposed to have caught the words, not with his head turned and the way he'd spoken under his breath. It was her good fortune to have excellent hearing, honed from years of listening for an employer's call, anticipating their every need. Or back at the orphanage, when a footstep in the hallway late in the evening sometimes preceded punishment.

She lifted her chin. "Thank you for your help." Not that he'd done much. "I'm certain I can find my way from here."

She wasn't certain of any such thing, but if there was one thing she hated, it was the feeling of being a burden. The only thing worse was being invisible. Perhaps she should be thankful the doctor had seen her on the train platform at all.

She started down the stairs, wondering where she might find assistance. Her stomach reminded her that she hadn't eaten since a meager breakfast of weak coffee and a stale biscuit. If she could only warm up, she could think this through.

The doctor caught up to her on the boardwalk in only a few long-legged strides. "I'll take you to the preacher's house. Maybe he and his wife will know what to do with you."

How magnanimous of him.

She wanted to snap at him, prick his feelings the way he'd pricked hers with his impatience. But she swallowed back the impulse. The local doctor was likely an important figure in town. She didn't want to be an embarrassment to Mr. Black before they even got to the altar.

"Thank you," she managed before following him in silence.

~

Jed was keenly aware of the pocket watch ticking away in the inside breast pocket of the vest he wore beneath his coat.

He needed to check on Mrs. Farraday, who was forty-one-and-a-half weeks pregnant with her third child and due to deliver any day. Any moment really.

The five-year-old son of the blacksmith was recovering from whooping cough. Jed should stop in and check on him again.

And he'd promised Jamie he would be home for supper. His twelve-year-old son had been sullen and tight-lipped when Jed had to leave to meet the new nurse at the train station. Jed had reminded his son that Miss Plum would provide some much-needed help for the thriving clinic.

Jamie had only scowled and turned his back while Jed had shrugged on his coat.

His son probably had a right to his anger. Jed had been working longer and longer days. He couldn't remember the last time they'd eaten supper together. Roderick and Helen, an older, childless couple who ran the mercantile, took pity on the widower doctor and his son and fed Jamie when Jed was seeing patients.

And tonight—thanks to a no-show Miss Plum and stumbling upon Wilhelmina Bannister—he was going to miss supper again.

Jamie wouldn't be heartbroken. Or maybe he would. He just wouldn't tell Jed.

Jed was bone-tired of the sulky attitude. Where had his curious, jovial little boy gone?

Jed ground his teeth. There was nothing for it. He didn't want to give Jamie another reason to resent him. Not at Christmas.

"I need to make a stop," he said. He didn't wait for an answer because he'd nearly passed the storefront for the clinic. It was closed and dark, no lamps lit inside.

Miss Bannister gave the window a dubious look.

"My son thought I would be returning from the train station right away."

When her expression softened, he felt a tug in his gut that he ignored. "Of course. He must be worried."

Worry was likely the last thing on Jamie's mind.

Jed pushed through the door, trying to keep his thoughts off the young woman he gestured to follow him inside. "You'd better come in out of the snow."

She hesitated just beyond the door. The stove wasn't lit in

here, but being out of the wind and snow made it so much warmer.

He could see a line of light beneath the door that separated the clinic from his and Jamie's rooms at the back of the building. "This way."

"I don't want to drip all over your floor."

That was thoughtful, but unnecessary. He waved her forward, his steps clacking against the wood floor in his hurry. At this rate, he would be up into the wee hours making notations in his patient records.

"Jamie?" he called out as he moved through the hall and into their small kitchen and dining area.

His son poked his head out of his bedroom door. His hair was tousled, and he looked like the boy Jed remembered. A surge of love for his son filled his chest.

Until Jamie spoke. "Thought you weren't coming back. Where's your Miss Plum?"

Jed frowned. Nurse Plum wasn't his in any sense of the word —just a woman he'd hired to work for him." She didn't arrive on the train."

But Jamie's gaze jumped to the hallway behind Jed, where a slight movement from Miss Bannister must've given her away.

"This is Wilhelmina Bannister. Miss Bannister, my son, Jamie."

The young woman gave a slight wave, still clutching her carpetbag. Jamie raised one imperious eyebrow.

Jed sighed. "Miss Banister arrived on the train. We need to take her to the Owens's house. Get your coat on."

Jamie scowled. "Why?"

Jed sent a prayer for patience winging heavenward, but before he could formulate any words that wouldn't sound like a growl and provide further friction for his relationship with his son, she spoke.

"I've come to marry Mr. Black, but he didn't meet my train."

Jamie's eyes goggled, flicking from Miss Bannister to Jed.

"Your father was kind enough to offer to escort me to the preacher's home."

Something flickered in Jamie's expression. "That's the doc for ya," he muttered. At least he reached for his coat from the peg on the wall. "Kindhearted to a fault."

Jed's face heated at the blatant sarcasm in his son's mumble.

He should correct Jamie. Punish him for the disrespect.

But he hesitated for a moment too long. Jamie popped his arms through the coat sleeves. "You really gonna marry that old coot?"

Jed glared at his son, who missed the look entirely.

The woman's brows crinkled for a brief moment. "Old coot?"

Jed squeezed his son's shoulder before the boy could say anything more. He motioned for her to lead the way back through the clinic and outside. "That's none of our concern," he said to both his son and himself.

The door closed behind them. Back in the swirling snow, the icy bite of the air stung the inside of Jed's nose.

"But—"Jamie cut himself off when Jed shook his head.

His jaw worked and then his chin jutted out stubbornly. "What kind of name is Wilhelmina?"

"Jamie!"

Her laugh covered his exclamation and almost stopped him cold on the boardwalk. The sound was so alive. So full of joy. She obviously wasn't offended by his son's insensitive question.

"You can call me Minnie. Everyone does."

Jamie shot a triumphant look at his father.

Jed felt his lips pinching in a frown. If everyone called her Minnie, why hadn't she invited him to do so?

"How old is Mr. Black?" Minnie—Wilhelmina—directed her question to Jamie.

"At least twenty years older than you. Maybe thirty!"

Jed bit back the urge to shush his son. She'd asked.

He couldn't help himself, though. He glanced at her face. She wasn't disappointed or angry. She was almost expressionless. Her eyes moved from side to side as if she was thinking.

What on earth would prompt someone to answer an ad for a mail-order wife? He couldn't fathom it. At least, not when that someone looked like Wilhelmina.

On the platform, he'd been struck by her petite size, the blue eyes that made one feel as if she could see right inside him.

He'd even had a stray thought that she would be a temptation, working alongside him in his practice.

He'd quashed the thought quickly. He was a professional. He would never—

But she isn't going to be working alongside you, his traitorous brain offered now.

Wilhelmina had asked how much farther to the preacher's house, and Jamie was pointing down the boardwalk.

The wind seemed to muffle it, but he heard a sound that didn't belong.

He shushed his son, straining his ears to hear. The snow muffled everything. But it came again, louder this time. An ominous creak.

He looked across the street. Two blocks down, a dangerous amount of snow had accumulated on the flat roof of one of the buildings. The storefront was split into two shops, a leatherworks and a dressmakers. Both families had their residences in rooms at the rear of the building, just like he and Jamie did.

He held his arm to stop Jamie's forward progress as a loud crack split the air.

Then he watched in horror as the roof collapsed into the building.

CHAPTER 2

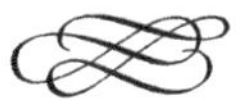

Shock and terror coursed through Jed as he ran toward the rubble. He didn't realize until he was searching for a way inside that Minnie and Jamie had followed him.

"Is Grover in there?" Jamie asked in a trembling gasp.

"I don't know. I need you to stay here on the boardwalk." He waved to Mr. and Mrs. Peterson, who lived above the grocery, and Mr. Wilder, who owned the saloon, urgently motioning them to come and help.

When he glanced back at his son, he saw that Minnie's hand rested on Jamie's shoulder. A pang hit deep in his belly. She was comforting his son.

Good. He tried to breathe through the stark terror. He was going to have to go inside. What would he find? Surely the families had been at home on such a cold night. Would there be any survivors?

It was impossible to budge the front door, even putting his shoulder into it. He gave up and rounded the side of the building, where a window had broken from the force of the collapse. He knocked the remaining glass free with his elbow and then reached inside to pry the sash open.

He saw movement at the corner of the building. Were others coming to help? "Hurry! Come on," he called out.

He didn't wait to see if they would follow but crawled inside through the window. The roof here had landed on two tall shelves, providing a pocket of empty darkness. He turned back to the window and shouted, "Bring lanterns!"

He edged his way into the room, conscious of motion behind him—someone else coming in to help—and a soft moan from somewhere toward the rear of the building. Glass and other debris crunched beneath his feet as he slowly moved forward. It was a mess, store items and furnishings scattered and jumbled all together.

"Ellie Jane? Grover? Pieter?" His voice echoed strangely in the confined space.

And then there was a cold pocket of air, and he found himself stepping onto part of the roof that had fallen to the floor. Snow spilled across his shoes.

It was slightly lighter, open to the night sky. Light enough that when he heard a rustling behind him and turned to caution the man following him, he could see it wasn't a man at all.

It was Minnie, and she looked as frightened as he felt.

"What are you doing?" he demanded. He didn't have time to wait for her answer. He surged forward, stumbling when the broken roof buckled beneath his weight. "Get out of here. It's dangerous."

"You need help," she said clearly, though he could hear her teeth chattering.

He heard her advancing behind him.

When another pained moan came from somewhere to his right, he forgot about Minnie. "Ellie Jane? Is that you?"

A soft, broken sob answered.

Debris and a large chunk of wood from the roof blocked his way. He reached out with his gloved hands to try and feel the edge of it.

And then light flashed from behind him. Bobbed and became clearer.

"Over here," he commanded.

The sound of scuffling came from somewhere in front of him, somewhere behind this piece of wall. Then another soft sound of pain.

"Doc?" a wavering voice called out.

Suddenly Minnie was beside him. He didn't have time for frustration that she hadn't listened to him, only gratefulness that she had obtained a lamp. The flickering light showed the edge of the wide plank, still covered with snow. It was wedged at an angle, impossibly heavy with all that snow packed together on top. And at least one person was behind it.

"Over here," Minnie called out, and more bodies joined them. Two men, Mr. Wilder and the local blacksmith, Mr. Vickers.

"There's someone on the other side," he told them in the flickering lamplight.

"It's too heavy to lift." The blacksmith had recognized the situation in only a moment's time.

Minnie crouched near a dark crawlspace he hadn't noticed on the other side of the big board. "What about here?"

Mr. Wilder took a second look at her. "Who are you?"

"She's new in town," Jed mumbled. He pushed past the other men to see the place she indicated. "It's too small." Disappointment flared. They needed to get the family out.

"I can crawl through," she said. She was pale in the light, clearly frightened, but her voice was calm and her hand holding the lamp was steady.

Another soft sob broke the beat of silence.

"Here." Minnie pushed the lamp toward him. He took it.

Without hesitation, she dropped to her knees and crawled into the dark. "Ellie Jane? Grover?"

She didn't know anyone in town—she'd told him so herself

—but she'd remembered the names he'd called out only moments ago.

"There's someone here!" she called out.

In a soft murmur of voices, he thought he could make out Minnie's, encouraging and steady.

"Doctor, it's a boy!" Her voice was more of a grunt. He heard a rattle as if she'd bumped into something. She didn't cry out.

And then Grover was crawling out of that small space, dragging one leg behind him. Jed did a quick pat down and determined that his worst injury was a broken ankle.

"Can you carry him out?" he asked Vickers, who didn't hesitate to scoop the boy up.

Minnie hadn't reappeared.

Jed leaned down to speak into the crawlspace. "Minnie?"

There was no answer, only the distant scrape of her shoe.

This was dangerous. No place for a lady.

But she hadn't turned back.

There were distant shouts from outside. He could only hope that someone had found a way into the Ratcliff's part of the building. The leather craftsman and his wife had four children.

He should be thinking about where to set up triage. If there were multiple people wounded, he would need to attend to the most dangerous injuries first. His clinic wasn't big enough. And there was only one of him.

He needed a nurse.

And that's when Minnie's face appeared, dirt-smudged and worried.

"There's a woman," she spoke quickly. "I couldn't rouse her, there's... there is blood from a wound at her temple." Her voice trembled. He found himself kneeling beside her, his hand clasping her shoulder, comforting her the same way she'd done for Jamie.

She took a breath and her voice evened out. "Something

heavy—maybe part of the wall—fell on top of her. I can't move it."

"Where?" he asked.

Wilder hovered behind them, ready to jump into action.

She pointed to an area where the roof had broken into pieces.

"I'll see if I can find something to use as a lever," Wilder said.

"Is it safe to move her?" Minnie asked.

"I don't know. I need to see her." He eyed the darkness around her. "Does it open up?"

"A little."

"Can you show me where she is?"

Minnie crawled away. He followed her, pushing the lamp across the floor ahead of him. It was a tight fit, and he had to angle his shoulders just so to get through the first bit, but Minnie led him to Ellie Jane. Blood matted the hair at the crumpled woman's temple, but it was the heavy bookcase that rested on her midsection that worried him. Had it caused internal damage?

Ellie Jane's eyelids fluttered.

"We've got to keep her still," he told Minnie.

She was watching his face, and seemed to understand the seriousness of the situation.

"What do you need me to do?"

~

Minnie took the cup of coffee from the preacher's wife, whose name she couldn't remember. She thanked her with a smile because she was too exhausted to do much more.

Taking a deep breath, she moved down the aisle of wooden pews until she reached the last one, where Grover sat.

"How's my ma?"

She'd learned that Grover was the son of the man and woman who ran the dress shop. He was the first person who'd been pulled from the wreckage. And he was going to be the last one to receive treatment.

"Doctor Jed has been with her. I'm sure he'll come to tell you himself."

"How much longer, d'you think?" He shifted on the wooden bench, unable to hide the wince that crossed his features. It was well past midnight, hours since Grover had been rescued.

Jed had begun moving patients to the church building—the only building with enough space to house the two families—as soon as they had pulled Ellie Jane, Grover's mother, from the wreckage.

Minnie had felt such a rush of admiration and fear as Jed had carried the woman out of the building in his arms.

Admiration for Jed's calm leadership, how he'd jumped in so quickly to try and help the people who'd been injured. She could see why everyone in town seemed to look up to him.

Fear for Ellie Jane. Jed had been grim at her prognosis. She still hadn't come to.

"When will Doc come?" Grover asked.

She looked up just in time to catch Jed's eye. He'd been bent over a patient on one of the benches at the front of the sanctuary and now straightened. And looked right at her.

She couldn't read his expression. She knew he must be as exhausted as she was—if not more. He was the one who'd been putting in stitches, examining head wounds, giving instructions in a quiet, commanding voice.

She knew he probably didn't need it, but she tried to offer him comfort through her expression.

"I think he's headed this way. I bet he'll have news about your mama."

The boy smiled ruefully. "Grownups never tell kids anything."

"It's true," Jamie complained. She hadn't even realized he was close, but he'd brought a cup of water to his friend. He sent a sideways smile to Minnie. "My pa never tells me anything. Like when he'll be home late from work. Sometimes I don't even see him before I go to bed."

She felt a pang of familiar loneliness for the boy. There were many nights when she had prayed for one friend. One person to care whether she was all right. Her heart went out to him. "That must be hard. Do you have to make your own supper?"

Jamie blushed a little and toed the floor under his feet. "Nah. Mrs. Vickers watches over me and feeds me supper."

"Your pa can't help it," Grover said. He tipped his head so it rested on the back of the pew. "He's out helping people. You should tell Miss Minnie how he saved Old Man Hummerts's hand. Old farmer nearly cut it all the way off chopping wood."

Jamie's expression soured.

Her stomach twisted. "That's all right."

Grover picked his head up. "Jamie said you're supposed to marry Adam Black. I said he was pulling my leg, just trying to distract me while I waited."

A flush stole into her cheeks. "Jamie's right. I am going to marry Mr. Black."

Grover wrinkled his nose. "What for? He mistreats his animals, y'know? You should marry Doc instead."

She gaped at him, completely aghast at his suggestion.

How should she respond? Luckily, she didn't have to say anything because the doctor arrived at Grover's pew, his shadow falling over the boys.

"You two quit trying to meddle in adult affairs."

Grover had the grace to look abashed. Jamie's chin jutted out defiantly, but he held his tongue.

Minnie wished the doctor had been present to shut down the questions from others a bit earlier. She'd taken it upon herself to help, especially when Jed had been giving orders as the injured were brought into the church. She'd found herself making introductions to help keep people's minds off their injuries. And in her nervous state, she'd babbled too much about why she was here.

She'd heard about Mr. Black's temper from the saloon-keeper as she'd pressed a cloth to his head while waiting for the doctor to administer stitches. He'd bumped his head during the search for survivors.

Mrs. Peale, who'd fetched clean linens from the clinic and her house nearby, had whispered that Mr. Black was known to be months behind on the mortgage on his land.

And now Grover.

Jed seemed to be the only one in town who understood decorum. Was everyone in Cooper's Hollow a terrible gossip? Or had she misjudged the man who'd sent for her?

"It's going to hurt when I set your leg," the doctor told Grover now. "But it must be done."

He carefully laid two pieces of wood and some cloth on the floor within easy reach. "We'll splint the leg for tonight. Tomorrow we can put a plaster cast on."

Grover nodded gravely. "I ain't afraid."

But she saw his white-knuckled grip on the back of the pew.

"Can you lie flat on your back?" the doctor asked.

Grover did as he was told, but he couldn't suppress a gasp when the movements made it necessary to shift his leg.

Jamie looked on, wide-eyed.

Minnie touched his shirt sleeve. "You don't have to watch." The boys were clearly friends, and this wasn't going to be easy on Grover.

Jed glanced at his son. "She's right. You should be home and in bed."

Jamie wore that stubborn look again. He crossed his arms over his chest. "I'm stayin'."

Something flickered in Jed's expression. "Fine. You can help hold Grover's shoulders down. Really pin him in place."

Jed motioned Minnie to his side. "Can you hold here?" He showed her with his hands where he wanted her to press down on Grover's thigh.

She did as he asked but couldn't watch as he moved to Grover's lower leg to set the bone. The boy held a cry behind a clenched jaw.

Jamie's compassion showed in the shine of his eyes.

It only took a matter of moments. The doctor set the bone and put the splint in place while she spoke to the boys. When Doctor Dawson's gaze flicked to his son, she realized he wanted to reach out but held back.

And then she left the three of them, went to stand in the vestibule. It was colder here, and she wished she had a shawl, but she settled for wrapping her arms around herself.

She closed her eyes, trying to shake off the anxious feeling slithering down her spine.

"Are you all right?" She startled, not realizing anyone had followed her.

The doctor stood nearby, wiping his hands with a cloth.

"I'm fine." She wasn't fine. And his knowing gaze seemed to say as much.

"I've seen grown men break down in tears tonight," he said.

Something about his dry delivery made her eyes fill. She turned away to hide her emotion. What they'd been through tonight had been frightful and intense and pierced with poignant moments. It almost made her forget that they were strangers.

But that's what they were. Strangers.

She sensed him come close. She didn't know what she would do if he reached out and touched her. It had been so long…

Growing up in the orphanage had been lonely, and she

hadn't had a parent figure, only a caretaker. She couldn't remember a time when someone had held her.

But he only stood close, offering comfort through his silence and warmth.

"You were incredibly brave tonight."

His words were like a snick of a match being lit, a little flame coming to life somewhere deep inside her.

He thought she was brave, though she'd spent most of tonight terrified.

It made her strong enough to swipe a hand over her cheek to clear any fallen tears. She turned to nod at him."Thank you, Doctor Dawson."

He stared at her, his eyes dark and unfathomable. "After everything we've been through tonight, I think you'd better call me Jed."

CHAPTER 3

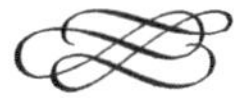

Christmas Eve dawned cold and gray. It wasn't snowing, so that was something. But the skies were full and heavy as if it might start again at any time. Minnie didn't mind the quiet, hushed feeling in the air. There was something comforting about being in the doctor's quarters on a day like today.

"Why are you boiling those?" Minnie asked.

Jamie had already washed the different needles Jed had used to put in sutures after last night's disaster. She'd helped him with the hot, soapy dishwater. Now he stood over the stove with a deep pot of boiling water and a pair of long-handled tongs.

"Pa wants them sanitized before he uses them again."

She nodded as if she understood, but wasn't something clean after it'd been washed?

She kept one eye on Jamie as she hung linens on the lines crisscrossing the room just under the ceiling. She and Jamie had toted the armfuls of soiled linens back to the clinic this morning.

She'd slept for a few hours on one of the pews, waking when

she heard an unfamiliar noise or when the hardness of the pew cut into her hip or back or shoulder. Sometime in the darkness, she'd heard Jed speaking in low tones. Had he gotten any sleep at all?

She'd lain awake in the quiet of the morning before anyone else had woken. She couldn't stop thinking about the doctor.

About Jed.

Everyone else had something to say about Mr. Black, about her plan to marry him. But not him. Why?

When Jed had sent Jamie home from the church an hour ago, she'd seen the vulnerable look on the boy's face before he'd firmed his jaw. Jamie might be old enough to take care of himself, but he was still a boy. She'd heard herself offer to accompany him before she'd even thought about it.

There was something about the preteen that called out to her. She felt connected to him. Didn't she know what it was like to be on her own for hours at a time—days at a time? To feel invisible.

Now there were only a handful of small towels left in her pile of damp, clean laundry. Her task would be complete. Then what would she do?

"I still need to find someone to drive me out to Mr. Black's place," she said.

Jamie grunted, shaking his head from where he stood at the stove, over the pot.

From the front of the clinic, doors opened, voices rose in conversation. She could hear the cadence, or maybe it was the command in the words, and recognized the doctor's tone.

"Might not be safe," Jamie said.

It took her a moment to come back from her distraction.

"Why wouldn't it be safe?"

She was ashamed to admit she'd let all the gossip stir misgiving about marrying the man she'd never met. Did he truly have a short temper?

"Horse could flounder in the snow. Step in a drift and hurt itself. Then you—and whoever was taking you—would be stuck out in the freezing cold."

Oh. He wasn't talking about Mr. Black.

She flipped the last towel in the air to spread it. "Are you telling me no one comes to town during the winter?"

She'd grown up in the city, but she wasn't afraid of farming. At least, she didn't think she was. But she was trying to imagine being isolated for months at a time—and she couldn't.

"Naw." Jamie put the tongs on the counter with a clank. "Some of the snow'll melt off in a few days. Unless it snows more."

A few days.

Where was she supposed to stay for these few days?

She'd planned for Mr. Black to meet her train. For them to be married before she accompanied him to his farm. It wasn't ideal to travel to him without being married—she didn't know whether anyone out here cared about reputations, but she'd been careful with hers. What if she—what if they... wintered at his isolated farm and then in the spring he refused to marry her?

She'd be in the same plight she was right now. Only worse off.

Jed had seemed sure the preacher and his wife would put her up for a few days, but that was before the building collapse. Two families had been displaced. Everyone except Ellie Jane had recovered enough to stay with friends. But it was a small town. With no hotel, no boardinghouse. Which meant that any place Minnie might've hoped to stay was now occupied by someone who belonged here.

She felt a little like Jesus's mother arriving in a strange town, nowhere to sleep. Maybe someone had a barn she could shelter in? The thought made her chest feel tight, and she visually searched the room for a distraction. There was a pine bough stretched on the windowsill above the kitchen counter, strung with red ribbon. A reminder that tomorrow was Christmas.

"Do you think Mr. Black decorates a Christmas tree?"

Jamie looked skeptical. "Prob'ly not."

"Oh. I've never had one." She squeezed water from the last of the linens.

She'd never received a Christmas gift, either. There'd been no money for that at the orphanage. And she'd been lucky if an employer gave her a small monetary bonus at Christmas, much less a gift.

But this Christmas was supposed to be different. A new start for her.

"Will you give your pa a Christmas gift?"

It was an innocent question, but Jamie scowled and then shrugged. "I dunno."

Movement from the doorway caught her attention. Jed filled the portal with his broad shoulders.

"I'm finished," Jamie mumbled and darted into his room, slamming the door behind him.

Minnie was left to stare after him. She straightened and looked to Jed, who was watching the closed door.

"I think I said something wrong," she murmured. Maybe she shouldn't have mentioned Christmas at all.

"Saying something wrong is a daily peril."

She might've expected the words to sound dry, but all she heard was the exhaustion in his voice. A closer examination showed tiny white lines fanning his mouth and eyes.

She ducked beneath one of the towels to go to the stove and retrieve the coffee pot she'd put on earlier. "Did you get any sleep last night?"

He shook his head.

She brought him a cup of coffee.

"Thank you." His gaze wandered the kitchen. "You didn't have to wash all this."

"Jamie gave me good instructions. We used boiling water—"

He waved off her explanation as he swallowed and lowered the mug. "I wasn't questioning the quality of your work."

He wasn't?

"I should've said thank you, instead."

Oh.

"I like being useful." She didn't know what to do without a job for her hands. She'd always been pushed to keep busy ever since she'd been a child.

Something she couldn't name jumped into his eyes as he watched her, then he broke the moment and took another sip of his coffee. He raised his other hand and rubbed it over his face. She couldn't help but notice how his elegant fingers trailed along his jaw, now dark with stubble.

A bolt of attraction shivered through her. That was no good. She ducked her head and shifted so that she was half-hidden behind one of the hanging towels.

She'd felt the same beat of attraction—was it only last night? —on the train platform. When she'd thought he was Mr. Black, come for her.

But he wasn't her intended husband. And she had no business feeling anything other than friendship for this man.

She tried to smile and hoped her lips weren't trembling. "I suppose it's time for me to go. Do you know if the livery is open?"

~

Jed sipped his coffee again, hoping it would wake him up. He felt like he was moving through molasses. His thoughts weren't coming as quickly as needed.

"The livery? I don't know. It's Christmas Eve. And after last night..." He shrugged. The only reason she would ask was because she still intended to marry Adam Black.

And that was her business. He'd told his son and Grover the same last night, along with Helen Vickers when she'd whispered, "You can't let that young lady marry Adam."

It wasn't his business. Jamie was his business. The clinic and the people of Cooper's Hollow were his priority.

And all of that was more than enough for one man.

His mind had been working between patients all night long. Cogs shifting, searching for answers. But he had none. Only an idea.

"I have a proposition for you," he said.

She made a soft noise that might've been distress. He needed to see her, so he batted one of the clean towels out of the way and stepped closer.

"My nurse didn't show up. She isn't coming." Roderick had handed him the telegram from Miss Plum on his way up the boardwalk not long ago. It had arrived late yesterday. Jed had discovered he wasn't all that surprised. Only resigned. "I know you're anxious to see Adam, but the conditions are still dangerous. And I need help. I'm worried about Ellie Jane. I don't like the bruising on her abdomen."

Between the head injury and the contusions to her torso, it was something of a miracle she was still alive. "I need to keep her under constant surveillance," he said. "Pieter will help tomorrow, but his own injuries meant he needs rest today. And Grover needed him." He paused. "There are others that will need to be checked on now. And an expecting mother who might give birth any day."

He didn't mention that he'd treated minor burns every Christmas since he'd arrived in Cooper's Hollow. Too much holiday frivolity mixed with cooking extravagant meals—as extravagant as his neighbors could afford—meant at least one person was bound to need treatment. "If you could stay on for a few days, it would be a great help to me."

She looked shocked. "But—I'm not a nurse."

"That's true. But you were a Godsend last night."

She'd been invaluable. Not only crawling into that horrible, dangerous building but fetching and carrying, talking in low tones and keeping his patients calm.

Now she looked astounded. Her mouth hung open slightly and the absurdity of her expression made him want to laugh.

He didn't.

He didn't have the energy.

"Stay through Christmas," he said. "If Adam hasn't made it to town by now, he's probably decided to wait for some of the snow to melt."

He wasn't going to say the rest of it, but he saw the hesitation on her expression, the way her lips were beginning to form the word, "no."

"Jamie could use the company," he blurted.

He really must be tired. He rarely lost control like that.

"It's Christmas and he shouldn't be alone. I have no choice but to see patients, though I'll try to spend as much time with him as I can. The two of you have made a connection." He had lingered in the doorway before either of them had known he was there, watching. He'd seen the smiles and camaraderie, seen a side of Jamie that hadn't been present in months. Maybe not since before Veronica had died. It was only after Jamie had spied him in the doorway that his thundercloud frown had appeared, and he'd gone off to sulk in his room.

Jamie was the reason Jed had put the wheels in motion to hire a nurse. His son was growing up. It wouldn't be long until he would be out of the house. And Jed was missing it.

They hadn't been close in a long time. Jed didn't know whether that was something they could get back.

"Last Christmas was the first without... without his mother. It didn't go well." He couldn't hold her eyes now, too full of nervous energy. He moved to the counter and put down his coffee cup, reached out to touch the tongs Jamie had used earlier. "I don't want my working to ruin his Christmas."

He kept his face averted. A natural response would be to say, *then don't work this Christmas*. But Jed had taken an oath, sworn to use his training as a doctor to heal those who needed it. Grover needed Ellie Jane. So did Pieter. Jed couldn't turn his back, not when she might not survive.

He cleared his throat, rubbed one hand on the back of his aching neck, forced himself to turn to Minnie. Why had he told her all of that? He was tired, that was all. There was nothing magical about her, only that she was kind and seemed easy to talk to.

She watched him with a considering look in her eyes. Veronica had often worn a look like that, usually just before she suggested a compromise or told him something he wouldn't like. But Minnie only said, "I'll stay."

A rush of relief stormed through him. "You will?"

She blushed a little and averted her eyes. Maybe she sensed his gratefulness, the extreme reaction he'd tried to hide behind a stoic facade.

"I'll stay through Christmas. I suppose I should listen to you and Jamie when you say it is too dangerous to travel out from town."

It wasn't a long-term solution. His brain was cruel enough to remind him of that. In a few days, he'd be back where he started. No nurse. A stubborn, irascible son. But for now, he had an ally.

She moved over to the stove. "When's the last time you ate something? You should sit down."

She was right. He felt even more sluggish than he had a few moments ago.

"You don't have to cook. Mrs. Peale will be by later with a meal. Other families will bring food." It was what their community did when his workload was overwhelming.

"It won't take but a minute for me to scramble an egg and toast bread."

He didn't even know if there was bread in the larder. He did take her suggestion to sit down. He propped his head on his hand, elbow on the table, as mannerless as that was. "Ellie Jane is sleeping in the front exam room. She'll need to be checked on..."

"I can check on her." Minnie's murmur was reassuring, and he didn't even realize he'd nodded off until a gentle touch on his shoulder startled him awake.

"You should go lie down." She looked like she'd jumped back when his eyes snapped open.

A plate with fluffy scrambled egg and a toast slathered with jam sat right in front of him. She was right. If Ellie Jane needed medical assistance right now, he would be useless.

He took the plate with him to his bedroom. Only after he'd closed his bedroom door did he realize he should have told her that he didn't need this. That she wasn't here to take care of him. That's not why he'd asked her to stay.

But it didn't stop tears from pricking his eyes as he wolfed down the eggs and toast.

Veronica had been the last person to send him to bed when he'd been practically asleep on his feet. He hadn't realized until now that he missed having someone to look after him.

CHAPTER 4

Jed woke with no sense of how much time had passed. He rubbed both hands over his face as he sat up. His mouth felt like cotton. He could still feel the warmth of Minnie taking care of him.

A glance at the pocket watch from his nightstand showed it was lunchtime. He'd slept for several hours.

Not enough, but it would have to do.

Voices murmured behind the door. Jamie's. And then Minnie answered. Her voice was both new and familiar. And comforting somehow.

Responsibilities intruded. He needed to check on Ellie Jane. If she remained stable, it wouldn't hurt to make a call on Mrs. Farraday to see how she fared. Surely someone would've called on him if she went into labor.

He splashed water from the basin onto his face, rubbed vigorously with the towel to dry it. That only made him think of Minnie and the laundry she'd done—of her own accord—this morning.

The hot scent of a hearty stew. His stomach rumbled, mouth instantly watering.

Jamie and Minnie were at the kitchen table, an open book in front of each of them. Minnie sat back in her chair, sipping from a mug. Jamie was leaning over the table toward her, motioning with one hand.

"No, he wouldn't say that! He hasn't been visited by the spirit of Christmas present yet."

"But his attitude has already started changing," Minnie argued right back, a smile playing around her lips. She was the one who glanced up and caught sight of him in the doorway. Her eyes widened.

And then Jamie saw him, too, and closed his book with a thunk.

"What are you doing?" Jed asked.

Jamie ducked his head so Minnie answered. "Playing a game." She stood from the table and moved toward the stove, where a bubbling pot rested. "Do you want something to eat?"

He did want something to eat, but he felt a pull to the clinic to check on Ellie Jane. "What kind of game?" he asked. His feet hadn't moved.

Was it his imagination, or was Minnie blushing? "Oh. Just something I made up to pass time. Sort of combining two books together."

Jamie's fingertip traced something on the tabletop. "You take characters from one book and imagine they are facing all the obstacles or going through life from another book."

How creative. "I suppose you're putting Mr. Scrooge through the wringer?"

Minnie looked slightly surprised that he'd recognized the reference in the short time he'd been in the doorway. "We've put him on the deserted island of Mr. Crusoe."

A short laugh barked out of him at the absurdity of it. "Have you really?"

Jamie's eyes widened with surprise.

Maybe Jed's laugh was a little rusty. He actually couldn't

remember the last time he'd laughed with his son.

Minnie was wiping her hands on her borrowed apron. She hadn't dished out any stew.

"I've been in to check on Ellie Jane." She said it in a rush, like he might've been disappointed to find her in the kitchen instead of at Ellie Jane's bedside.

"Every fifteen minutes," Jamie chimed in. For once, he wasn't wearing the fiery frown.

"Has she been awake?"

"Once," Minnie answered. "She said her stomach hurt. I gave her a bit of water and that seemed to settle her. I don't know if that was right. I should've woken you."

She was doing a favor for him. And she wasn't a nurse. He hadn't even given her any instructions before he'd fallen comatose. "That's fine. You probably wouldn't have been able to wake me anyway."

"Pa could sleep through a tornado," Jamie said. He grinned, but it was so quickly there and gone that Jed couldn't even be sure he'd seen it.

"Do you remember when Ma would tell the story of when I was born—?"

Jed must've flinched. Jamie cut himself off, chastened even though Jed hadn't said a word.

It was the first time he'd brought up Veronica in months. Jed's throat was suddenly dry. Words failed him.

And then a soft cry from the clinic diverted his attention.

He didn't say a word to Minnie or Jamie, just took off past the table and through the hall, into the exam room.

Ellie Jane's face was flushed. One touch of his hand at her forehead confirmed the ravaging fever.

Minnie must've followed him. She hung back in the doorway. "She wasn't like that before."

Her words trembled, and Jed felt the urge to reassure her. "I believe you."

Ellie Jane moaned again, her head thrashing on the pillow. "Hurts," she gasped. "Stomach."

Jed and Mrs. Owens had put her in a nightgown after she'd been cleaned up from the rubble. He lifted it now to see the mottled bruising, getting darker by the second, on her stomach. When he barely pressed the area, she cried out.

"She's bleeding inside," he muttered.

He turned to Minnie in the doorway, for the first time noticed Jamie hovering behind her. "I'll need to perform surgery or she could die."

Minnie's face went white.

"Can you assist me?"

She nodded, though she was clearly terrified.

"I need some hot water. Jamie, can you put on a big pot and then run and tell Pieter what is happening? He can wait in the front room, but I don't want him in here."

He saw the faint tremble of Jamie's mouth. "Okay, Pa."

Jed's thoughts were clicking faster than a steam locomotive, more orderly now—each step laid out neatly in front of him—than they would've been if he hadn't slept.

But as he turned back to the exam room to start prepping, Minnie tugged on his arm, pulling him to a halt. He opened his mouth to tell her that every moment counted, but she had her other hand on Jamie and was pulling the boy in close.

It was awkward, made more so because it shouldn't have felt right to have her under one arm and Jamie under the other. He wouldn't have thought to hug his son, wouldn't have felt the shudder go through the boy, lanky and bony as only a pre-teen could be.

"Everything will be all right," Minnie whispered.

When Jamie stepped back, he was steadier. His eyes met Jed's evenly before he turned and rushed for the door.

And maybe Jed's own hands were the slightest bit steadier, too, as he turned to ready the room.

Had Minnie done this to him?

~

"Can you hand me that clamp?"

Minnie pointed to a strange, small type of scissors after Jed jutted his chin in that direction. There were several instruments on the small table he'd pulled next to Ellie Jane's exam bed. She must've guessed correctly because he nodded.

She quickly passed them to him, trying not to look at the place where he'd cut into Ellie Jane's stomach, just beneath her ribs. There was so much blood. Minnie glimpsed the gore, and her stomach took a tumble before she averted her face.

"Can you count her breaths? How many does she take in ten seconds?"

Jed had put a stopwatch near Ellie Jane's shoulder. Minnie had already done one count. Now she leaned close, thankful for the distraction of turning her head.

"Five—no, six."

It was easier to focus on Jed's face. He wore a look of fierce determination and complete focus.

“The forceps.”

This time she handed the tool to him quickly.

"How did you think up that game you played with Jamie?" He asked the question in an offhand way, while still completely focused on Ellie Jane. Maybe talking helped focus him?

"I used to play it with myself, sometimes."

"What do you mean?"

Her cheeks grew hot. This man was a professional, had been through medical school. She was a nobody who'd come from nowhere.

"When I worked as a maid, the hours were long and the work repetitive. But I could go anywhere in my imagination. Playing that game with characters and book settings was a way for me to pass the time."

"It's very creative."

That sounded like a compliment, and her cheeks grew hotter.

"Can you hold the laudanum over her mouth and nose for a count of five?"

She did.

"You're well-read then, I suppose? Did you go to a good school growing up? Or perhaps your family prized reading?"

"Neither." She straightened the pile of small towels on the counter to give her hands something to do. "I never knew my parents. I was brought to a city orphanage when I was three years old. I don't remember anything before that."

He didn't say anything. Her nerves grabbed hold of her throat and made her babble. "We were supposed to have regular schooling, but the orphanage had a hard time employing teachers. I am still terrible at arithmetic. Reading was my escape."

He made a motion with his hands. Was he stitching up a wound inside Ellie Jane? One Minnie couldn't see?

"Reading was my escape, too," he said.

It was? "What did you need to escape from?"

He frowned. It was an impertinent question. Maybe she shouldn't have asked it.

Or was he frowning at what he was doing with his hands?

"Boredom, mostly. My father worked long hours in his medical practice, and my mother liked socializing with friends. She still does."

"Your father is a doctor, too?"

"Mmhmm." He handed her one of the clamps. "For awhile, I thought Jamie would be the third generation of Dawson doctors. When he was younger, that's all he talked about. Being just like me. Being a doctor."

He shook his head slightly. "Last Christmas, I gave him a small bag, like mine, with some instruments. A stethoscope, reflex hammer. He barely looked at it. A few weeks later, when I asked him about it, he said he never wanted to be like me."

She could imagine the words in Jamie's voice. No longer a boy, not yet a man. It would've been his first Christmas without his mother.

Jed reached for a towel and used it to dab his face before he tossed it into the corner on the floor.

"I work too much," he admitted. "That's why I sent for a nurse. I remember feeling the same when I was Jamie's age. I didn't want to turn into my father, but it seems to have happened."

"He will come around. It's obvious he still needs you."

She might've been the one to initiate the hug between the two men, but both had needed it. The tension between them instantly dissolved when they'd touched.

Jed gave a wry look. "It's obvious he needs a woman around. You've done more for him in twenty-four hours than I have in weeks." There was a hint of bitterness in his voice.She didn't know him well, but she knew he cared about his son.

"I know what it's like to be overlooked," she said.

"What do you mean?" He bent over Ellie Jane, pausing to look closer at something.

Why had she said that? Minnie was grateful for his distraction. But now she tried to backtrack. "I could tell he was feeling in the way last night, so I engaged him with Grover. And today, I saw how his hands were shaking. He's worried about his friend."

He muttered something under his breath, and she didn't know if he was still listening.

Nearly a half hour later they were washing up. She hadn't

realized the way blood could get everywhere. She was grateful for the full-length apron he'd provided for her. She pulled it over her head as he scrubbed his hands in the sink.

Pieter was sitting with Ellie Jane.

"Will she make it?" The question had been bouncing around her head since she'd seen Ellie Jane in such awful pain earlier.

Jed sighed deeply, moving to dry his hands with a towel. "I don't know. I believe I stopped the bleeding, but there's always a risk of infection when I have to perform surgery."

Gone was the determination she'd seen in his expression during the surgery itself. Now he only looked tired. Worn through.

"The stew will still be warm on the stove," she said.

He'd been leaning against the counter, staring at the floor. Now his gaze flicked to hers.

She didn't know what he saw when he looked at her, but she was sure she looked as exhausted as he did. Her sleep last night had been broken and hazy on that church pew.

"Thank you. For staying. For helping today. I was glad for your steady hands."

She couldn't bear the intensity of his gaze and dropped her head. "I barely did anything."

He stepped toward her. She looked up, surprised.

"You've got a little—" He motioned to her cheek. She swiped with her hand but he shook his head. Reached forward and brushed his thumb over a spot on her jaw.

His touch was warm, and that thrill of attraction she'd felt earlier came rushing back.

Jed was close now. Only a breath away. She couldn't help it when her gaze fell to his lips.

She'd never been kissed before. She knew it wasn't right, but for a heartbeat, she wanted Jed's kiss. His lips parted as if he'd had the same thought.

A door opening and closing from the other room broke the

tension of the moment. She exhaled a shaky breath, took a step back. Nothing had happened between them. But she'd wanted it to. She'd wanted Jed's kiss and had spared no thought for Adam.

What was wrong with her?

CHAPTER 5

Minnie slept on a narrow cot in the second exam room. It wasn't a real bed, but it was better than a wooden church pew. Which meant she should've slept better than she had the night before, but she tossed and turned.

Jed had almost kissed her.

She had almost kissed Jed.

She had wanted his kiss. It hadn't mattered that she had promised to marry Mr. Black. What did that say about her?

She woke to muffled voices in the exam room next door. She had been in several times during the night to check on Ellie Jane, tiptoeing around Pieter, who'd elected to stay with his wife. She'd heard Jed's tread on the wooden floor more than once, no doubt doing his own checks. Was it Jed in the room now?

It was quiet and dark. She didn't have a watch or clock, but her intuition told her dawn wasn't far off. The voices in the exam room were quiet but sounded excited. Or agitated. Was something wrong? What if Jed needed help? She thought about the sadness in Jamie's voice when he spoke of his mother, of

Grover's worry for Ellie Jane, and dragged herself from the warmth of the woolen blanket.

She slipped out of the exam room door and hesitated just outside the doorway of the room next door. Jed wasn't in there. He'd been the one who had left a lamp lit, turned down to its lowest wick. When she'd asked him why he'd hidden it behind a standing screen on the counter, he'd told her that if there was an emergency during the night, he wanted to be able to quickly see the room and evaluate his patient. The screen was meant to block the light so Ellie Jane could sleep.

Now it gave just enough illumination that she could see Pieter had pulled a straight-backed chair up to the side of the examination bed—the very one where Jed had performed surgery yesterday.

Ellie Jane was awake, her head turned toward her husband.

"I wish I had asked Mrs. Vickers at the mercantile to hold the gifts I'd bought for you and Grover," Ellie Jane whispered. "They were hidden under the bed."

"Your favorite hiding spot." Minnie saw that their hands were clasped between them on the edge of the bed, and Pieter's flexed like he was squeezing. "The bed was pretty sturdy—I can go and recover a few things."

Ellie Jane shook her head on the pillow. "It's too dangerous. They were only trinkets. Please don't—"

"Okay." He brushed a reassuring kiss on her forehead. "I won't. I won't go into the building."

Ellie Jane seemed to breathe easier at that. A tear slipped down her cheek.

Pieter brushed it away. "You getting better is the only gift I want." His hand rested on the top of her head.

The touch was so tender, the words so intimate and private that Minnie felt like the worst intruder. She slipped back into the shadows, crept to the doorway of the exam room she'd slept in. She felt as if trapped beneath a ton of rubble. Her chest was tight and, for some reason, her eyes stung with tears.

It couldn't be more obvious that Pieter loved his Ellie Jane. That's what Minnie wanted. Wanted so desperately that simply witnessing that kind of love brought on tears.

She'd told herself that it would be enough to have the security of a safe home, someone that could give her companionship, and food on the table. She needed those things. Safety, food, friendship. But she couldn't lie to herself. They weren't enough.

She longed for someone to love her like Pieter loved Ellie Jane.

They didn't have a house anymore. Their business was gone. They would have to rebuild. Start over. Where would they even get the money—?

But none of that mattered to the man sitting at Ellie Jane's bedside.

When Minnie hugged herself against the chill of the room and squeezed her eyes closed, she could only see Jed as he'd looked last night.

Part of her had wanted him to reach for her. She'd wanted to know what it felt like to be in his embrace, to have his kiss.

But Jed didn't love her. He barely knew her.

How could she have fallen for someone she'd only just met?

It was ridiculous, wasn't it?

She'd written to Mr. Black for months. He knew far more about her than Jed did. She even knew a little of him from his letters.

She'd promised to marry him.

But now that promise felt... heavy. Like she was the one trapped underneath a beam, not Ellie Jane.

Because she wanted to be loved.

And the arrangement with Mr. Black was simply that—an arrangement. They didn't love each other.

But Jed hadn't reached for her last night.He wasn't looking for a wife. He'd needed her help as a nurse.

The first rays of light slipped over the horizon, visible out the front window of the clinic. She suspected Jamie would wake soon. It was Christmas morning, after all.

Pieter had gotten his miracle. Ellie Jane was awake; Jed had saved her life with that surgery. But Minnie knew there would be no Christmas magic for her. There never had been.

She had promised Jed she would stay and help through Christmas. One more day to be with him and Jamie. And then she would go to Mr. Black.

There was nothing else for her here. She had nowhere else to go. No money for another train ticket. But could she ever be happy with Mr. Black?

The sound of movement in Jed and Jamie's rooms cut off her ruminations. No time to dwell on what she didn't have. She'd enjoy one more day with them.

But what if...?

What if she could make Jed fall in love with her?

The thought galvanized her, even though it didn't make sense. She'd never been enough for one of the couples who had come to the orphanage looking for a child to love. She must've met hundreds of prospective parents during her years there. None of them had ever chosen her. Not like they had the other children.

And there was still the problem of Mr. Black. Even if she somehow managed to catch Jed's eye, Mr. Black was the one she'd promised to marry.

But in the early morning light, with resolve wrapped around her like a shawl, neither of those problems seemed insurmountable.

It was Christmas morning.

Maybe there wasn't magic waiting for her.

But what if she could make her own Christmas miracle?

~

Jed slipped into the clinic as the rays of dawn illuminated the horizon. He'd hoped to return before Jamie woke, but noise from the kitchen told him his hopes hadn't come to fruition. He paused in the entryway of the clinic, listening. He could barely make out the murmur of voices.

Would Jamie be angry that Jed hadn't been there when he'd woken up on Christmas morning? Jed wished he knew. These days, mornings could go either way. Pleasant or ugly. And Christmas was meant to be a morning of togetherness with family. A celebration of Christ's birth.

He hated that he might be disappointing his son. If only babies would time their births to fit Jed's needs.

He'd been awakened by Mr. Farraday in the early morning darkness, the clinic silent around him. The baby was coming. It'd been only a matter of hours before a healthy baby girl had been born. Jed had held her in his hands, seen her mouth open and heard that first cry, and he'd been hit with the miracle of Christmas all over again.

His Savior had been born on a night such as this. One filled with terror and uncertainty. Jed's fears were different than what Mary and Joseph experienced. He still didn't know whether Ellie Jane would survive. And yet he'd felt a sense of peace.

And now his stomach was coiled tight because he wasn't sure that peace would last. He wasn't sure that Jamie would understand.

No use standing here, delaying the inevitable.He moved through the clinic to his rooms at the back, heard a shuffle and a muffled, "Shh," as he pushed through the door to the kitchen.

Jamie stood at the table, where a steaming batch of biscuits and gravy waited. His son wore a look that managed to be both vulnerable and stubborn, his chin jutted out slightly but his eyes searching.

"Good morning," Minnie chirped. Jed allowed his gaze to encompass her, saw her wrapping a small package in brown paper secured with twine, tying a bow. "Jamie made you breakfast."

His gaze flicked back to his son. That was the vulnerability. Jamie worried that Jed was going to reject his offering.

"It smells amazing." Jed's stomach gurgled as if to punctuate the statement. A small smile pulled at Jamie's mouth.

On a normal morning, Jed would've gone to the washbasin first. But he couldn't stop thinking about Minnie pulling Jamie into that hug yesterday. Jed took a tentative step toward his son, reaching out with one arm. Jamie slipped under his arm to receive the embrace.

Jed's eyes were hot when they flew to Minnie, catching her stare above his son's head. Her eyes looked both happy and wistful before she blinked.

Jed let Jamie go. "Merry Christmas."

"Merry Christmas, Pa."

He moved to the washbasin now.

"Did Mrs. Farraday have her baby?"

"A little girl," he confirmed over his shoulder.

"Please tell me they didn't name her somethin' silly and Christmassy like Holly," his son said.

When Jed turned to face the room, wiping his hands with a towel, Jamie was sitting at the table eyeing the biscuits.

"Holly is a perfectly fine name," Minnie said. She finished tying off her string with a flourish and set the small package in front of one of the empty plates at the table.

Jed's stomach jumped. Was that meant to be a Christmas gift? Perhaps it was for Jamie, not for him. But then he noticed an identical package in front of Jamie's plate.

It was Christmas, after all. But he had been saving lives,

catching what little sleep he could in between. And he hadn't even known Minnie existed before they'd met at that train station.

"What about Carol?" Minnie asked.

Jamie grimaced.

"Noelle? Joy?"

Jamie's expression grew more disgusted with each suggestion, and Minnie finally dissolved into giggles. Jed stood apart from their pretend argument, worry gnawing at his stomach. What if Minnie's feelings were hurt because he hadn't thought to provide a Christmas gift?

"I should check on Ellie Jane," he murmured, interrupting their merriment.

Jamie's expression fell. It was slight, but there.

"I won't be long," he said. "You don't have to wait."

Jamie immediately pulled the serving plate toward himself. Jed could almost feel the disappointment radiating off of his son.

Minnie said something as Jed went back into the clinic proper. Jed could feel the expectations of his son and the community weighing on him.

This was his life. He was always pulled in too many directions. He'd thought having a nurse to help with his patient load would solve the predicament. But he was the problem. He could never be what everyone needed him to be. He peeked into Ellie Jane's room and found her awake, Pieter holding her hand. They looked up when he entered.

"Morning, Doc. Merry Christmas," Pieter said.

Ellie Jane smiled.

Emotions boiled up inside him. Last night, he wasn't sure he'd see her smile again.

"How are you feeling?" he asked as he moved toward the table.

"Everything hurts."

He didn't doubt it. He took her pulse at her neck. Her skin was cool, no sign of fever. That was a miracle in itself. If only it would last.

He caught sight of a plate near Pieter's feet, scraped clean.

The man followed his gaze. "Minnie brought me some breakfast. She checked on Ellie Jane, brought another blanket."

His helper had been busy this morning. Breakfast, checking on his patients, somehow finding gifts, making Jamie smile.

"She sure is something," Ellie Jane said.

Jed stepped to the counter to find his stethoscope. He wanted to listen to her lungs.

"Be a shame if she married Adam," Ellie Jane murmured.

He turned back to the table with his tool in hand. "Don't go getting any ideas. Minnie can make her own decisions."

Ellie Jane pursed her lips. A familiar expression that reminded him of Veronica when she'd thought Jed was being particularly unreasonable. "You've spent hours and hours alone with her," Ellie Jane whispered. "Seems like her reputation might be compromised."

Jed frowned. "Folks out here don't care about that kind of stuff. Nothing has happened between us."But his neck grew hot thinking about the near-kiss from last night. He'd wanted to kiss her. Just to see what it would be like.

Ellie Jane was staring at her husband now. Pieter cleared his throat, his eyes widening at his wife. He coughed. "Umm, Minnie helped you in the surgery, didn't she? Maybe you need a wife who could help in the clinic."

"Maybe you need a wife who isn't so much of a busybody." Jed said the words mildly. He was happy that Ellie Jane had enough energy to think about matchmaking—as futile as her efforts were.

He finished his examination and, thankfully, Ellie Jane didn't say anything more.

After putting away his instruments, he hesitated in the hallway. Ellie Jane hadn't said anything he hadn't been thinking. He liked Minnie well enough. He saw how Jamie responded to her. She'd brought back his son, not the recalcitrant boy who'd grown to be a stranger while Jed had been busy with his patients. Yet she'd only agreed to stay through Christmas. Jed couldn't ask her to stay longer, not when she'd come all this way to marry Adam.

It didn't matter what the folks of Cooper's Hollow thought. Minnie and Adam had written letters. She must have some feelings for the man if she'd come all this way. But suddenly the thought of hiring a nurse wasn't enough. A nurse wouldn't make Jamie light up from a silly argument. Wouldn't play a character game with him to make everyday chores lighter.

A nurse wouldn't cause the slow flip in Jed's stomach every time she brushed by him in the hallway. She'd prepared breakfast, even though Jamie had taken the credit. His son might've helped, but Minnie had prompted it. Jed was sure of that. She'd made his life easier, more pleasurable these past short days they'd been together. She made him see the positive side of things.

But it wouldn't be fair to ask her to stay.

CHAPTER 6

Late the next afternoon, Jed entered the clinic after he'd stomped snow from his boots on the boardwalk.

They'd had two days without snow, and slightly higher temperatures meant that the packed snow on the ground was slowly beginning to melt. Minnie would be able to leave, to go to Adam in a day or two if she still wanted to.

He didn't know how to ask her to stay.

And time was running out.

The clinic was quiet inside. Ellie Jane had fervently campaigned to be allowed to move to her sister and brother-in-law's home, a ranch at the edge of town. Jed knew that while the clinic had been quiet on Christmas Day, and so far, this morning, it wouldn't stay that way. Ellie Jane seemed much improved after the emergency surgery. And the ranch was close enough that he could still check on her once a day.

He'd spent the afternoon helping Pieter and Ellie Jane's brother-in-law bundle her up and move her in a wagon they'd padded with blankets. Being comfortable would aid in Ellie Jane's recovery. Being around family she loved. But the more

Ellie Jane had talked from the back of that wagon, the more Jed wanted to be home with Jamie. And Minnie.

When he returned, the clinic, and his rooms, were awfully quiet. While walking past the exam room where Ellie Jane had recovered overnight, he caught sight of movement inside.

Minnie.

She was on her hands and knees scrubbing the floor, a bucket of sudsy water just in front of her. She looked up at him. Her hair was escaping its pins. She blew a strand off her forehead. "Hi."

"You didn't have to clean up in here."

She kept scrubbing. "It's the least I could do in exchange for giving me a place to sleep for a couple of nights."

"Where's Jamie?" He might not have expected his son to be helping, except that he'd helped yesterday when they'd been cleaning up from the collapse.

She shook her head, her focus still on the floor. "I don't know. He left after lunch."

Disappointment rankled. Jed had promised to play Jamie and Minnie's character game after lunch, but the Holman's wagon had pulled up during the meal and he'd been called away. He hated that he'd missed Christmas afternoon with his son. The sun would be setting soon.

Where—?

The door slammed. Jamie stomped inside, loosing snow from his pants legs as he moved toward Jed.

Jed looked at the woman working to get a blood stain off the wood floor then at his son, who in that moment seemed not to care about cleanliness at all. It made his voice harsh. "Where have you been?"

Jamie's chin jutted as he skirted Jed in the hallway. "Out. Like you."

Jed followed him a few steps, stopping in the kitchen. Jamie unwound his scarf from his neck. Why was his son being evasive? "That's not good enough. Where were you?"

"What do you care?" Jamie muttered as he hung his coat on the peg. "You weren't here either."

"I'm your father. It's my business to know." Another pang that he'd missed the chance to play a game with his son, time they would never get back.

Jamie had turned, his shoulders hunched. Was he hiding something?

Minnie had come into the kitchen behind him. "Jed, let him—"

He knew she was trying to help, but he was Jamie's father.

"Turn around," he ordered.

Jamie twitched. And then he threw his shoulders back and turned around. He was holding something wrapped in his sweater. A tiny orange kitten. His expression was defiant.

"Where did you get that?" Jed had a niggling suspicion and prayed he was wrong.

"He's Grover's, and he can't take him out to his aunt and uncle's because they've got a big, mean dog." Jamie's eyes slanted to the side.

Maybe he thought Jed wouldn't notice that he hadn't answered the question.

Minnie brushed past Jed, already reaching for the tiny thing. "Oh, look at him. Her?"

Jamie nodded.

Minnie took the kitten into her arms, held it against her middle. "You're wet and cold, little girl."

"You know we can't keep it," Jed said. "No animals allowed inside the clinic. It isn't sanitary."

Jamie glared. "Just until Grover can take her back."

He understood his son wanted to help. Jamie had begged for a dog when he'd been younger. Jed had thought he understood why they couldn't have one. But a bigger issue remained.

"Where did you get it?" Jed asked again.

He held Jamie's stare until the boy lowered his eyes. "Me 'n Grover went over to the store. She was cryin'—"

"Did you crawl inside the wreckage?"

He hadn't meant to speak so tightly. Minnie, at the counter pouring a tiny bowl of milk, darted a look over her shoulder.

Jamie's eyes flashed. "We were careful."

"That was incredibly stupid. Do you know how much danger you put yourself in?"

He didn't mean for the words to burst out like that, but the rubble was unstable and imagining Jamie trapped beneath a beam and bleeding out like Ellie Jane had been two nights ago had his heart thundering in his ears and head pounding.

"You didn't tell me not to," Jamie muttered.

"I shouldn't have to—"

"Because you weren't here. You're never here."

"I have a duty to the people in town." He heard his father's voice emerge from his mouth.

Jamie scowled. "That's all you care about. Your duty."

"Son—"

Jamie ran into his bedroom and slammed the door. Jed stood there, air sawing in and out of his lungs as if he'd slogged through knee-high snow for an entire block. Minnie remained at the counter, that kitten in her arms, looking as if she wished she could disappear.

He couldn't take the hurt in her stare. For Jamie?

He turned away, pushing his hand through his hair. Humiliated that she'd witnessed them blowing up at each other. Broken inside because he had turned into his father after years of vowing he never would.

"He doesn't realize now," she whispered, "But he's lucky to have a father like you. I didn't."

He knew she was an orphan. She'd told him earlier. But

before he could respond or even think, there was pounding on the front door.

The muscles in his shoulders tightened. The timing couldn't be worse. But he didn't have a choice. Snow blew in the door when he wrenched it open.

Adam Black stood on the other side. "I'm here for my wife."

~

I'm here for my wife.

Minnie heard the words as if she were buried in a snowbank, muffled and fuzzy though she stood only steps behind Jed in the hallway.

Mr. Black was here.

She couldn't quite see him. Jed, broad-shouldered and tall, blocked her view.

She was still breathless from witnessing the fight between Jed and Jamie, still aching because of what she'd almost told Jed. She, who could talk up a storm when uncomfortable, but had never spoken of her loneliness.

Maybe it was for the best.

She didn't hear a response from Jed over the pounding of her pulse in her ears. He moved to one side and Mr. Black stepped inside.

She felt the kitten trembling, still wrapped in Jamie's sweater, where it rested in the crook of her arm. Or was she the one trembling?

Mr. Black was shorter than he'd purported to be in his letters. When he swept the hat from his head, she saw the receding hairline, the wrinkles and age spots. He'd told her he was forty. Was this forty?

His scraggly beard was streaked with gray, and when he smiled, he was missing one tooth on the top. "I'm sorry the snow kept me from meeting your train."

His gaze swept her up and down, and was it a might... possessive? She wasn't sure she liked the uncomfortable feeling that choked her.

"Minnie," he said. "I'm Adam Black."

Wilhelmina. She wanted to correct him. Wanted to put some distance between them. She'd come all this way, but it suddenly felt wrong.

Behind Mr. Black, Jed towered silent and watchful. Somehow, his presence made this moment feel exponentially more charged.

"How do you do?" Her words sounded like a breath; she could barely get them out.

Mr. Black didn't seem to mind. He smiled again. Jerked his finger over his shoulder. "I've got my sleigh out front. We can hop over to the preacher's and get hitched right now."

Leave. Right now.

"If we hurry, we'll make it home by midnight."

Her chest felt tight, her eyes suddenly hot.

Jed stood silent behind Mr. Black.

She'd thought... she'd thought she had at least one more day with Jed and Jamie. Twenty-four more hours to dream of what it would be like to share a life with them. To prove to Jed that she could be a helpmeet.

But she didn't have one more day. She had a matter of minutes.

"I will need to gather up my things," she said quietly.

"You can wait here." Jed directed Mr. Black to one of the hard-backed seats in the tiny front room of the clinic.

Minnie whirled and slipped into the exam room where she'd left her carpetbag tucked beneath the cot she'd slept in last night. Her Bible was on top of the cot.There wasn't anything else to pack. Her coat hung in the kitchen, next to Jamie's. Her meager possessions somehow seemed smaller than ever.

A sound at the door brought her head up. The motion

unleashed a tear she hadn't realized had been gathering. It slipped down her cheek.

Jed moved into the room, closing the door most of the way.

She brushed away her tear and waited, words she'd heard about Mr. Black filtering through her mind.

Adam has a short temper.

A mean streak.

He's unkind to his animals.

He doesn't keep up with repairs on that shack of his.

But Jed had never added a disparaging word about her intended. Even now when she ached from wishing that he'd say something, anything, he stayed silent.

His arms were crossed over his chest and a muscle jumped in his cheek. The tilt of his head reminded her of Jamie.

Jamie.

In her shaken state these past few moments, she'd almost forgotten about the fight between father and son.

And suddenly, Jed's stare was too much.

She turned and shifted the kitten into one arm so she could reach down and pull her bag from beneath the cot. She set it on top of the mattress and opened the clasp.

"Jamie loves you." Her voice trembled almost as badly as her hands. "That's why he's been acting the way he has."

"Is that your bonafide opinion?" She didn't know what his tone meant.

"He was so excited to prepare Christmas breakfast for you. To give you your gift."

She hadn't expected to receive anything but after a whispered conference, the two males had gifted her a beautiful, knitted scarf. She suspected by the squint of Jed's eyes when she'd wrapped it around her neck that it had belonged to Jamie's mother.

Jed exhaled, the sound loud in the silent room. "I... don't

know what to do," he said quietly. "How to be in two places at once. People need me, need the care I can provide."

"And Jamie needs you, too," she said. She couldn't quite look at him. "Have you considered taking him on some of your calls?"

He was quiet for a long moment. Maybe it had been a silly idea. She felt time ticking away. Her smile was tremulous when she looked at Jed again.

"Growing up, in the orphanage, I..." It was so difficult to talk about this. The words felt as if they hit a stopper in her throat. She cleared it. "Prospective parents would visit on Sundays. Every child in the orphanage, myself included, would scrub ourselves clean, put on our nicest clothes, and line up to meet the people who might want to take us home. Who might see in us their son or daughter."

She had to swallow the aching knot in her throat to go on. "I wanted so badly to be chosen."

The words shook her. She'd thought she was only talking about Jamie, but now her eyes were swimming with tears again. She wanted Jed to choose her. For him to say he felt the same thing she did. They hadn't known each other long, but there was something between them. If it wasn't love yet, then maybe it could grow.

Whether she marries Mr. Black or not is Minnie's business.

How many times had he said that, or something similar, over the past two days?

Jed had had ample opportunities to speak up, just like everyone else had. To tell her why she shouldn't marry Mr. Black. And right now, this moment, he could choose her. Ask her to stay.

But he didn't.

Somehow she found the words inside. "Choose Jamie," she whispered roughly. She laughed a tiny, tearful laugh. "It's clear to everyone how much you love him. Maybe he needs you to say the words, and to show him."

There was nothing else for her to say. He'd asked her to stay through Christmas. Ellie Jane was back with her family. There was nothing for Minnie here now.

She picked up the carpetbag, juggling the kitten, who had gone to sleep tucked against her. She only stopped long enough to hand the kitten to Jed before she fetched her coat. The scarf hung in plain sight after she lifted the coat away.

She looked at it for a moment too long. And left it there.

CHAPTER 7

"Aren't you going after her?"

Jed looked up from where he'd propped both hands on the exam table. Jamie stood in the doorway, watching him.

The kitten sat tiny in the middle of the table, licking its front paw.

Jed sighed and straightened. His muscles felt heavy and sluggish. One too many nights without sleep. "What?"

"Aren't you going after Minnie? You can't let her marry Adam Black."

No one chose me.

He shook his head to dislodge the memory of her pale face, her eyes just a little too big.

His chest felt tight. Was he coming down with a lung complaint?

"She came here to marry him," he reminded his son. He moved to the cabinet on the far wall and dug around until he found one of the older blankets he kept there.

Jamie made a sound like *pfft*. Jed turned to see his son

bouncing on the balls of his feet. Like he was ready to run out into the night and get Minnie himself.

"Adam is a no account, lying, lazy fleabag. She don't belong with him."

"Hey. We don't talk about people like that."

Jamie's chin took on that stubborn tilt. And he wasn't wrong.

Jed had been so careful to tiptoe around the subject in his mind, but now he couldn't avoid it. Adam Black wasn't a good person. Nevertheless, Minnie had traveled out here to marry him. Made promises in her letters.

It wasn't Jed's business.

But Jamie was.

"We need to talk."

Jamie's eyes flashed as he crossed his arms over his lanky chest.

Jed didn't even know where to start. Then Minnie's voice popped into his head, and his gut panged. He supposed somewhere was a better choice than nowhere.

He tossed the blanket to Jamie, who had to unwind his arms to catch it. "Make a bed in your room for the cat."

Jamie's eyes lit up with cautious hope.

"It's only for tonight," Jed said. Jamie's shoulders slumped. "Tomorrow, I'll help you find a safe place for the kitten to stay. Somewhere close so you can check on him every day."

It was the best he could do. Animals brought in dust and pollen from outdoors, not to mention their dander and germs. He couldn't have an animal in the clinic.

"But—"

Jamie had been staring mulishly at the floor; now his gaze jumped to Jed. "But what?"

"I know you've wanted a pet for a long time. The clinic and our rooms here are barely big enough for the two of us."

Jamie nodded, still listening. He moved a half step forward to reach out and pet the kitten.

"The Hursts and Ratcliffs will have to rebuild. There's space on the block for a two-story building. I could use another exam room. And having our rooms on the second floor would mean some separation from the clinic."

"Enough for a pet?" Jamie barely breathed the words. He was vibrating with excitement.

"Enough for a pet," Jed said.

Jamie's face relaxed into a smile. "Thanks, Pa."

Jed's gut pinched a little for the boy who once would've thrown himself at Jed, hugging his knees. Jamie was past that stage now, on his way to being a man. Jed would never get those years back.

His throat felt as if he was at the onset of a bacterial infection. "About what you said before—"

"I'm sorry." Jamie interrupted, hanging his head. "I know I shouldn't have spoken to you like that."

Jed pushed his hands into his pockets, and his right index finger brushed against something wrapped in paper—the peppermint candy Minnie had given him. His hand closed over it.

"We've had a rough patch lately," Jed said. His voice felt gravelly. "Since your mother passed."

She'd been the one that had connected them. For the few hours that Minnie had been a part of their lives, she'd taken that place in the dynamic. But it wasn't hers to have.

Jed needed to find a way to connect with his son on his own. In a few more years, Jamie would be grown and on his own.

"I haven't said it enough, but I love you. I'm proud to have you as my son. Whether you grow up to be a doctor or a cowboy or whatever."

Jamie glanced up from the kitten, his mouth a wobbly line.

That gave Jed the courage to go on. "Maybe instead of a nurse, I need to add another doctor to this practice. It could take months—"

Jamie shook his head. "Do you really think it'd make a difference? If someone needed help at dinnertime, you'd see them."

Jed felt helpless at the certainty in Jamie's tone.

"It's who you are," Jamie said. "Someone I'm proud to be related to."

What? Jed stared at his son, who dropped his chin bashfully.

"Maybe I could go with you sometimes," Jamie muttered. "On your house calls."

"I'd love that." Jed didn't try to hide the emotion in his voice. "Minnie suggested the same."

"I know," Jamie said wryly. "I could hear through the wall."

Jed's hand closed around the candy in his pocket. Minnie had somehow slipped out and charmed Mrs. Peterson into selling her the candy on Christmas morning. She'd spent what little of her hard-earned money she had left to give Jamie and Jed a gift.

"You gotta go after her," Jamie said, urgency in his tone. "You can't let her marry Adam Black."

She wasn't Jed's business. Even if he wanted her to be.

"What would she do if she didn't marry him?" He shouldn't have posed the hypothetical question because Jamie jumped in with a quick answer.

"Marry you."

Jed froze, his stomach knotting, all the blood draining from his face. Because the idea hit home. He shook his head. "I don't have time for a wife."

Jamie scoffed. "What I said before? I was wrong. You aren't like Grandfather. You've got time enough. Besides, you love her."

Jamie's words hit like a punch to the solar plexus. He didn't love Minnie. Did he?

It was too soon. They barely knew each other.

But she didn't know Adam Black at all.

Jamie was right. Surely he was a better choice than Adam.

And Jed suspected she had feelings for him too. If she didn't love him now, surely those feelings could grow.

He winced. He was no prize. He was impatient and over-worked and...

"Why would she want me?" He hadn't meant to say the words out loud.

Jamie looked at him with a smirk. "Why don't you go after her and ask? She didn't want to go with Adam, did she?"

No one chose me.

Had she been trying to tell him something? The vulnerable look in her eye, the tip of her nose turning pink.

Nervous energy coursed from his spine out through his extremities.

"I have to go," he told Jamie.

Who grinned.

Jed stopped only to hug his son and grab his coat.

"Tell her you love her," Jamie hollered after him as he went out the front door.

Jed would.

If it wasn't too late.

~

"We don't need no fancy, long ceremony," Mr. Black said to the preacher.

Minnie sat on a chair in the minister's parlor, her carpetbag in her lap. She had tucked her hands beneath it to hide their trembling. The fire in the grate, only a few feet away, was crackling merrily, but she couldn't seem to feel it. The short drive in Mr. Black's sleigh had chilled her to the bone.

Or maybe she'd been frozen inside before that. When Jed had let her go.

"Miss Bannister has made several friends in her short stint in town," the parson said. "Surely she'll want to marry with her friends around her. To celebrate."

The older man seemed to be trying to delay the ceremony. She couldn't understand why. They were here now.

"I've got to get back to the homestead," Mr. Black said. "Things to take care of. You understand."

Neither man asked her what she wanted. They spoke as if she wasn't even in the room. As if she were invisible. Just like she'd been all those times prospective parents had come through the orphanage and overlooked her.

Her heart beat fast and painfully in her chest. Then Mrs. Owens appeared at her side. She held a coffee cup in her hands, but after one look at Minnie, she motioned her up.

"Your bride needs a moment to refresh herself," Mrs. Owens said in Mr. Black's direction.

Minnie hadn't said a word, but Mrs. Owens was right.

She followed the woman down a short hallway and into a bedroom with a neatly made bed beneath the curtained window. Someone had lit a lamp on the desk in the corner and it illuminated the looking glass on the wall.

Minnie caught her reflection and held back a gasp. Her face was pale, dark smudges under her eyes. She looked like a frightened mouse.

What was she going to do?

At Mrs. Owens's urging, she sat on the edge of the bed. The older woman sat beside her and pressed the cup of coffee into Minnie's chilled hands.

"Thank you," she murmured. She braced herself. She didn't know whether she could sit through Mrs. Owens telling her she couldn't marry Mr. Black. Everyone else had.

Everyone except Jed.

"We're so thankful you came to town," Mrs. Owens said, surprising her into raising her gaze.

The older woman looked sincere. And warm. Like how Minnie had always imagined a mother would look.

"If you hadn't arrived in town when you did, Jed would've been overwhelmed with his patients."

She shook her head. "There were others who helped."

"Maybe so, but you were the one who crawled through the rubble to reach Ellie Jane."

Warmth seeped into the pit of her stomach, unfurling the tightness there by a tiny bit. Mrs. Owens thought she'd done a good job.

"Jed would've found a way to rescue her. And take care of everyone else. He's an amazing doctor."

When it grew too hard to hold Mrs. Owens's gaze, Minnie plucked at the skirt on her lap.

"Everyone with working eyes can see the way Jed looks at you when he thinks no one else is watching."

Minnie shook her head. That wasn't right.

"I admit I hoped you'd end up being stuck in town for a few more days. Give that boy a chance to chase after you himself."

That boy? It took Minnie a moment to realize she'd meant Jed.

Mrs. Owens thought Jed would want Minnie?

Jed was the only one who hadn't warned her off Mr. Black.

Jed was a man of honor.

"I'm not good enough for him." She whispered her deepest fear. "I'm a nobody from nowhere." She'd been thrown away. Never chosen.

"Hogwash," Mrs. Owens said fiercely, startling Minnie. "That's a bunch of nonsense, and whoever told you that deserves a good smack for their trouble."

Minnie couldn't help but laugh at the outlandish statement. More warmth unfurled inside her. The heat from the mug she held between her hands had also started to warm her.

"You might not have a lot of book learning," Mrs. Owens

said, "but many of us are the same. You've got a kind heart and a strong work ethic. But most of all, you're a child of God."

Her words settled deep inside Minnie. She'd sat in church pews all her life, heard the words preached from the pulpit. Sang the songs. Become a baptized follower of Jesus. But no one had ever said those words to her before.

Mrs. Owens put her hand on Minnie's shoulder. "It doesn't matter where you come from. It matters that you're His."

The realization unleashed the last of the tightness in Minnie's middle. It freed her.

She was a Daughter of the King. Adopted into the only family that mattered. God's family.

No matter what happened, no one could take that away from her.

Her shoulders straightened and she sipped the coffee, enjoying the warmth sliding down her throat.

Mrs. Owens must've seen the change in her. "What're you going to do now? Are you still going to marry Adam?"

As if on cue, a knock sounded at the door.

"Where's my bride?" Definitely Mr. Black's voice, but this time the demanding whine sent a shiver of unease down Minnie's back. She didn't know the man. And at first glance, he didn't seem to match the description of himself that he'd given her in his letters.

She exhaled the last of her tension and opened the door.

She was taller than him, she realized as they faced off in the doorway. Mr. Owens hung back in the hallway.

"We barely know each other, Mr. Black," she said. Was it only the second thing she'd said to him? And he had been okay with her silence? "I think the wise choice is for us to delay the marriage for a bit. Get to know each other. Find out if we truly suit."

"We agreed on immediate marriage," he said, frowning.

"So we did. But I don't want to marry in haste and have regrets later. Do you?"

Something ugly glittered in Mr. Black's eyes. "You can't go back on an agreement. You gave your word."

"I'm not going back on my—"

"Either we marry tonight, or we don't marry at all." His lip curled as if he thought fear would choose for her.

A man who would use words against her, twist them, make ultimatums and threats before they were even wed?

There was no choice.

She tucked her trembling hands against her stomach. "I'm sorry. I can't marry you."

CHAPTER 8

Jed left the clinic less than an hour after Minnie had gone with Adam, but when he arrived on foot at the parsonage, there were fresh tracks in the snow and no sign of Adam's sleigh.

Was he too late?

His breaths puffed out clouds in the bracing cold. Snow started to fall. Tiny flakes that felt like nothing when they brushed against the exposed skin of his face.

Everything was quiet and still. The sun had set, but lights shone from the buildings and houses down Main Street. He thought he heard the jingle of a harness, but when he strained his ears to listen, it was only his harsh breaths in the stillness.

If they'd only just left, should he go to the livery and fetch his horse? Go after her?

But what could he do if she was already married?

Nothing.

The answer twisted his stomach with dread.

And then the parsonage door opened.

Mrs. Owens motioned toward him. "You'd better come inside."

His feet carried him up the stairs and onto her porch before he'd given it a thought.

He felt raw, like a scrape where several layers of skin had been shaved away. If he'd been a bit quicker to come to terms with what he was feeling, would things have been different—?

He stepped onto the top step of the porch and a curtain of snow from the roof fell behind him. He was only peripherally aware of it because he'd glimpsed the room behind Mrs. Owens.

Minnie was there, standing in front of the sofa as if she'd just risen from her seat.

Suddenly his skin was tingling as if he'd doused himself in a bath of disinfectant. He could feel each heartbeat pounding beneath his skin.

He wasn't sure how he got inside, if Mrs. Owens moved aside to let him in or if he just ran her over.

He couldn't seem to look away from Minnie. She watched him silently, cautious hope in her eyes.

"You're here," he breathed.

"You're late." A soft, barely-there smile twitched on her lips at the echo of the first words they'd said to each other.

Had it been only three days ago?

His world had shifted on its axis when he'd met her on that train platform. As if he'd been reborn, given another chance at happiness.

But intrusive thoughts didn't stay silent for long. He broke the glance with Minnie, glanced around the room. "Where's Adam?"

"He went home."

Mrs. Owens had faded away in silence. Soft murmurs from down the hall made him guess she and the parson were giving him a moment of privacy with Minnie. Bless them.

"So you're not married yet?"

She shook her head. "No."

His heart jumped into his throat. Even though she'd teased him, he wasn't too late.

He couldn't seem to look away from her, and she seemed to be having the same trouble.

"What are you doing here?" The question cost her, vulnerability lighting in her eyes.

"I couldn't let you marry Adam. Jamie set me straight."

She glanced away. He keenly felt the four paces between them. Awkwardness threatened, his mind betraying him, whispering *what are you doing*? He shook the thoughts away.

"That came out wrong." He took one step toward her.

She fiddled with the edge of the sofa arm, not looking at him now. But he had the sense she was still listening.

"When you arrived on that train three days ago, I was desperate. I thought I needed help at the clinic, but you opened my eyes to what my life really needed. You."

He caught her tiny gasp before her eyes flew to his face.

He crossed another step toward her. One more and he'd be close enough to reach for her.

"You showed me how to connect with Jamie. Worked by my side tirelessly."

She'd taken care of him. Something he hadn't even known that he'd missed.

"I—" *I love you*. For a moment, insecurity threatened. The words remained trapped in his chest. What did he have to offer her? Life with a husband who was rarely home? In this remote place?

"What are you saying?" she asked, her voice a murmur.

"I know you've made promises to Adam." He didn't know why the other man had left. Didn't care. "But we've spent the past forty-eight hours together. Enough of that time spent without a chaperone that your reputation may be affected."

Folks out here didn't put as much stock in a soiled reputation as the society people he remembered from his younger years. But he didn't say that.

"The easiest way for us to fix that would be to marry."

Her face fell.

He'd been ready to cross the last bit of space between them but hesitated when she wrapped her arms around her middle, a defensive posture he recognized from Jamie.

And then she shook her head again. "I can't."

His stomach bottomed out. For a moment, his ears rang as if he'd been socked in the jaw.

I can't.

More words tumbled over themselves in his throat. His jaw worked.

He couldn't seem to get his thoughts in order.

He'd thought she had some feelings for him.

Had he been wrong?

isappointment surged through Minnie, making her tremble.

Jed had come for her.

He'd offered to marry her.

For all the wrong reasons.

The hope she'd felt moments ago, seeing the determination in his eyes, the stare that twisted her stomach so deliciously... it was all gone. But beneath the disappointment, resolution stirred inside her like red-hot embers glowing in a fire. She wasn't the same woman she'd been yesterday or even earlier today. The difficult decision she'd made in Mrs. Owens's bedroom not long ago was still right.

Jed looked both flummoxed and hurt. He was so dear to her. She couldn't stand for him to be hurt. She took a big breath.

"When I turned away Mr. Black, I did it because I realized I couldn't let fear dictate my choices. Not any longer."

Jed watched her, a frown pulling on one side of his lips. He was trying to understand.

"I came all this way to marry a man I didn't even know because I wanted to belong somewhere. And because I was running from my past. I was afraid of being alone, being vulnerable with no one to help." She could still feel the echo of that fear. But it didn't live inside her any longer.

"When I arrived here, you and everyone else in Cooper's Hollow taught me about community. People that take care of each other." She wanted to be a part of it. But she also couldn't sacrifice the deepest dream inside of her.

Her chin wobbled, but she steadied it. "My choices led me here, but I can't marry out of desperation. Or for convenience sake."

Tears pricked her eyes. She wanted to accept him. Oh, she wanted it. But it would be pure torture to be married to Jed, to love him so desperately and know that her feelings weren't returned, that he had been trapped into the marriage.

She couldn't quite meet his gaze now, so she stared at the top button on his shirt. "I still want someone to choose me. Someone to love me. And maybe that means I'll be waiting forever, but—"

She was distracted by the single tear that slipped down her cheek. At the same moment she reached up to brush it away, Jed crossed the last bit of distance between them.

He swept her into his arms, and she didn't try to push him away, weak as that made her. Not when she'd wanted to be right there for so long.

His left hand came up to cradle her jaw. "I've made a hash of this, but there's one thing you can be assured of. I love you."

He didn't give her time to register the words, only dipped his head to kiss her.

The first brush of his lips was tentative, exploring. Her hands—how had they come up to rest on his shoulders?—flexed, and maybe she even tried to clutch him closer.

His kiss grew more sure, his lips more fervent against hers. The arm that wasn't tenderly holding her face banded around her waist. He kissed her like he was trying to prove what he'd just said.

He loved her?

He pulled back slightly to rest his forehead against her. His breaths were uneven and she felt a strange kind of satisfaction in that.

"I love you," he whispered. "I should've said it before you walked out the door with Adam. I should've chased you down the street, yelling it at the top of my lungs. It should've been the first thing I said when I stepped into this room. I was frightened, too. That you wouldn't want to be with someone who is so busy he can't even keep his life straight."

He loved her.

She believed him. And as the certainty settled over her, she realized that he needed to hear it, too.

"I love you," she whispered in return. "The man who cares so much about his friends and neighbors that he doesn't have time to take care of himself."

His eyes closed in what she suspected was relief. He squeezed her tighter, and she let herself be folded into the warmth of his body. They held each other for long moments, murmuring their love, reassuring each other that this was real.

And then he stepped back. All the way back.

Her breath caught and her heart started pounding when he knelt on one knee. He held both her trembling hands in his.

"Minnie, my heart. I love you. I want you to be my family, mine and Jamie's both. Not because of anything you can do for us and not as a matter of convenience. Because you are the most beautiful, kind-hearted, infuriating woman I know."

She couldn't help smiling through the tears gathering in her eyes.

"I offer myself. As poor a choice as that might seem to some. Flawed and impatient as I am. I ask you to choose me. Marry me."

Her wobbly voice answered, "How can I refuse? Yes."

He rose to his feet and swept her into his arms once again.

"I love you," she said just before he kissed her again.

A throat being cleared from nearby interrupted the private moment. Mrs. Owens was peering around the corner of the hallway, Mr. Owens just behind her.

"I believe congratulations are in order," Mrs. Owens said.

A blush heated Minnie's cheeks, but Jed seemed unperturbed, happy to keep his arm around her shoulders as they faced the older couple.

"Can you marry us now?" he asked the preacher. Then tilted his head to Minnie as if he'd just had second thoughts. "Unless you want to wait for Sunday, when everyone will be gathered at the church for worship?"

He was giving her the choice, not pushing like Mr. Black had. He wanted her to have the special day that she wanted.

"I don't want to wait to become your wife."

His face eased into a smile.

"But maybe we should fetch Jamie. And perhaps we could have a small celebration with everyone on Sunday."

His eyes warmed even more, if possible. Because she wanted to include Jamie?

"He'll be proud of himself for months, claim he set me straight."

A smile twitched on her lips now. "Did he?"

"Maybe a little. I like to think I would've gotten there on my own."

He squeezed her shoulders then donned his hat and coat to go back into the cold. He and Jamie returned within minutes.

Minnie found herself standing in the middle of the p
parlor, facing Jed, holding both of his hands.

I take thee to be my wife.

Tears pricked her eyes as Jed repeated his vows. Words of promise. Words that meant she'd been chosen. That she was loved.

She recognized his emotion when he swallowed hard as she repeated her own vows.

And then the simple ceremony was over.

Jed brushed a chaste kiss across her lips. The parson and his wife offered their congratulations as Jamie hugged her tightly.

"Let's go home," Jed said, holding her coat for her to slip her arms inside.

Home.

His eyes glinted as he read the emotion she couldn't hide from him.

Home was Jed. And Jamie. Wherever they were together, that was her home.

Her Christmas miracle.

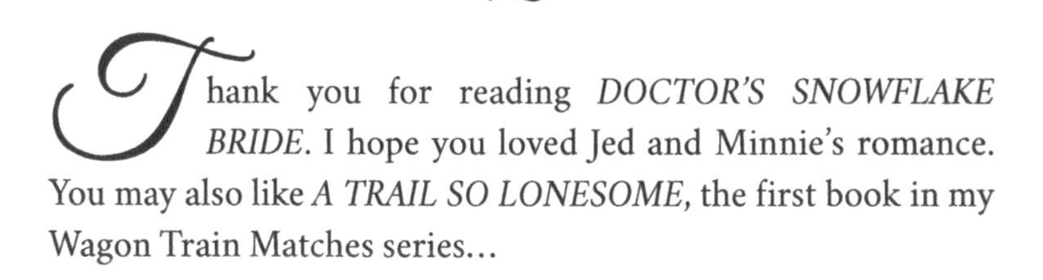

Thank you for reading *DOCTOR'S SNOWFLAKE BRIDE*. I hope you loved Jed and Minnie's romance. You may also like *A TRAIL SO LONESOME*, the first book in my Wagon Train Matches series...

"What do you mean, she's gone?" Evangeline whispered the words, standing outside the wagon with her father. "How could Mrs. Fletcher just abandon us?"

Sara was still asleep in the tiny pallet Evangeline had created inside the wagon, atop all their supplies. Sara had outgrown her crib months ago in their stately townhouse back in Boston. But this was different. Aware of how high the wagon bed was from the ground, Evangeline had put Sara's pallet in between two trunks, with a barrel of salt pork and a smaller one of sugar barricading the girl in.

How could Sara sleep through all this ruckus? The thin line of silver at the horizon was the only sign that the sun was rising, but the camp was bustling and had been for some time.

It didn't seem possible that so many of their neighbors were awake after the raucous celebrating that had gone on long into the night. But the teenaged boy two wagons away was working to get his oxen into their braces one-by-one. The family just beyond him were eating breakfast. If Evangeline remembered correctly, their name was Fairfax. An older brother barely twenty, a sister in the middle, and a teen brother. And their aunt. Evangeline's nose twitched at the scent of fried ham.

Her father was loading the last of the crates into the rear of the wagon and she realized their time was short, but she couldn't wrap her mind around what he'd just informed her. Their cook, a long-time employee and one of the only women in Evangeline's life after her mother had passed, would not accompany them to Oregon.

"She didn't want to go in the first place," Father said without looking up.

"I know that," Evangeline returned. "But she promised. You *paid* her." Her father had offered the cook an exorbitant amount to come West with them. For good reason. Evangeline had never learned to cook. Father and Mother had always employed a cook. And a housekeeper, a groom for their horses, two maids.

Evangeline had spent almost a year preparing for this trip. Reading about what to expect on the trail. Making lists and buying what they needed. Taking riding lessons. Sewing lessons.

But she hadn't spent any time in the kitchen because Mrs. Fletcher was coming with them.

"It's not too late to rethink this plan of yours."

She kept her smile in place, though Father's words stung. Actually, it was too late to change her mind. Almost four years too late.

We have to go. She didn't give voice to the words. *Sara needs Oregon.* There was no future for Sara back in Boston. No future for Evangeline, either, but she'd resigned herself to that a long time ago. She could change things for Sara.

Evangeline knew how to win her father. "Just think of all the timber in Oregon," she said. "Every family on this wagon train will want lumber to buy to make a new house. And you'll provide it for them. Along with the families that come next year, and the year after."

Her father was a shrewd businessman, and they both knew she was right. Her father had built a series of successful mills under the tutelage of his father. The number of families traveling to Oregon with them was just the beginning. If there was a fortune to be made in Oregon, her father would be the one to make it.

He had listened to her opining about Oregon and the adventures—and the money—awaiting them on the other side of the country at the dinner table for nearly a week before she had won him over to the idea. She had been desperate, and he had finally seen the possibility.

He only glanced briefly at Evangeline. She ignored the pinch of hurt. "What will we eat for five months on the trail?"

"I'll cook."

It was still too dark to read her father's expression, but she could well imagine the skepticism she would see if there was light. Father didn't understand why this trip meant so much to her. "I'm certain I packed a cookbook."

He grunted. "Probably more than one," he muttered. "I'll start hitching up the oxen."

Evangeline had once been a spoiled girl, only worrying about the next fancy dress she would purchase for the next party. But that Evangeline had expired a long time ago. She straightened her shoulders and buoyed her resolve. How difficult could it be to cook over an open fire?

She took one last look at the skyline of Independence, now coming into relief as the first silver rays appeared on the horizon. She wouldn't let herself be frightened of this. There was no place for fear. Only courage.

"I don't suppose you've got an extra cord of rope." The oldest Fairfax brother was speaking to the neighbor between his wagon and Evangeline's.

She'd seen folks of all shapes and sizes in the meeting the other night. Stephen Fairfax seemed shy, had kept his head down during the brief introductions she and Father had made last night at camp.

She saw the slump of his shoulders and called out, "I have some extra rope."

She had packed the wagon meticulously, planned for a scenario just like this one. She and Father were perhaps at a disadvantage being from the city. But if she could help their neighbors and perhaps garner goodwill, surely it would make their journey easier at a later date.

She carefully stepped up into the wagon box, doing her best not to jostle the conveyance. She glanced to where Sara slept, though it was too dark inside the wagon to see anything other than a shadowy lump where she lay. Evangeline would have to wake the girl in a few minutes. They couldn't afford to stop for her to wash up as the wagons rolled out.

Evangeline reached into the small box that held the odds and ends she had packed as extras. She got back down from the wagon, waving the tied up rope like a prize.

"Thank you." His voice was fervent, though softer than she expected. She got her first good look at his face and realized he was younger than she'd thought. Much younger.

The smooth face with no hint of whiskers might belong to a 15-year-old. Surely she was mistaken. Maybe he was older but cursed by the fair skin he seemed to share with his sister. Some men didn't grow whiskers until an older age, right? Maybe he was even as old as seventeen. Not eighteen, surely?

He ducked his head and she realized she was staring. She cleared her throat. "You're welcome. I'm happy to help a neighbor."

He was gone before she could say anything else. She moved around to the back of the wagon, where the item she needed right now was packed away. She had to unlatch the tailgate and drag a box of ammunition out of the way before she found the crate she was looking for. It was packed with books, and she let her hand run over the spines of those at the top. She had packed and re-packed three crates just like this, her own personal library. She had filled every inch of space in each crate, re-arranging the books until not even a sheet of paper would fit between. She just knew there was a cookbook here.

"Pulling out in half an hour."

She nodded idly at the voice relaying the message, not looking up from what she was doing. Where was it?

"We won't wait if you're not ready. Half an hour." This time the starch in the male voice made her raise her head and look at him.

Leo Mason, the man who had been elected to captain for this first month of the journey. He had seemed resigned the other night; this morning he wore a stormy expression.

She abandoned her search for the cookbook and wiped her hand on her skirt before sticking it out and taking a few steps toward him. "I am Evangeline Murphy. My sister Sara is still sleeping, and my father is going to get the oxen. We'll be ready."

He stared at her hand doubtfully before he gave a limp handshake. "You have any problems, you can come to me."

"Or Owen. I remember."

His jaw tightened at the mention of his half brother. She had spent far too long last night remembering the tension between the two men during the meeting. Owen had seemed to take an ornery delight in announcing to the room that Leo was his half brother, as if anyone with eyes couldn't have seen the resemblance between them. She was an only child. When she had been young, she had often longed for a brother or sister. A companion to play with. Perhaps that was why she had spent so much time wondering at the broken relationship in a family of strangers.

"You'll want to keep the little one up in the wagon till we get clear of the creek." He pointed to a line of trees in the distance.

She didn't see a creek, but maybe he knew the landscape she didn't.

He started to walk off—without giving her a chance to say anything else—but seemed to change his mind. "It's not too late for you to decide to stay."

She bristled. "What does that mean?"

"You don't look like you belong here."

The nerve of the man.

ONE-CLICK A TRAIL SO LONESOME NOW

Want to connect online? Here's where you can find me:

GET NEW RELEASE ALERTS

Follow me on Amazon
Follow me on Bookbub
Follow me on Goodreads

CONNECT ON THE WEB

www.lacywilliams.net
lacy@lacywilliams.net

SOCIAL MEDIA

ALSO BY LACY WILLIAMS

WAGON TRAIN MATCHES SERIES (HISTORICAL ROMANCE)

A Trail So Lonesome

Trail of Secrets

A Trail Untamed

WIND RIVER HEARTS SERIES (HISTORICAL ROMANCE)

Marrying Miss Marshal

Counterfeit Cowboy

Cowboy Pride

The Homesteader's Sweetheart

Courted by a Cowboy

Roping the Wrangler

Return of the Cowboy Doctor

The Wrangler's Inconvenient Wife

A Cowboy for Christmas

Her Convenient Cowboy

Her Cowboy Deputy

Catching the Cowgirl

The Cowboy's Honor

Winning the Schoolmarm

The Wrangler's Ready-Made Family

Christmas Homecoming

SUTTER'S HOLLOW SERIES (CONTEMPORARY ROMANCE)

His Small-Town Girl

Secondhand Cowboy

The Cowgirl Next Door

COWBOY FAIRYTALES SERIES (CONTEMPORARY FAIRYTALE ROMANCE)

Once Upon a Cowboy

Cowboy Charming

The Toad Prince

The Beastly Princess

The Lost Princess

Kissing Kelsey

Courting Carrie

Stealing Sarah

Keeping Kayla

Melting Megan

The Other Princess

The Prince's Matchmaker

HOMETOWN SWEETHEARTS SERIES (CONTEMPORARY ROMANCE)

Kissed by a Cowboy

Love Letters from Cowboy

Mistletoe Cowboy

The Bull Rider

The Brother

The Prodigal

Cowgirl for Keeps

Jingle Bell Cowgirl

Heart of a Cowgirl

3 Days with a Cowboy

Prodigal Cowgirl

Soldier Under the Mistletoe

The Nanny's Christmas Wish

The Rancher's Unexpected Gift

Someone Old

Someone New

Someone Borrowed

Someone Blue (newsletter subscribers only)

Ten Dates

Next Door Santa

Always a Bridesmaid

Love Lessons

NOT IN A SERIES

Wagon Train Sweetheart (historical romance)

MARRYING THE MOUNTAIN MAN'S BEST FRIEND

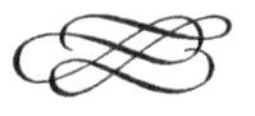

MISTY M. BELLER

Marrying the Mountain Man's Best Friend

MistyMBeller.com

Unless otherwise indicated, all Scripture quotations are taken from the Holy Bible, Kings James Version.

CHAPTER 1

DECEMBER, 1868
VIRGINIA CITY, MONTANA TERRITORY

An icy wind whipped against Two Stones's cheeks as he strode along the row of shanties, aiming toward the one second from the end. Callum Morgan lived there, and if the man's plans had played out the way he hoped, his daughter would have joined him here in Virginia City by now.

Two Stones gripped the leather pouch tighter. She must be a young woman, for Callum himself showed only a few gray hairs. Yet the man had said his daughter had suffered a loss, which was why she'd come to live with her father in this wild village of miners.

And also why he'd asked Two Stones to find such a delicate gift.

There weren't trading posts in these mountains that stocked blue sapphire pendants hanging on gold chains. He'd found the chain in Missoula Mills and a ruby brooch in Helena, so he'd had to go to the Coulter ranch for the right stone.

Sampson and Jude Coulter had worked together to cut and polish one of the sapphires from their mine, then fit it in the brooch in place of the ruby. Sampson had sawdered another gold loop on the brooch so it hung properly from the chain. The price wouldn't be cheap for Callum, but he'd said he would gladly pay anything Two Stones required.

This gift must be important to him.

He eyed the narrow shanty that was Callum's. One board had popped loose at the end, leaving a wide gap where heat must be pouring out and the winter wind blowing in. The plank must have just come loose, for Callum would not have left it undone for long. Especially if his daughter had come as expected.

Maybe Callum would finally take Two Stones up on his offer to help build a house outside the town, away from these rundown huts that stretched in a long mismatched row of loose boards. Each shanty shared walls with the structure on either side or behind, which allowed heat from their warming fires to spread through the cracks from one dwelling to the next.

The stench flowed freely between them too. And the noise.

Beyond the foul buildings in front of him rose the grandeur of the stony mountains that loomed in the distance, their snow-capped peaks reaching heavenward. This picture of two places so different felt like his own life—split between the serene village where his Salish family resided and the raucous, unpredictable world of the miners he traded for.

Neither was a home to him, never had been. The closest thing he had to a home was the trail between the worlds, and riding through these soaring mountains was where he spent most of his time.

He moved to the door and reached for the latch string, but then paused. Callum was one of the few white men he knew well enough that he could enter without knocking, as was normal among his people. But if the man's daughter had come, Two Stones should follow the white man's customs.

He lifted his hand and rapped on the wooden door. The flimsy barrier rattled. Perhaps he should have used a lighter touch.

A moment later, the latch shifted, then the door pulled open to reveal the shadows inside. A woman stood there, her skin much lighter than Callum's. The shadows darkened her wide eyes as she stared at him.

She didn't scream, though, as some white women did when they first saw him. Maybe Callum had spoken of him, and she'd known he would be coming. Maybe she even knew about the gift in the pouch.

She didn't speak, not even a greeting. Just stared at him.

He dipped his chin. "You are Callum's daughter."

She blinked. Had he said something that should surprise her? Maybe Callum *hadn't* spoken of him.

Disappointment pinched.

At last, she spoke. "You know my father?"

The disappointment nudged harder, but Two Stones pushed it down. Callum must not have mentioned him, for surely she would know him if her father had described him even a little—a man of the People who dresses as a white man, traveling throughout the mountains, locating trade goods that were hard to find. He'd built a reputation for this skill. For his ability to seek out what others could not.

He nodded. "I am Two Stones. I bring what Callum asked me to trade for." He used his best English, clearing away as much of his accent as he could. Why he did so, he couldn't have said. He shouldn't want to prove anything to this woman. Especially if Callum—a man he considered one of his nearest friends—hadn't seen fit to mention him to his daughter.

"Come in." The woman murmured barely loud enough to

hear as she stepped back, allowing him room to enter. "My father is hurt."

Two Stones stepped inside. Callum's injury must be what kept him from greeting Two Stones at the door. He would find something to help his friend recover before he left Virginia City.

The air inside pressed down on him—the scent of sickness. She'd said injury, though, hadn't she?

She led him toward the back room, where faint light barely filtered through the darkness.

"Two Stones." The voice rasped with weakness but held an unmistakable warmth. "Come closer, my friend."

Worry needled through his chest as he moved toward the corner where Callum lay on a cot, his face creased with pain. Two Stones knelt by his side. Only his face and one hand showed above the blankets. Were his injuries covered?

Two Stones met his eyes. "You are hurt?"

Callum glanced toward his right shoulder. "A small cave-in. Timbers hit my shoulder. Broke the bone, I think. Can't seem to get my energy back." His eyes held no strength. And the stench of sickness was much stronger here.

Two Stones frowned. "The bone is not mending. Will you let me see it?" He was no healer, but he needed to know how bad this was. He needed to know whether the man who called himself doctor in this town could help. It might take the touch of a wiser one.

Too bad this place was so far from the Coulter ranch. Jericho's new wife could help. God had given her the gift of healing in greater measure than any other Two Stones had met.

Callum's eyes drifted shut, as though he didn't have the strength to hold them open any longer. "Don't worry over me. But tell me, did you bring it?"

Two Stones swallowed down his worry. "I have it here." He held out the pouch, and Callum's eyelids parted.

He didn't lift a hand to take it though. Did he want Two Stones to open the pouch and hold up the necklace? Or maybe just press the gift into his hand. After all, the man's daughter was watching them from the doorway. Perhaps he wanted to surprise her with this token when they were alone.

Callum's voice finally sounded, more weak and rough than before. "Open it."

He pulled the string to loosen the tie, then lifted the leather flap and took out the chain and pendant. The gold setting gleamed in the dim light, and he lifted it up for Callum to see.

The man's eyes widened, and he let out a hoarse breath. "It's a beauty. Thank you." His voice had dropped nearly to a whisper but strengthened as he called to his daughter. "Heidi?"

The woman stepped forward, moving to stand by his feet. "What is it, Papa?"

"This...for you." His voice dipped again, losing strength.

Two Stones held the necklace and its leather holder out to her.

She studied the jewelry with wide eyes, but didn't reach for it.

"Your mother had one...like it." Callum's raspy whisper didn't tear his daughter's focus from the gift. "She wanted you...have it. But...lost in...the fire."

Callum had to pause for breath between words, and his daughter's gaze shifted back to his face, worry marking her pale brow.

"Take it. Please." Callum had closed his eyes again, but he was probably attuned to every sound that would signal whether his daughter accepted the token.

In the years they'd known each other, Callum had spoken a great deal about his life here in these mountains, traveling from one mining camp to another. He'd even spoken of the wife he'd had back east, how she'd died when their lodge burned in a fire. How much he missed her.

He'd spoken of a daughter who'd stayed behind, learning to be a woman from others. But he'd said no more than that. A pain had always settled in his eyes when their talk leaned close to her, so Two Stones hadn't pressed. Now, he had no knowledge of why she would refuse this gift.

Finally she stepped forward and took it from his hand. Her movement seemed awkward, as though trying not to touch Two Stones. Was she frightened of him? Or did he repulse her?

A shift from Callum drew Two Stones's focus back to his friend's face. The man was looking at him through barely opened eyes. "Wood. Will you...stock...?"

"I will." Two Stones always did work around the place when he was here. Restocking the pile of firewood outside the shanty. Refilling the water barrel from the creek. Picking up a load of supplies from the trading post. Whatever he could do to ensure Callum would have enough to manage for a while. Callum should know this without asking.

Two Stones hadn't planned to tackle such tasks until the morning, but perhaps Callum wanted time alone with his daughter now. Time to tell stories of her mother and the necklace that had once belonged to her.

"I will see to all you need, friend." Two Stones pushed to his feet. "Then I will return to sit with you." They'd developed a habit of sitting by the fire, Callum telling tales of his time in the mountains and the colorful men he'd met. Maybe Two Stones could offer stories this time. Something to bring a smile and strength to his friend. Warm food from one of the hotels would help too.

As he left Callum's side, he glanced at the daughter, who stood motionless by her father, the leather pouch and necklace still lifted in her hands. Her gaze was fixed on Callum, though, with an expression not easy to define. Worry, yes, but much more.

She was older than he'd expected. A woman grown,

according to the look in her eyes, but the pallor of her skin and hair made her look younger than she likely was. No wrinkles anywhere.

He turned his focus toward the front door. He would make sure these two had warmth, water, and food, then he'd see to Callum's injury, whether the man wanted him to or not.

CHAPTER 2

"Sit."

Heidi's feet felt like blocks of iron as she stood near her father. He was so weak. How had he declined so quickly?

He'd already been injured when she reached him a week ago. He'd been favoring that right shoulder but said the bone just needed a little longer to heal. Over the next few days, it hadn't seemed to heal, and she couldn't tell how much pain he was covering. He clearly hadn't wanted to talk about it, and her time married to Winston had taught her not to press when given a command.

But yesterday her father hadn't risen from his pallet. He'd allowed her to send for the local doctor, but the man clearly knew little about actual doctoring. He'd left a bottle of medicine and taken some of Papa's gold dust in payment.

Today, her father hadn't even gotten up to relieve himself. And he wouldn't eat more than a few sips of broth. He wouldn't let her get the doctor again either, not that she could blame him there.

Something had to be done. What, though?

"Heidi. Sit...please."

His awful rasping whisper drew her from her spiraling worries, and she forced herself to obey. To sink to the ground beside his blankets. This hovel didn't even have a wood floor or proper beds. They slept on a stack of furs, using dingy wool blankets for cover. She'd been cleaning as much as she could since she arrived, but when she'd boiled her bedding with lye soap, the covers had shredded in several places. She'd not yet attempted to wash her father's. He needed new blankets, but the trading post had none left. Hopefully, next week's shipment would contain a few.

Her father's good hand fumbled over his chest, reaching toward her. Did he want to hold the necklace? It was such an extravagant gift—not something she needed at all.

Her independence was gift enough. And safety from Winston's family.

She held out the leather pouch and necklace, touching it against his fingers so he could take hold. But he wrapped his hand around her palm instead. She moved the gift to her other hand so he could hold this one.

His grip was stronger than she would have expected. Coarser too, like rough-cut wood.

Still, she hadn't held her father's hand in so long. Not even at her wedding. He'd not been there to give her away, as he should have. No, he'd given her away from another land.

From *this* land. These mountains had stolen him long before that day when her name and her life had forever changed.

She pressed down the bile that tried to rise into her throat. Forced back the burn in her eyes.

Did her best just to enjoy this moment. Papa had apologized for leaving her when she was only a girl. For abandoning her to a boarding school when she needed him most. He'd moved thousands of miles away, stepping out of her life. At least, that was what it had felt like when she was only thirteen and heart-broken after her mother's death.

He'd said he thought he was doing the best for her, giving her the life he thought she needed. She'd not believed him back then, believing he only wanted to be rid of her. But when he sent her the letter inviting her to come to him in the Montana Territory after she wired about Winston's death, the chance to reconnect had brought a morsel of hope. And when, after she'd arrived, he apologized for abandoning her all those years ago, she could see he meant the words. He'd been heartbroken too, having just lost the woman he loved more than life itself. They'd both been hurting then, but now they had the chance to start over.

They had much time to make up for. Like this simple touch. The joining of hands.

His throat worked, eyes parting. His mouth opened, dry lips cracking with the movement. "Heidi...my girl." Even in that hoarse whisper, the words brought a new round of tears surging to her eyes. "I...am not long for...life."

She had to strain to understand him. Surely she'd not heard right. He thought he would die from a broken shoulder? The pain—and probably the effects of whatever had been in the bottle the doctor left—made him tired and weak.. But he wasn't dying, was he?

"I want you…to go…with Two Stones."

Her heart skipped a beat. Go with the Indian? To where? For supplies? It seemed unwise to leave her father here alone.

He kept talking though, and she leaned in closer. "When I...die..." He paused often to breathe, and rest. "Do as he...says. He's a...good...man. Trust him."

Dread twisted her middle. Papa really thought this was his end.

"You're not dying. And don't worry about me." She was

finally getting the chance to build her own life. The way she wanted.

"You can't...stay...here." His chest barely rose and fell when he breathed. "Not...safe."

She kept her mouth pressed so she wouldn't argue with him. She could protect herself. And surely he wouldn't die. She needed to find a real doctor for him.

She gave his hand a gentle squeeze. "I'm going to inquire about a different physic. You'll recover. I'll make sure of it."

She tried to pull away, but his grip tightened. "No." He croaked the word, and it seemed to take everything in him.

She stilled. "Papa." What could she say to ease his fears?

"Promise me." He opened his eyes farther now, his grip on her hand still tight. "Promise me, Heidi. You'll go with him." His eyes were nearly wild, desperate for her answer. Despite his weakness, he'd infused his voice with strength she couldn't ignore.

She swallowed. She had to say yes, even if she didn't mean it. If she found a chance to build her new life in a nearby town, maybe she could pay Two Stones to accompany her.

So she nodded. "I will."

He held her focus another heartbeat, then eased out a rasping breath. The air seemed to take away half of his substance too, leaving him only a shadow among his blankets.

"Bring...Two Stones...here. Please."

~

Two Stones dropped the armload of logs on the ground beside the stack, then reached down to organize them neatly on top of the others. Four more loads tonight at least. Then he could bring more in the morning before he left.

The door to the shanty opened, and he glanced up to see

Callum's daughter standing in the opening, her expression tense. Had something more happened?

"He's asking for you." Her voice pinched as tight as the lines at her eyes.

Two Stones straightened. "Is he worse?"

She shook her head. "He thinks he's dying."

The knot in his chest twisted tighter, and he strode toward her. She stepped aside to allow him entry, and he maneuvered through the dark space into the back room.

Once more, the stench of sickness nearly smothered. Was it death he smelled too? *Lord, You can't take him. Not this good man. My friend.*

At least Callum knew Creator Father. He didn't often speak of his faith, but his quiet convictions held strength. If this was his time, Callum would be taken to a far better place.

Yet what about his daughter?

He knelt by his friend's side. Callum looked like barely more than a corpse now. How had he dwindled this much in the time it took to bring three loads of firewood?

Callum's eyes cracked again, so Two Stones spoke. "I am here, my friend. What is it you need?"

The lines of his face shifted, like he was mustering the strength to speak. Callum's gaze flicked toward the doorway.

Two Stones looked back that way, but the man's daughter wasn't there. A wheeze brought his focus back to his friend.

"Heidi. Please...will you...marry...her?"

Two Stones frowned. He must not have heard right. "Speak the words again. I did not hear." He leaned closer, edging his head sideways so he could better hear and still study Callum's lips.

Callum blew out a hoarse breath with the first words, but they were louder than before. "Marry...my daughter...please. Make her...your wife. Take her...to live...in safety."

The air lodged in Two Stones's chest.

Marry Callum's daughter? Take her as his woman? He'd hardly spoken to her. And he was an Indian, a Salish warrior. Though his own people rarely seemed to think of him so, since he spent so much time among the white men.

What kind of life could he offer a woman? And she'd just come into this land, and from a very different place. She wouldn't know his ways. Likely she wouldn't even want to enter his world.

But as he looked into Callum's eyes, the desperate fear gripped his throat. This was a dying man's last wish. Whether he wanted a wife or not, he could agree to take care of Callum's daughter. She wouldn't be safe in this den of rowdy miners. He could take her to his parents. She could live in the quiet village tucked in a peaceful valley.

White Bear and Running Woman would love to share their home. She could be the daughter they'd always wanted. A replacement for Two Stone's sister, who'd died when only a girl.

He wouldn't need to take her into his own lodge, not in the way of a man and woman. She would be safe with his family, and Two Stones could provide her with everything she wished for. A much better life than she'd have in this hovel, surrounded by men who wanted her for only one thing.

"Please." Callum rasped the word, his fingers grappling across the dirt floor toward Two Stones.

Two Stones gripped it in a solid clasp. "I will, my friend. I will take her to safety and give her a good life."

Callum clutched tighter, his bony fingers like a claw. "As your wife. You'll...marry her." He sounded like he could barely breathe, and he was expending the last of his energy with his desperation.

Two Stones dipped his chin and placed his other hand over their joined grip. "I will. As my wife."

Callum eased, but only a little. "Find Turner. He was...a

preacher. Ask him...to speak...words over...you both. A real...ceremony."

Two Stones swallowed down the roiling in his belly. Callum was making too much of this. Two Stones would see his daughter to safety. See that she had a good life. Why did he wish the marriage ceremony to be such a significant part? "I will marry and give her a good life as my wife. Rest easy."

Callum's eyes opened a little wider, pinning Two Stones with their earnestness. "A real...ceremony?"

He had no choice except to dip his chin again. "I will find Turner and ask him to speak the words of promise. I will make sure your daughter is safe and happy."

Callum's eyes finally closed, the fire fading from his features along with the color. But he managed a few final words in that hoarse whisper. "I trust her to you."

CHAPTER 3

Heidi couldn't help the anger coursing through her from the request she'd just heard her father make of Two Stones, yet panic wove with the emotion, propelling her forward. He was lying so still. Almost...lifeless.

She dropped to her knees by her father's head. "Papa?"

He couldn't have died. Surely. Yet he was so pale. Unmoving.

She pressed her fingertips to his neck, the action bringing back a memory too fresh. She'd done the same thing to Winston. That that time, part of her had wished for the worst to be true. She could be free from him.

And she *was* free now. Finally loosed to live the way she chose.

This wasn't the way it was supposed to happen. Father wasn't like Winston at all. She could be free *and* live here with him. She finally had a chance to start fresh with her father and she didn't want him to leave her. Again.

She forced herself to focus on the sensation under her fingers. Was there any movement? Anything at all?

Nothing. No thrum in his neck. No lift of his chest.

She gripped his uninjured shoulder and shook it. "Papa?" Her voice rose with the panic flaring inside her.

His head wobbled with the movement. Like he could no longer control his limbs.

She pulled her hand back and clapped it over her mouth to stifle a sob. This was happening too fast. She'd just found him. Just finally started to repair what had been broken eight years ago.

He couldn't be gone now. Not like this.

The next sob wouldn't be quelled, bursting from her like vomit. Her body wretched as tears flowed freely down her face.

She lowered her head to rest on her father's arm, covering her mouth to hold back her moans. The scent of sickness and death clung to everything. Too much like Winston. She couldn't bear it.

A presence approached behind her, and a hand landed on her shoulder. She ignored it, pinching her eyes shut. But when the grip continued, she looked up at Two Stones.

He knelt beside her, his expression grave. "I am sorry."

Her breath expelled in a sob, and she couldn't speak.

"I will prepare him for the burial."

She nodded, but only because she had to. In truth, she didn't want to prepare for anything. She wanted her father back.

~

The weight of Callum's request pressed on Two Stones's chest, making every breath a challenge as he stood beside Callum's daughter at the graveside the next day. They'd prayed over the grave. Or rather, *he'd* prayed, at her request.

He'd like to use these final moments to remember the man, or maybe share his own pain with the Lord. But he couldn't wrench his thoughts from what lay ahead.

Callum's daughter turned from the mound of dirt and the cross marking one end.

Two Stones followed, moving beside her toward the shanty.

She walked slowly, as though she knew this was the time for words to be said. The cold wind whipped across the open land between this yard of graves and the shanties lining the edge of town.

He slid a look at her. She studied the ground, the skin around her eyes red. She wasn't crying now though. Some might honor her for holding back tears, but it did not feel right in his spirit.

Callum had loved his daughter. He'd been a good man. A good friend. He would be missed in this world, though he'd been welcomed into a much better land.

His daughter should mourn him now, as she had when he first passed. Perhaps she would let herself do so again in time.

The moment had come to tell of the promise he'd given her father. *Lord, give me strength.*

He swallowed to prepare himself. "Your father asked a promise of me."

Her head jerked toward him. Before he could check her expression, the intensity of her voice made her thoughts clear. "You are relieved of your promise. My father clearly didn't know me well." Her eyes flared, and her chin came up. "I don't need your name or your protection. I can care for myself. I came out here to forge my own path, not to subject myself to another man."

The weight pressed harder on Two Stone's chest, wrapping around his throat now too. She must have heard Callum's request. Or maybe she only assumed her father had asked Two Stones to watch over her. He should make his responsibility and his intentions clear.

He tried to meet her gaze, but she glared steadfastly toward the town ahead. He spoke anyway, keeping his voice kind and steady. "I do not wish to make your grieving harder. Your father asked me to take you as wife. This was his strongest wish, and he would not rest easy until I gave my promise."

She flinched, like she was gathering to fling angry words at him, so he pushed ahead quickly.

"I will take you to Turner, the man of God, as your father asked, but after that I will not act as a man with his wife. We will go to my people, a quiet village in a valley rich with game and all we want. You will be safe there. My parents, Running Woman and White Bear, will welcome you to their home. I will make sure you have all you wish. And you may live free of me. The only time you will see me is when I ride into the village to bring you supplies. We will be as friends only."

He paused, waiting for her to say something. But she only stared ahead, her eyes unfocused. Finally, the same words came out again, but in a much quieter tone. "You are relieved of your promise. My father didn't know me very well."

Even if she refused, that didn't mean his promise could be forgotten. Callum must have had a reason for pressing so hard for the ceremony.

He glanced toward the town. The shouts and music from the saloons had already started, though the sun had only just begun to slip behind the western mountains. A shot rang across the distance.

Two Stones's middle clenched. Gunshots sounded so often in this place that he'd learned not to flinch anymore. But tonight was different. Tonight, he was responsible for a woman's safety.

And this place would offer her nothing but danger.

Callum was right. Two Stones had to take her away from Virginia City. And marrying was the only way to do it correctly in the eyes of other white men. Even he knew this.

Maybe he could explain it better so she would understand too.

He took a deep breath, steeling himself to continue. "This

town has men who will think you do not belong to anyone. That they can do as they wish with you. But if we are married, none will bother you. I will not force you to do this, but I made a promise to your father. And I give you another promise now—to keep you safe and to give you anything you wish. You want to live a life with no man speaking over you. Allow me to keep my word to your father, and I will give you this life in the village of my people. I will give to you and take nothing. Your life will be your own."

She studied him, her gaze cool yet piercing.

He met the look, doing his best to let her see she had nothing to fear in him.

At last, she said, "I think you are a good man. I see why my father trusted you." Her voice gentled a little yet kept it's determined tone. "Even so, I wish to stay here. My father is gone, but if I could speak with him, I would have him take back his request, to absolve you of the promise you made him. He's not here, so you'll have to accept it from my own mouth. You are free from your vow. You can go on your way. Thank you for being such a good friend to my father."

With a firm nod, she turned and strode toward the shanties. The ramshackle row seemed to sag deeper into the earth, as if sharing the weight of sorrow for Callum's loss.

Two Stones let her go, but he couldn't accept her words. Callum must have known his daughter would be contrary. That was why he'd been so insistent.

Two Stones would have to approach it a different way. Maybe with time spent in prayer, the Father would show him what was best.

~

As Heidi trekked along the main street of Virginia City the next morning, where most of the businesses resided, the air hung thick with the aftermath of a rowdy night in the saloons. She wrinkled her nose against the scent of stale whisky mixed with the sharp tang of sweat and cheap perfume that clung to the damp morning air. The distant sound of clinking glasses, punctuated by slurred curses, drifted through the streets, a reminder of the revelry that had ended a few hours before.

She'd blocked most of the noises out as she fought for sleep. It came in snatches, though waking and sleeping both held their own forms of misery.

She stepped off the boardwalk to maneuver around a man's body. He lay face down, but his slurred words showed he lived and likely had no worse injuries than a roaring headache.

A mangy dog limped down the road, pausing to sniff at a shattered whiskey bottle. When she reached out to call it toward her, the animal moved farther away, as if even it understood this was no place to linger.

Debris littered the dusty street ahead—broken glass, discarded playing cards, and even a lost boot. This place really was uncivilized. A far cry from the cobblestone streets and flower-lined residences in Savannah. Of course, behind many of those front doors lived men just as crude and vice-ridden. They only hid it better.

But surely good people lived here, too, decent souls who would help her find footing in this strange world. She maneuvered around a rut filled with horse droppings and stepped onto the boardwalk..

This town certainly wasn't Savannah. But then...that was exactly what she wanted.

She eyed the businesses ahead for any sign of promising work. She'd planned to find employment soon after arriving in

Virginia City, but then Papa had been injured and weak. She'd worried about leaving him home alone all day. Now...she had to secure something soon.

She would likely find an eager employer in one of the saloons, but she wouldn't stoop to that life. She already had to hide herself from the men when they began imbibing each day. Their calls and suggestive offers made her ears flame, but it was easy enough to tuck herself inside the shanty once the rowdies began filling the streets.

Now though, she had a clear path to search for gainful employment. Well...clear except for the trash littering the street.

As she turned her gaze from the mess, a figure stepped from the shadowed doorway in front of her.

She stumbled back before catching herself. The man stood tall and broad-shouldered, his leathered face bearing the marks of a life spent outdoors. He wore a buckskin vest over a white shirt, and his blue eyes glinted in the morning light.

"Good morning, miss." He tipped his hat. "You look like you could use a hand."

Why would he think that? "I'm fine, thank you."

"Are you new to town?" Though he didn't take a step, it seemed like he edged closer. "I don't recognize you."

"I am new." Should she mention her job search? He wasn't dirty enough to be a miner and didn't have the look of a saloon owner. Nor did he seem intoxicated. Maybe he owned one of the respectable businesses—the trading post or the dry goods store. Or maybe the exchange. This could be her chance to begin her search. "I'm looking for work." Should she qualify the comment by mentioning the types of jobs she would be willing to do? They could be summed up in a single word—respectable.

"Well, I might be able to help with that." The corners of his mouth tipped in a friendly expression. "I've been looking for a bright young woman. What experience do you have?"

She swallowed. "I'm quite capable of running a household with servants. But I'm also happy to do menial tasks, such as cooking or sewing or assisting customers." She managed a pleasant smile.

His lips pressed together and he tapped his chin, his brow gathering as he thought. "I do need someone who's good with customers. A woman willing to do whatever is necessary to ensure they're pleased with our service." He frowned as he studied her. The look was so severe, she almost couldn't bring herself to ask what kind of business he owned.

But that *was* an important detail. She squared her shoulders and lifted her chin.

Before she could open her mouth to speak, he straightened and snapped his fingers. "I think you'll do. Can you start right now?"

She blinked. "Now?" What kind of business would have her start immediately without even discussing wages or details of the job? But if she would be working in daylight hours, it wasn't likely to be anything untoward.

Still... She offered a pleasant expression. "What type of work will I be doing?"

The man's eyes creased in a friendly smile. "It's probably easier to show you." He gestured for her to follow him down the boardwalk.

Her middle twisted, but she stepped forward. It wouldn't hurt to at least know the location. She had to find work, and she shouldn't turn down this opportunity until she knew for certain what it was.

But then he motioned her down the alleyway between the building he'd stepped out of and the next. It was a path barely wide enough for the man to walk down without turning sideways.

She halted, her heart pounding faster. "Where are we going?"

"Just a shortcut." He looked back at her over his shoulder, his expression still friendly. "It's one street over. This will be much quicker than going down to the corner. Don't worry." But something in his tone set off a clanging bell within her.

She took a step back.

He spun and grabbed her wrist. His teeth flashed in a skin-tingling grin. "Come, now. Don't be difficult."

Panic surged through her as she fought to pull from his grip.

He was too fast, flinging her around so he stood behind her, one hand clamping over her mouth and the other wrapping around her chest and arms.

CHAPTER 4

Heidi lifted a leg to slam her heel into the man's shin, or maybe even higher in his kneecap. Her skirts tangled around her boot though, muffling the force of her blow.

Before she could try again, a roar sounded behind her. Not from the man. From farther away.

Then he jerked her back...and released her?

She scrambled forward, spinning to see what had happened.

Her attacker was on the ground, a figure looming over him with hands wrapped around his throat.

Two Stones.

Heidi's heart hammered as she backed farther away, onto the edge of the main street.

Two Stones glanced at her. "Are you hurt?" He was breathing hard, and fire sounded in his voice.

She shook her head, her own breaths coming in short gasps. "I'm all right."

He turned back to the man and released one of his hands from the cad's neck. In a fluid movement, Two Stones pulled a pistol from his waistband and stood to his feet, towering over the scoundrel lying on his back. "If you come near her again, you will breathe your last breath."

He took a step back, his gaze locked with her attacker's, even while the fellow scrambled up and away from the fierce brave. Once he'd gained his feet and retreated from the alley onto the main boardwalk, his eyes darkened into a glare so full of hatred, she took another step back.

Thankfully, Two Stones stood between them, his back to her like a mountain no man could conquer.

Just before the scoundrel stepped into the same shadowed doorway he'd appeared from before, his gaze moved past the brave to focus on her. "I'll have you, girlie. Ain't no injun gonna stop me." Then he disappeared into the darkness.

She wrapped her arms around herself even as Two Stones backed toward her, his pistol still aimed at the place the villain had last stood.

When he reached her, still with his back to her like a shield, he spoke just loudly enough for her to hear. "We should return to your father's house. I do not think he will give up so easily."

Heidi shivered, the memory of the man's leering gaze still fresh in her mind. Two Stones was right. Men like him didn't take rejection well.

She started forward, retracing the steps she'd taken such a short time before.

Two Stones stayed at her side as they passed the building her attacker had entered, then moved behind her as she lengthened her stride to the quickest walk she could manage without drawing too much notice.

Who was she fooling, though? Her very presence drew notice. There were so many men in this wilderness city, and her father had warned that the few women here all worked for the brothels and saloons.

How had she ever thought she would manage to keep herself safe and find respectable work? No other female had been able to. Surely not all of them had come west already entrenched in disreputable careers. How many had been innocent, accosted by the man who'd tried to drag her down the alleyway—or another just like him?

By the time they reached the shanties, she'd begun to tremble. The awful event had passed. Two Stones had saved her. Yet her body didn't seem to believe she was safe.

She slapped the door open and stumbled inside, then paused to take in the dim room.

Her father's tobacco pipe still sat on the rough-hewn table next to the leather-bound Bible he'd read aloud from every night since she arrived here. Those last few nights, she'd done the reading while he lay in his bed pallet. On the wall hung the frying pan he'd scorched their breakfast in just a few days ago.

Heidi blinked back the burn that rushed to her eyes. She couldn't cry. Not now.

Two Stones entered behind her, and the door thumped closed. Quiet descended over them as they stood, side by side.

She had to face him, this man who'd risked his own safety to help her. Who'd appeared when she needed him most.

She didn't look at him yet, but she ventured words into the quiet. "Thank you."

"I'm glad I was there."

The feel of that man's grip around her wrist flooded back, but she pressed it away, fisting her hands against the memory. It felt too much like the things Winston had done early in their marriage.

She was no longer that woman, though. No longer the weak wife controlled by the men around her. She made her own choices now.

Yet, did she really?

At the moment, she couldn't stomach the thought of stepping out of this shanty.

Two Stones turned to her, his tone gentle. "It is not safe for you to walk through town alone." Something flicked in his eyes. Like uncertainty, but it disappeared so quickly she couldn't be sure. "Come with me. My village is quiet and you will find peace. I will not bother you there. And this will keep my promise to your father."

Indecision gnawed at her.

The picture his words painted sounded wonderful. A quiet Indian village where she could live her own life. She could learn to hunt and cook the way his people did. It would likely be vastly different from what she was accustomed to, but if it allowed her a peaceful life where she was fully in control, it might be quite pleasant.

But... "Will your people accept me? A white woman? Or will they wish me to leave?" She wouldn't go where she wasn't wanted.

He nodded without hesitation. "They will see you mean no harm. My mother will embrace you as a daughter."

The longing his words released in her would make her too prone to emotion, so she pushed it away. His village did sound like a good place to start this new life.

But what if it didn't work out? What if she wanted to move on? "Will you make me stay there if I'm not happy? You say we would be married, but once we reach your village you won't bother me. What if I don't like it there? Can I leave on my own?"

His brows gathered, and a line creased his forehead. Concern filled his eyes, but was that sadness too? She couldn't let his emotions manipulate her decision. Not like before. She had to know she would be free to make her own choices if she went with him.

At last, he nodded. "I think you will like the village of my people. But if you do not, you may leave. I only ask that you tell me if this is what you want. I will not stop you, but I will see you there safely and make sure you have all you need for your new life."

How could she say no to that? This man seemed noble, but Winston had spoken pretty words to convince her to wed him. They'd all been lies—some he'd likely believed himself. But every one of his promises had been trampled on, over and over, by his own polished boots.

This man would likely do the same. But if she agreed to marry him, that didn't mean she had to submit to abuse from him.

In Savannah, Winston'd had all of society and the police department to ensure she remained securely in his grip.

In this vast Montana Territory, she could leave Two Stones in the night and disappear forever. She would still be married and certainly wouldn't seek out another man. But she wouldn't subject herself to constant demeaning and punishment for offenses she didn't commit.

On the other hand, if he turned out to be speaking the truth now, she might reach a place where she could truly find the peaceful life she craved, a life where she would be free to make her own decisions.

He stood quietly. Not pushing. His presence solid, but not intruding while she worked through her decision. Was it because he believed he'd already won?

Either way, her chances were better with this man than if she stayed in Virginia City alone.

So she nodded. "All right. I'll come."

She could only pray she wasn't making the second worst decision of her life.

~

As dawn turned the horizon pink and orange the next morning, Two Stones knelt beside the cold creek, splashing the icy water over his bare chest and arms. He could do with a full washing on a day this important, but the biting chill of the water kept him at the edge. At least he would be wearing a new tunic and leggings.

He'd sought out Turner yesterday after Heidi agreed to the marriage, and the three of them decided to hold the ceremony just after first light this morning. Turner could start his work at the mine straight after, and Two Stones and Heidi could head southwest toward the Mullan Road.

And home.

Home.

He always felt a little empty when he tried to use that word, even though his people had camped in that quiet valley for five winters now. It was the place he came back to when he had a lull between trips, though not as often of late. Still, was it home?

He pushed to his feet and slipped the tunic on, pulling it over his damp skin. Did Heidi regret her choice yet? If he gave her more than one day before the ceremony, she surely would, just like the others had.

This would be his third attempt at marriage. Neither of the first two betrothals had reached the day of the ceremony. He'd thought he loved Standing Kettle, but when her family chose another over him, she'd withdrawn her affections without a backward glance.

That had been a good lesson for him. He'd learned not to allow his heart to enter friendship with a woman. So when his parents tried to arrange a union between him and Yellow Mouse, he'd not been hurt when she refused to even look his way.

He'd made it clear to his father then that he would forge his own path, and that journey would *not* include a woman by his side. What would they say now when he brought Heidi to them?

And she was a white woman. Seeing that she was his choice for a wife would surely strengthen his family's belief that he was more white than Salish now. They'd not said such in several winters, but he could still see the truth in their eyes.

His chest tightened, but he scooped up his satchel and rifle and turned toward the shanties at the end of town. He'd given his word. He couldn't turn back now.

Of course, she would only be with him for this week they'd be traveling. After that, she wanted her freedom. And he'd allow her to keep it. In a way, this truly was the best situation for both of them.

God must surely have brought them together for this reason. *Thank You, Father.* Maybe if he offered thanks enough, this marriage living apart would feel more like a gift and not just one more rejection.

As he walked, he squared his shoulders. He had given his word to Callum. No matter his doubts, he would not break his promise. Heidi needed him, and he would be there for her.

Turner strode toward him from another row of shanties. As he neared, he lifted a hand. "Morning. Are you ready?"

Two Stones nodded as they fell into step together. "I am."

Neither of them spoke again until they reached Heidi's door. He paused to knock. Would he ever reach a friendship with this woman where he could be himself and simply walk in?

A longing slipped in his chest as he waited for Heidi to open the door. He *wanted* a friendship between them, like what he'd had with her father. Or maybe more like what was between him and Jericho Coulter. Both as equals, knowing each other well and accepting all parts.

As the door opened and Heidi stood in the frame, any thought of Jericho pushed to the back of his mind. How could he have ever compared her to that overgrown bear of a man?

He'd rarely been drawn to white women, probably because most of the ones he'd met were loud and coarse, working in saloons and saying whatever necessary to lure the men into handing over their gold.

He preferred a quiet woman, and he usually found them only among his own people. *The unfading beauty of a gentle and quiet spirit,* the Bible called it. A woman didn't even need to possess much beauty if her manner was kind and her spirit joyful.

Heidi Morgan had far more outer beauty than most. She was quiet too. But not, he believed, in a peaceful, contented way. It felt like more like intentionally holding back, afraid to be who God made her to be.

He offered a smile. Or what he hoped she would see as a smile. Many years had passed since he last tried to win over a female. "Are you ready?"

She nodded, any hint of joy leaching out of her expression, leaving her features pinched. Shadows under her eyes showed she hadn't slept well. Which weighed heavier on her—grief for her father's passing or being forced to marry him?

That thought would do him no favors, so he pushed it aside and followed Heidi into the shack to see what he should carry.

"We'll come back here to load the horses after...?" She didn't seem to want to speak the name of the ceremony.

His middle clenched tighter as he nodded. "After we are married, I will bring the horses here to load our supplies." He wouldn't allow their union to grow into a silent mountain between them. He would pledge himself to her before God. Whether she wanted him or not, he would do everything he could to gain her friendship.

They walked with Turner past the edge of town and stopped at a grassy area. The mountains in the distance rose up to the clouds, easing his spirit even as he filled his chest with a strengthening breath.

He glanced at Heidi to see if the view did the same for her.

She was paler than usual, her eyes downcast and her posture rigid. Though she held her chin high in a show of courage, her fingers twisted the fabric of her dress.

When she saw him watching her, her features smoothed into a stoic mask. He could do nothing to ease her worries other than offering an encouraging smile as they faced Turner.

The preacher cleared his throat. "Shall we begin?"

Two Stones nodded, and Heidi must have too, for Turner opened his Bible and began reading the marriage liturgy in a steady voice that carried in the still morning air. Two Stones had heard this service twice before, and the meaning of the words swelled through him.

When it came time to exchange vows, Heidi's voice barely rose above a whisper. But she spoke the words clearly. "I, Heidi Morgan, take thee, Two Stones, to be my wedded husband, to have and to hold from this day forward, for better or for worse, for richer or poorer, in sickness and in health, to love and to cherish, as long as we both shall live."

To love and to cherish. Was she still completely set against those? If that was what she wanted, he wouldn't press her for anything at all.

But when he repeated the vows in turn, he spoke them as a silent prayer to the Father. *Show me how to love and cherish this woman in a way that makes her feel safe and treasured. Without going back on our agreement.*

When Turner grinned and said, "It's customary for the bride and groom to kiss now," Two Stones wanted to glare at him.

The memory of that at the end of the other ceremonies slipped in, though. He couldn't shame Heidi by refusing, yet by the wariness in her gaze, he feared she'd bolt faster than a frightened fox.

He took one of Heidi's hands instead and lifted it to press a kiss to the backs of her fingers. It seemed the only way to keep his distance and still honor her.

The relief easing her face showed he'd chosen right, and the corners of her mouth even curved in the slightest of smiles.

Maybe this wouldn't be as hard as he'd imagined. The two of them might be walking into an unknown future, but if they worked at it together, they could make a good life.

He would do all in his power to make sure she never regretted choosing him.

CHAPTER 5

Finally. They'd put Virginia City behind them.

Heidi couldn't even see the town now that she and Two Stones had crested a slope and were descending the far side. Clusters of lodgepole pines dotted this side of the mountain, but she could see through gaps to the long valley below.

Other than the clop of the horse's hooves and the squeak of the saddles, the only sounds of life were the occasional cries of a hawk circling overhead. Probably searching for rodents among the trees.

Two Stones hadn't spoken since they rode past the last mine outside of Virginia City. Was he lost in his thoughts, or did he always ride in complete silence? She didn't like much talking either, but she couldn't stand days of this.

Also, she needed to know more about what lay ahead in their journey. She could no longer follow a man blindly. That had become the only way to survive life with Winston, but she had control of her path now. If she chose to set out on her own, she needed to know more details.

When the trail leveled off a little, she ventured a question.

"How far until we reach your village?" It was several days at least, but she didn't know exactly.

He eyed the skyline ahead. "A week." Then he slid a look at her. "My people measure time in sleeps. We should reach my parents in six sleeps." He turned forward again. "If the weather doesn't slow us. The sky speaks of snow. I do not know how much."

She jerked her gaze upward, pulling her coat flaps closer together. Already, the thick wool wasn't keeping out the cold as well as she'd hoped. She and Papa had planned to get her a fur coat from the trading post in Virginia City. She should have thought to do that yesterday. In truth, she'd not been able to think of much, not with her father's burial and then her impending marriage to a Salish brave. Even now, thinking those words made her situation—and her decisions—seem too ridiculous to even contemplate.

But as she glanced over at the strong, steady profile of the man riding beside her, a peace eased her spirit. She'd taken a step of trust with him. Of every man she'd ever met, he was one of the few who just might not fail her.

His voice interrupted her thoughts. "Before we reach the village, we'll stop at the ranch of my friends. The Coulters are brothers to me. Jericho has married a doctor, and she asked me to bring medicine from Virginia City."

She studied Two Stones as a flurry of questions whipped through her. The names sounded like they belonged to white people. A bond as close as brothers...how had he come to know them? And a woman doctor? That was even more unusual. Had she set up practice in the wilds of the Montana Territory? Apparently so, if she had sent for medicine.

Two Stones looked her way, drawing her from her thoughts once again. "We'll reach them just before Christmas. We can stay a few days if you wish. Dinah and her sister will be happy to meet you."

Christmas. How could it only be a week away? She'd been relieved to reach her father in time to celebrate with him. She'd planned to cook his favorite foods.

Two Stones still watched her, his expression a little hopeful as he waited for an answer.

She nodded. "Christmas with your friends will be nice, if that's what you want. Will your parents want you home? Or... do they celebrate Christmas?" Two Stones had made it clear in various comments that he shared her father's faith, so that was likely why he observed the holiday.

But if his parents weren't Christians, they might want nothing to do with it.

He shrugged. "They do, but it is not the feast the white men have on that day. They are used to me sharing the meal with my brothers."

"That's good." She wasn't sure what else to say. Clearly, his faith meant a great deal to him, and familiar Christmas traditions would be nice.

The terrain steepened again, and she had to rein her mount behind his to maneuver the slope. Two Stones continued talking, though, speaking of the Coulter family. Six brothers, he said. Jericho was the oldest, the one who'd recently married the doctor. The doctor's sister and her young babe also lived with them, as well as the Coulter brothers' niece and nephew, who sounded like they must be school-aged. She did her best to memorize all the names, but Two Stones said little about what each was like.

Would the two of them be expected to share a room in that house? She could perhaps manage that, but what about the same bed?

The numbing thought stopped her breath. He would introduce her as his wife, no doubt. Would he also explain they slept separately?

Her heart hammered, but she breathed a slow breath in. As

long as Two Stones honored his promise and didn't try to touch her, she could manage. And if he did cross the line, she would have her father's pistol ready. She tapped her coat pocket, where she'd tucked it so she could reach it easily.

If he indulged in strong drink or some other vile thing that made him less trustworthy, she would be ready to defend herself.

~

The first flakes drifted down an hour after they left camp the following morning. Heidi scrunched her nose as another crystal pricked her skin with an icy poke.

Two Stones had said he expected snow this day before the sun reached its zenith. Those were some of the only words he'd said during their quick meal before they'd packed their bedding that morning.

He'd been a gentleman through the entire experience of camping with him. He managed the animals and bore the brunt of the work to unload their supplies. She'd cooked a simple meal over the fire he made, but he'd carried the water for her, along with load after load of firewood.

Bedding down had been awkward, at least for her. He'd not shown signs of feeling the same. Because of the lay of the land, their blankets couldn't be on opposite sides of the fire as she'd hoped. But they'd been positioned end to end with enough space between them that she couldn't have touched him if she'd tried.

Once he lay down in his furs, he never rose again until the first gray of dawn lightened the eastern sky. She'd lain awake several hours, listening for any rustle that might signal he was coming to her. But that sound never came, and at last, her weary body succumbed to the call of sleep.

She kept her gaze on him now, riding ahead and a little

downhill. Already, the flakes were thickening to a curtain, though each was still small. He'd not said anything about stopping when the snow came, so he must intend to continue despite the weather.

As they left the shelter of the mountain they'd descended to ride through a pass between two peaks, the wind picked up, swirling the ice pellets and sliding them into all the openings of her coat. She shivered as another gust crept down her neck, seeping into her bones.

Ahead of her, Two Stones raised his hand for a halt. He reached around to the bundle of bedding he'd fastened behind his saddle. He must need to retrieve something.

Her horse shifted beneath her, stomping a hoof as they waited. She patted the gelding's neck. He must be one of Two Stones's animals, for he had similar markings as his mount and pack horse—dark coat with flecks or small spots of white across its rump. She'd not seen markings like these back east.

Two Stones pulled out one of the fur coverings he used for sleeping and held it out to her. "Wrap around you for warmth."

She hesitated. Use his bedding? The fur looked soft from many nights tucked around him. It likely carried his scent too.

But she'd begun to shiver more than she could control, and she would only grow more miserable as the snow dampened her wool coat. So she accepted the offering. "Thank you."

The pelt was even softer than she'd expected. She pulled it tight at her neck, snuggling into the comfortable warmth. It did smell of him, a familiar musky scent that made her feel safe and relaxed. Or maybe the warmth did that, but she was grateful as they continued their trek.

The snow began to thicken on the ground. By the time they stopped for a midday rest, at least a foot of thick crystals covered the trail, and the sky showed no sign of easing.

They'd dismounted to let the horses rest and now sat on a boulder Two Stones had wiped clean of snow. She handed him a biscuit and a chunk of sliced meat from their food stores, then bit into her own hard bread. It was almost too stale to eat, but she hated to waste food. Out here, there was no bakery on the street corner to purchase fresh goods.

She slid a glance at Two Stones beside her. Did he approve of using every last bit of food? Or would he rather have the best she could offer in this frozen mountain wilderness? As he bit into his second stale bite, and he didn't look angry or frustrated.

In truth, he didn't seem to be thinking about the food at all. His brow furrowed, his eyes staring through the snowflakes, his mind seeming far away.

"Are you worried about something?" The question slipped out before her mind had decided to voice it.

He slid a sideways look at her, a warm glimmer in his gaze. Not angry about the stale food at least. "I am thinking where to camp. We will not make the cave where I usually sleep." He turned forward again, his focus shifting back to that distant place. "I think better to stop at a cliff that hangs over." He bent his fingers at a right angle like a lean-to.

Heidi studied his hand motions. "An overhang?"

He nodded. "The snow will not cover us." Once more he tipped his face to look at her, but this time his forehead creased with concern. "It is not the place I wish to bring you. Not the way I wish to care for my wife."

A rush of something that felt far too much like emotion surged to her eyes. Such a tiny comment shouldn't turn her head. Especially when he'd only said he *wished* to care for her. He wasn't actually accomplishing that service. She would be sleeping in a snowstorm with only a rock overhang to protect her from the weather. Probably open on both sides for the icy night wind to gust through their camp.

Yet the concern in his dark eyes held her. Even when Winston had tried to play the part of the conscientious husband, his eyes had always given him away. That diabolical glint that lay just under the surface. But Two Stones...could that earnest regard be genuine?

She turned away, facing forward as she struggled for another topic, something to distract them both. "How much farther will we ride today then?"

"A few more hours. We will make camp before dark."

She nodded. "That sounds like a good plan." Dark fell early in mid-December, so they would only have four more hours in the saddle at most. Every part of her ached, though she couldn't tell how much came from the discomfort of so many hours on horseback, and what part stemmed from the aching cold.

They finished their meager lunch, and she was more than grateful for the warmth of Two Stones's fur around her. But the snow had begun to seep through her boots, chilling her feet. She breathed out her relief when he moved to her horse and led the animal toward her so she could mount.

Once they set out, Two Stones guided them through the drifts. She could see no sign of a trail, but he seemed to know exactly where he was going. How many times had he traveled this path?

After a few hours, they rounded a bend in the mountain, and the overhang he had spoken of jutted out from the cliff on their right. The snow still fell—faster now, the wind driving it into their faces in stinging pellets. Her breath clouded in front of her, and she could no longer feel her feet, though they'd been burning an hour ago.

Two Stones dismounted first and helped her down. The snow crunched underfoot, and she had to lift her boots high to push through the thick crust.

Two Stones kept his hand at her elbow as though she needed help to maneuver final steps. Perhaps she did.

His voice rumbled low beside her. "It is not what I would wish, but it will provide some shelter."

She nodded. "It's good." She would be grateful for any protection from this biting wind and snow.

Beneath the overhang, only a thin layer of ice crystals covered the ground. He halted her in the protected area. "I will make fire, then settle horses."

He moved back out into the snow to get the tinderbox and wood he'd said he carried for occasions like this, when the firewood around them was too wet to start a fire. She could make the fire when he returned. Perhaps she was being lazy, allowing him to do all the work out in the thick snow. But he was far more accustomed to this weather than she.

When he approached with the armload of wood and the metal box that held the flint and steel, he also had the other fur he used for sleeping. After dropping the logs to the ground, he handed her the pelt. "Sit and get warm."

She took the covering with as much of a thankful smile as her frozen mouth could manage. It was strange being cared for like this, as though he truly was her husband and not just a man hired to escort her. "Thank you."

She reached for the tinderbox. "I can start the fire while you care for the horses."

He handed over the container, his gaze holding hers for a moment, concern marking his eyes. There was something else, too, but she didn't look deep enough to identify it. The fact that he would put himself out for her well-being was unusual enough in her experience. She still couldn't quite trust it.

As he turned away and strode toward the horses, she remembered what she'd meant to ask. "Could you bring my satchel, the one with the gold clasp?" It held her two extra skirts and some hairpins, along with the gift she still couldn't bring herself to wear.

The sapphire necklace.

It had seemed so important to her father. Probably because

it reminded him of her mother and that former life before their family was torn apart.

She'd done her best to forget that time completely though. To focus on the present and the life she wanted to build.

Maybe she would wear the necklace in time, but for now, it stayed safely tucked in the satchel.

As Two Stones nodded, then continued through the falling snow, she allowed herself to watch him another moment. He moved with an intentional stride, a man who knew his way around animals. His actions weren't rough, just deliberate, and thoughtful, the way he'd treated her since the moment she'd opened her father's shanty door to find Two Stones on the other side.

He'd proven himself dependable. A man of his word, there when she needed him every time. And that alone made her heart melt a little as she watched him disappear with the string of horses around the bend in the trail.

CHAPTER 6

Heidi was warming her hands in front of the small blaze she'd built by the time Two Stones returned with the supplies they would need that night.

He dropped his load against the rock wall. "I'll gather more wood now." He turned and strode back into the swirling snow.

Now that she had their supplies, she could ready a meal and warm drink for his return.

A quarter hour later when she handed him the cup of hot water, the smile he flashed as he dipped his face into the steam was enough to warm her insides.

"Thank you." He took a long draught, holding the cup with both hands to absorb the heat. "The warmth is good."

She turned to finish loading their plates. "Sit by the fire and warm yourself."

He obeyed, and when she handed him the plate, he patted the fur beside him. "Sit and warm yourself."

Those were nearly her own words. She glanced at the spot—far closer to him than she would have chosen. But this overhang would be tight. And she would have to sit close to stay on the fur. She didn't relish the idea of sitting on icy stone.

So she eased down beside him with her plate, keeping the soft fur he'd given her earlier tight around her like a cloak. As she ate, shivers coursed through her, and she leaned toward the fire. The icy wind still found its way under the rocky overhang, chilling her to the bone.

She glanced at Two Stones from the corner of her eye. His frame blocked some of the wind. If she scooted closer, he could protect that full side and she could glean some of his warmth. She shouldn't be so forward, though.

Yet when another gust swept through their makeshift shelter, she pushed aside her qualms. She might freeze to death before this night was over if she allowed her pride and propriety to choose.

As she leaned against his arm, he didn't seem surprised at all, just eased closer, shifting his shoulder so his hand rested behind her. Not wrapped around her waist as a suitor might, but propped on the ground, allowing her to shelter nearer his side.

The howl of the wind kept their silence from turning awkward. They were both still eating, too, and she took small bites to make the meal last longer.

When the food was gone, she pulled her fur tighter around her, closing off any gap at her neck as she snuggled deeper against his side. "Are the horses out in the weather?"

"I found trees near a cliff wall, so they will not feel much wind." The deep timbre of his voice rumbled near her ear. A delicious sound that made her feel protected.

She'd not felt protected in the arms of a man in so very long.

And hadn't actually been protected even then.

She'd need to remember to guard her heart. She might be married to this man in the eyes of God and in the town of Virginia City, but she would keep a wall around her emotions. She wouldn't let him hurt her—in body or spirit.

As they sat a little longer, the combination of his nearness, the fire crackling, the falling snow...they tightened her nerves until she could barely sit still.

Maybe talking would help.

"Tell me about your village. What was it like growing up there?"

Two Stones stared into the fire, the look in his eyes almost tender. "It is a small town. Set near the creek between two mountains. We have lived in this place five winters, and there is still good hunting. God has blessed my people with peace and plenty."

She studied him a moment, tipping her head just enough to see him. He didn't look her way. Maybe he'd told her of his village's current location because he thought she would want to know where they were going. But that wasn't what she'd asked.

And he needed to know she wouldn't be pacified or pushed aside when she asked a question. Not anymore. "You paint a lovely picture with your words." At least, she hoped so. "But if you've lived in that valley for five years, where did you camp before that? Where did you grow up?"

He slid a look her way. It didn't seem to hold annoyance, but not humor either. He focused on the fire again. "We moved nearly every year. Always searching. Sometimes the game would leave us. Sometimes the snows would be too heavy, our people dying from the cold, even with the animal skins. The Blackfoot and Gros Ventre, they pushed us from the good camps. From the places of shelter and plenty."

He paused, as though he was back in that time, staring at a memory that darkened his mood, even years later. Would he share it? Should she prompt him? As much as she wanted to prove she was strong and capable and not willing to cower to a man, she wasn't sure she had the courage to push if he didn't offer the story on his own.

"When I was eight winters old," he said after a long pause, "I went with my cousin to gather wood around the mountain. The snow began to fall heavily, so fast that I lost my way. I could not find my cousin, no matter how I called and searched."

Heidi's chest clenched as she waited for his next words. What awful thing had happened to him at such a tender age? From the tension in his voice, it must have been bad.

"I found shelter in the cleft of the rock that night and the next. The snow stopped, and I was hungry and feared for my cousin."

"And for yourself, no doubt." She hadn't meant to speak, but the story drew her in so, the words slipped out.

The tension in his eyes eased a little as he glanced at her. "A warrior is taught not to say so. But yes, I was afraid I would not ever find my way."

His gaze moved forward again. "For two more sleeps, I wandered through the mountains. I thought I would die there." He paused, eyes clouding with the memory.

She couldn't hold in her prompting this time. "What happened?"

"I met a boy on horseback. A few winters older than me. I was so hungry, I followed him. He took me to the cabin where he lived with his mother and father and brother. Though we could not understand each other at first, they took me in and cared for me."

Two Stones's brow furrowed. "I stayed with them, learning some of their language. They gave me food and were kind."

Heidi's heart ached for the lost little boy. "You must still have been afraid and missing your family. Did you try to escape?"

Again he was silent for long enough she wasn't sure he would answer. "I knew what it was to wander lost and hungry and cold."

So he'd been too nervous to leave. "How long did you live with them?"

The knot at his throat worked, as though he was struggling to voice his answer. "After one moon passed, they thought I would always be with them. They cut my hair. Made a mattress that was my own. Two more moons passed before the snow melted in the valley."

She barely kept herself from asking if he'd tried to leave at that point. He would tell her. She had to give him time.

As though he could hear her thoughts, he spoke again. "My uncle found me when I was with the older son, hunting. He told me to come with him, and would not let me tell the boy that I was returning home."

Something in his tone wrapped a longing around her. The white family had taken him in and helped him when he'd nearly died. Taken him almost as their own, it sounded like. But how relieved he must have felt to be reunited with his own family.

Did he worry what his white friends thought of his sudden leaving, without a word of farewell or thanks? She allowed herself to turn to him fully, so he would feel her studying him. "Did you ever see them again?"

He shook his head. "My mother would not let me leave sight of our camp until we moved to a different valley. She mourned the cutting of my hair. Mourned that I had been changed to a white man."

She fought to keep from stiffening. "Because you'd spent a few months with a white family? That didn't change who you are inside."

The slight lifting at the corners of his mouth showed no sign of a true smile. And her heart ached all the more. To be torn between two worlds at such a young age…

As she looked at him now, she could see the echoes of that lost boy still in him. A glimpse into the kind yet conflicted man before her.

"Did your mother keep you away from white people after that?" She asked the question gently.

He shook his head. "There were too many, and the English

I'd learned helped my people in trading. Everyone in our village called for me when they needed an interpreter."

She tipped her head. "Is that how you learned trading so well? That's what you do now, right? Find unique items for people, like specialty trading?"

A glimmer of a smile touched his eyes as he looked at her. "Something like that. I met many people when I interpreted. Most are not still here, but I do think that is where I learned to read men's intentions. To know where I could find the unusual things I am asked to search for."

He was still looking at her, but his thoughts seemed to turn inward as his mouth curved. Her gaze caught on that mouth longer than it should have. His skin was so smooth, his lips full. Not at all like Winston's thin mouth shadowed by a bushy mustache. Just one more way the two seemed as different as a Savannah summer and a Montana winter.

His voice called her back from that thought. "One of the white men I met changed me. Or rather, his God changed me." His gaze focused again, but the smile stayed at the corners of his mouth. "Dat Coulter was the first man who made me remember the English family who took me in when I was lost in the snow. He brought me to the mountain where his family was building a house."

The tenderness in his voice as he spoke brought out her own grin. "The brothers we're going to see. Those are his sons?"

He dipped his chin. "Six brothers. There was a girl, too, but she has gone from this life." Sadness touched his eyes. "Dat and Mum have left also, but they gave me much. They spoke of Creator to me, and of His sacrifice. That Jesus came to make peace between all men and Creator, making us brothers."

His expression turned earnest as he spoke of God. "I met Jesus and learned to follow His path. It is not always an easy trail—but the only place for peace. "

Heidi's throat squeezed at the intensity in his gaze. What

would it be like to believe so strongly the way he did, that God cared? Was it his faith that made him so...steadfast? He possessed a kind of quiet strength. Even when she sensed his uncertainty about being Indian among white people, he still seemed rooted, his character unchanging.

It made her want to lean in and take shelter at his side. Maybe that truly would be a safe place. Her experience told her that allowing a man power over her would only bring pain.

But could Two Stones be different?

CHAPTER 7

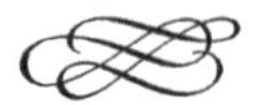

The icy wind bit into Two Stones's cheeks as he pushed his horse through the deep snow. Beside him, Heidi huddled under the fur he'd given her, face pale and pinched from the cold. Around them, the land lay bleak, drifts piling up in the lee of rocks and ravines.

Iron-gray clouds pressed down, promising more snow to come. They'd managed two days on the trail since the last storm. This new one looked like it could delay them again. How hard could he push Heidi through the cold and wind?

She'd endured so much this past week—losing her father, nearly being attacked in Virginia City, and now day after day in this miserable cold and snow. He'd promised to protect her, to take her to a safe place. He'd not made a good start of it, that was certain. Was she losing faith in the life he'd promised she would have when they reached his people?

If they could just make it to Jericho's ranch, she would have shelter in a warm home, surrounded by good friends. Three more days. As long as the weather didn't slow them too much.

When the road leveled out near the base of the mountain they'd been descending, he nudged his horse to pick up the pace. The wind whipped around them, swirling the flakes like a thick fog, the ice crystals so cold they nearly burned.

Ahead, a dark form appeared in the distance. Two of them—men on horseback, from what he could tell through the haze. As they approached, he could make out hats the miners wore, pulled low against the blowing storm. They must be white men, coming from the main road that stretched from Virginia City to Missoula.

He and Heidi had taken a different route—one many didn't know about. More direct, and usually faster than the road these men had traveled, though the snowfall had slowed them. This was the place the two trails joined and continued on as one.

The men had spotted them, reining directly toward them.

He tensed, his hand reaching to make sure the knife hanging at his neck was easy to reach. Then he lowered his fingers to brush the butt of his rifle in its scabbard.

He usually treated strangers as if he expected them to be friendly, but he was ready should a meeting turn dangerous. Should he do anything differently with Heidi at his side?

He glanced over at her. She was watching the strangers too, and her horse tracked close beside his own. As her gaze met his, he tried not to show any alarm.

He spoke quietly. "Stay close. I will speak."

She dipped her chin in agreement, so he turned his focus back to the men.

He'd never seen these two before, which didn't surprise him. Virginia City swarmed with new miners every time he had to travel there.

As the strangers drew near, he recognized the moment their curious expressions turned to glares. Had they just now realized he was one of the People, traveling with a white woman? Would that be enough to incite their fury? He'd seen men kill others for less. That must be it, for surely these two didn't know him individually.

One of the men reached for the rifle resting across his lap, lifting it to the crook of his arm. A position much easier to fire from quickly.

Lord, give me wisdom. The last thing he wanted was a fight. Not only for Heidi's safety, but the stories of it would do nothing good for her reputation, being associated with him if he killed a white man.

As they all reined in, the man who'd readied his rifle spoke first. "Afternoon." His tone seemed deceptively light. His eyes flicked to Heidi, lingering there far too long.

Two Stones forced himself not to react, only to nod, acknowledging the greeting. But his body tensed, ready for anything.

The other man—the younger of the two, if the smooth skin around his eyes could be believed—looked past Two Stones to grin at Heidi, his dirty teeth flashing. "Yer that girl Tyson couldn't get hold of, ain't ya? This must be the injun that saved you." He nodded toward Two Stones, but kept his hungry gaze on Heidi.

Creator Father, put Your response in my body. Every one of his instincts wanted to spring on the two of them and slice the grimy smiles off their faces. But that wouldn't be God's leading.

He was fairly certain.

He did nudge his gelding forward a step to shield Heidi from their view. He couldn't fully block her, but at least he would make his intention plain to these snakes.

He raised his chin. "We have no business with you." Then he started to rein his gelding away from them, motioning for Heidi to stay close.

"Maybe we got business with you." The older man's voice cut through the air before their horses managed a single step. The stranger kicked his mount hard enough, the animal leaped forward to catch them. Then the man jerked hard on his reins to stop the animal right in front of his and Heidi's horses.

Two Stones's gelding tossed its nose up in frustration, but Two Stones held his reins steady.

The fellow leveled a look on him as the younger man rode forward to position himself as back-up for his friend. "What you done to Tyson ain't right, an' I don't think we can let you leave without doin' our duty for our friend. Ain't that right, Fitz?" He tipped his chin toward his friend just enough to show those last words were aimed at him. But then his gaze slid to Heidi, and the gleam that lit his eyes made Two Stones coil to attack.

But he forced himself pause. *Should I, Lord? Is this Your way of protection?*

He sensed nothing in his spirit save a hesitation to touch these men. That might be from God, so he should try again to leave peaceably.

"I did not hurt the man, certainly not as he deserved. But I would not let him take this woman against her wishes." Should he mention their marriage? That was why Callum had wanted the ceremony, after all. To protect her in the eyes of white men. "She is my wife. I will not let you harm her."

The man's face flamed red, twisting into a foul glare. "Why, you dirty heathen." He lifted his rifle to aim.

Two Stones reacted on instinct, jerking his knife free. But he restrained himself before striking, holding back his fury by a thread. If the man moved his finger to the trigger or turned the weapon toward Heidi, he would strike.

The crack of a gunshot behind him made Two Stones jerk around. Not enough to lose sight of the two vipers, but to take in the new threat also.

His mind struggled to make sense of what he saw. The dusky haze of powder surrounded a pistol in Heidi's hand. He could just barely see her wide eyes that conflicted with the firm set of her jaw.

One of the men shifted, and Two Stones honed his focus on

their threat again as he raised his knife to fling it. The men would surely retaliate against Heidi's shot.

The rifle dropped from the older man's grip, his eyes widening as his hands rose to his chest, just below his throat. His mouth dropped open, maybe from pain *and* shock, for he seemed to be struggling to believe he'd been shot.

"Walker?" His friend's voice pitched high as he nudged his horse closer. "What's wrong? Are you hit? Is it bad?"

Both these men had lost their wits by half. If they didn't move quickly, Walker would bleed out in seconds. Maybe there was nothing they could do to save him, but there might be.

Two Stones slipped from his horse and moved to the injured man's side.

"Don't touch him!" Fitz's tone came out wild as he raised his own rifle.

Two Stones paused, letting the younger man see his hands were empty. "I'm not going to hurt him. We have to lay him down and stop the bleeding. He will not live long if we don't help."

"You've done enough. Get out of here, both of you. I'll tend him." At least his voice had lowered to a reasonable pitch now, though his eyes still looked wild.

Two Stones glanced at the injured man, who was leaning forward now, curling around his belly. He still clutched his chest, and his breathing had taken on a wheezing sound. If his airway had been hit, there was nothing they could do to help him.

He sent a quick glance toward Heidi to see how she was reacting. She'd shot a man, who would likely die from the wound. Her quick action might have saved them both from something worse, but he knew well how killing a man impacted a person.

She sat motionless in the saddle, her face stoic. At least she hadn't collapsed into tears like some women would.

He turned to the younger man again, keeping his hands out, away from his sides. "He needs help. We will leave if you wish. Or we will stay and do what we can for him."

Fitz's expression twisted into a snarl. "I told ya to git, didn't I? Get outta here before I kill ya both."

Two Stones moved back to his horse, keeping his eyes on the daft stranger. Once he'd swung into his saddle, he glanced at Heidi to make sure she was ready to ride.

She met his look with a hard set to her jaw, but he could just make out a tremble in her shoulders. She was holding together well, but she would need to release as soon as he could get her away.

He sent one more look at both men. Neither had changed position, but the injured one's shoulders rose heavily with each loud, wheezing breath. *Lord, draw him to You before his end comes.*

He motioned for Heidi to move her horse forward as he nudged his own. "Ride in front of me." He spoke just loudly enough for her to hear.

She did as he asked, and he edged his horse to keep himself between her and the men. The first time he glanced back, the younger man was pulling the other from his horse.

Two Stones eased out a breath. At least he was helping his friend. And it didn't appear he was planning to shoot them in the back.

It took far too long for them to reach the place where the path curved around a mountain, but as soon as they were completely out of sight, he moved his gelding up next to Heidi's. "There is a cabin not far from here. We can rest."

She nodded, her jaw still locked hard.

He pushed his horse into a lope, the pack horse trailing behind. The snow had been broken in this stretch by other riders, so the animals could move easier. They would get to rest soon too.

He'd wanted to cover so much more ground this day, but his

wife needed to free all the struggle that churned inside her. A dry place to warm herself would help, too, especially with the coming snowfall.

He had to watch carefully for the turn-off to the old shack. The building couldn't be seen from the main road, tucked behind a cliff so it would be hidden even in the winter when the tree arms were bare. Once when he'd ridden through here after a snowfall, he'd spotted horse tracks leading off the road. He'd been curious and looking for a place to take shelter, so he'd followed the prints to the abandoned cabin.

He should lead Heidi through the trees this time, so their tracks would not be easy to follow if the younger man came after them. For that matter, he didn't want another stranger to see their trail veering off the road and follow the prints, as he'd first done.

After they wound through a stretch of trees then rounded the edge of the cliff, the little structure stood before them, tucked against the mountainside for protection from wind and weather.

Heidi's face showed no change in her expression. She must be working to hole away her reactions to the shooting. He didn't want her to grow hard and bitter, though. Her spirit already held an edge that showed too much pain in her past. The last thing he wanted was to bring her more.

They reined in before the cabin door, and he slipped to the ground so he could help her.

She moved slowly, almost as if she was in pain. From the cold? Or the hardening inside her?

He stayed at her side as they moved toward the door. He wanted to touch her, maybe take her hand or press a palm to her back. To somehow let her know she wasn't alone. He would walk this hard path with her.

When he opened the door, it swung easier than the last time

he'd been here. Someone had replaced the leather hinges, something he'd intended to do when he had the right supplies.

The air inside smelled stale. But at least it didn't stink of animals that might have taken refuge here. He led Heidi to the place where he would build the fire. Since the cabin sat so close to the cliff, the floor was stone that extended from the base of the mountain. Someone had crafted a rock area in the corner where a fire could be built, including an opening for the smoke to escape outside.

He pulled off his coat and placed it on the cold floor. "Sit here. I'll bring in wood to make a fire."

She looked at him with a cloudy gaze. "We're stopping for the night?"

He nodded. "This is a good shelter for us. More snow is coming, and we can stay dry here."

She didn't question him further, just sat as he'd said to.

He went back out to the horses to unload their supplies, and he took the chance to lift his concerns to Creator Father. *Keep her heart soft. Do not let her close herself away from the pain. Nor push me away. You know I want to help her. I want to be the husband You would have me be to her.*

He knew nothing of how to do that. He'd spent little time with his parents for many winters now. Even in his childhood, though, he'd rarely seen his father and mother speaking as friends. Not like Dat and Mum Coulter did. Those two had spoken often, not caring who around heard them. Dat would ask her thoughts and follow her wishes in a way that brought honor to her. When Mum worried over something, he would ask her to speak of her concerns. The way they trusted each other had drawn Two Stones, even as a young man who craved a life of excitement and adventure.

He'd promised Heidi he wouldn't touch her as a husband, but he could honor her as Dat Coulter had done with Mum. *Lord, give me the right words.*

CHAPTER 8

When Two Stones finished bringing in the supplies, he knelt to build a fire in the hearth beside Heidi. She was shivering hard now but still hadn't made a sound. Hadn't really moved since she first sat. The cold likely had something to do with her trembling, but her fright even more.

As soon as he'd coaxed a flame to life, he filled the kettle with snow and nestled it among the logs to heat. He needed to see to the horses, too, and then warm food for Heidi. But maybe he could get her talking first.

He turned to face her, his knees nearly touching hers. She didn't meet his gaze, only stared past him, her body still shivering. She looked like a woman trying to be brave and fierce, but her trembling gave away the truth of her tender parts. His own chest ached to pull her close, to take on her fear and regret so she could be untainted. But she wouldn't allow that, he had no doubt. He would have to use words.

He honed his focus on her face. "You did the right thing." That wasn't quite what he'd intended to say, but it slipped out. Maybe this was Creator Father's message to her.

Her gaze flicked to his, then bounced away, her jaw setting even harder.

He pressed on, keeping his voice low and gentle. "I know shooting a man is not easy, but you saved our lives. I am grateful to you."

She turned to him then, her eyes shining and red-rimmed but still fierce. "Did you know I was married?"

He drew back a little. That was the very last thing he'd expected her to say. And why bring it up in this moment? He chose his answer carefully. "I did not. Callum spoke little about where you lived before, only how happy he was for you to come to him."

Her eyes flashed. And her chin lifted. "When my mother died, my father abandoned me at a girl's school. At least, that was what it felt like—abandonment. He took me there, then sold our house and came to this territory." She trembled so much, even her voice quivered.

But she kept going, her story twisting in his belly. "For five years I lived there. Then I caught the eye of a man from one of the best families. I thought I'd done well, forming a connection with so much advantage. He said all the right things, and my father wasn't there to tell me differently. I married him, and he turned out to be a snake. A man who took pleasure in controlling other people…me…and the men he did business with. He was only happy when we were at his beck and call." She paused for a heartbeat, her mouth pressing closed as though she were deciding what to say next.

So much he wanted to know. What had this man *done* to her to control her? Heidi seemed like such a strong, free spirit. How could anything hold her down, short of binding her with ropes? Everything in him wanted to find the viper and revenge her honor. Make him pay for every time he hurt her.

But he held his tongue so she could continue.

"He died in May." Her voice trembled again. "I'm finally free, and I *will not* be under any man's thumb again." With every word, her tone grew stronger, ringing with determination. Her eyes flared, nearly sparking now, though still rimmed red.

His anger dulled as realization spread through him. She was supposed to be safe with him, and yet she'd been afraid those two snakes were going to force her to...who knew what she thought they'd do. Take her back to the brothel owner in Virginia City maybe.

Two Stones wouldn't have let that happen, no matter what. But his delay in acting had made her think he wouldn't stand up for her.

He leaned in so he had her full attention. He waited to speak until her eyes focused on him. "I'm sorry I made you think you had to defend yourself. That I would not protect you from those white weasels on the trail." He tapped his fingers on her arm. "You are a woman who can do anything she sets her will to. But I promised to keep you safe, and to provide all you need."

He pressed a fist against his chest. "I want with all that is in me to do these things for you." He started to rein in the emotion that surged with his words. But maybe she needed to see the fierceness. To understand how fully he intended to carry out his promise.

So he let his eyes flash. "I hate what that other man did to you. If he were not dead, I would hunt him. I would bring his actions down on his own head. Make him suffer for every day you did not feel safe and happy." He lowered his voice, but kept it hard with his anger. "I promise you this. I will be a good warrior, a good husband. I will guard you with my life. As long as I have breath, you will live in peace and plenty. Even after I am gone, I will leave you with all I can."

He waited, barely breathing as he watched her face. She gave no sign of her thoughts, but she was certainly scrutinizing him.

At last, she spoke. "And what will you require in return?"

He had to work to keep in a snort. What had her other

husband required? He shook his head. "Nothing. I want only your happiness. I hope you will find it in the village of my people, but if you wish to leave, you are free to. I will keep my promise, protecting and providing for you." He might not be as free to travel for his trading if he needed to protect her in Missoula or one of the other mining towns. But he would do what he had to for her.

Not just because Callum had asked him. Not even as a matter of honor, since he'd taken her as his wife before God. But because Heidi needed him. She deserved to be safe and happy. He wanted her to be so. He *desperately* wanted it.

Maybe more than he should allow himself if he planned to guard his heart. He would have to ponder that later though. Now, Heidi needed his full support.

The sharpness of her gaze softened. She no longer seemed to be searching for the lie in his words, but maybe hoping they were true.

He let her search, not turning away as he waited.

At last, her mouth parted and quiet words slipped out. "Thank you."

Relief swept through him, nearly pulling the strength from his limbs.

She'd begun to shiver again though. Was there something he could say to ease her fears more? Maybe she simply hadn't gotten warm yet.

He reached out to touch the back of her hand. "Are you still cold?"

She nodded, a heavy tremble quivering her shoulders. "Will you...sit close? Like you did the other night?"

A layer of warmth eased through his chest. She was asking for help. Asking for him.

He moved next to her, settling close. Closer than they'd been the other night. That night, only her arm had touched his side. Now, he shifted so the length of their bodies touched. Maybe that was as far as he should go, but he wrapped his arm around her back, resting his fingers at her waist.

She didn't object, but she sat stiffly. At first. Little by little, as the crackling of the fire rose to warm the quiet around them, she eased her defenses, leaning into him.

He released a breath, letting himself enjoy the pleasure of her touch. Of her company. Of her trust.

The only problem now was remembering he'd promised to be a friend only, not a husband.

~

Heidi could still feel the memory of Two Stones's arm wrapped around her, though it had been two nights ago now. In the strength of his hold, she'd not had to face the fear of surviving in this world of men who took pleasure in hurting others. In overpowering people weaker than themselves. As she laid her head on his shoulder, she'd been free of the memory of watching the man jerk when her bullet slammed into him, the shock in his eyes turning to horror. Then pain.

Out here in the saddle, she had to squeeze her eyes shut to make the image fade. If only she could be tucked beside Two Stones again, wrapped in his comfort. But he was riding ahead of her as their horses tromped in a narrow creek. Tree-covered slopes rose up on both sides, and with the thick layer of snow concealing rocks on both sides of the water, the safest place for the horses to walk was in the creek bed.

The screech of a bird overhead drew her gaze up to where a black speck circled. After a glance at the sky, Two Stones turned back to her, his grin flashing. "We are nearly there."

He reined his gelding to the side and motioned for her to ride up next him. When she did so, he pointed to the bird. "That is Crowley, the raven my brothers keep. He sounds the presence of all who come to the ranch."

She squinted at the creature, though it was too far away to see much in the late afternoon sky. "They have a pet raven? I've heard of such, but I've never seen one."

"It's how we know when scoundrels like Two Stones are coming."

The strange voice made her jerk, and she spun to find its source in the line of trees. From the shadows stepped a man, maybe about her age. He wore a fur coat like Two Stones and a cap to match. Only his grin showed through as he came toward them.

Though he looked friendly and was probably one of the Coulter brothers, her body tensed and her hand moved to the handgun tucked at her waist. She wouldn't need it around this man. Hopefully.

Two Stones motioned for them to ride toward the newcomer, and she did so, letting her horse fall back a little as he led.

When they reached the grinning man, Two Stones reined in and slid to the ground, then stepped forward to clasp his hand. "It is good to see you, little brother."

The man pumped Two Stones's arm. "It's about time you showed up. Wait till you see what the women have planned for Christmas dinner."

His gaze moved past Two Stones. "I see you brought us a visitor."

Her mouth went dry, and her belly swooped. How would Two Stones introduce her? As his wife? Or would he simply give her name?

He stepped back, turning to include Heidi. "This is Heidi." His voice shifted both deeper and softer. "My wife." His gaze caught hers, its warmth drawing her so much that it took a moment to gather the strength to look away.

Two Stones managed it first, but the corners of his mouth tugged as he motioned to the other man. "This is Gil, one of the

Coulters."

She managed to nod at Gil. "It's nice to meet you." From what Two Stones had said, Gilead was the fourth brother in line.

Gil's eyes widened, but to his credit, his shock quickly changed to pleasure. He strode forward and reached up for her hand. "By jingo, I'm pleased to shake the hand of the woman who finally won Two Stones over."

He gripped her palm firmly, like he was welcoming an old friend. She couldn't help but grin back at his exuberance, but she slid a quick glance at Two Stones to check his reaction. His brows had gathered, though he looked half-amused. And half...perturbed?

Gil stepped back to take them both in. "Come up to the house then. Everyone will want to see you both."

After Two Stones remounted, they turned up the slope, riding through the trees. Gil disappeared for a minute, then rejoined them on horseback, leading the way.

At last, they reached a clearing where the ground mostly leveled out. A cabin sat near the upper edge, with a barn downhill from it. Fresh wood covered one half of the building, clearly a very recent addition.

Through the open barn door, a man stepped out, then a boy behind him. The lad called out, "Two Stones!" and trotted toward them. "Who'd you bring with you?"

Her husband dismounted again and paused to ruffle the boy's hair before turning to Heidi, holding her horse. He must mean for her to dismount here, so she leaned forward and slid to the ground.

"Sean." Two Stones glanced from the lad to her. "This is Heidi." He didn't give their relation this time, but maybe because it wouldn't matter as much to the lad.

She smiled at Sean, ignoring the others flooding from the cabin toward them. "It's nice to meet you." This must be the nephew. And the blond girl approaching with the woman must be his sister, Lillian.

She stood back a little as two more men greeted Two Stones with hearty handshakes and claps on his shoulders. Two Stones called one of them Jericho, so the pretty blonde woman beside him who held a baby must be Dinah, the doctor who'd married Jericho. She must not be the babe's mother, for he'd said the babe belonged to Naomi, Dinah's sister.

Once they'd all greeted Two Stones, their voices quieted as their focus turned to her.

Heat crept up her face, but when Two Stones moved to her side, she managed to square her shoulders and offer a pleasant smile.

"This is Heidi." Again, his voice took on that deep, almost tender tone. "She is my wife."

CHAPTER 9

Heidi held her breath in the wake of Two Stones's introduction.

A few murmurs immediately sounded from those surrounding them, but she couldn't bring herself to meet any gazes. These people were almost like family to him. Did they think her unsuitable?

The woman named Dinah thrust the baby into the arms of the large man beside her. Shock struck his expression for a moment before he caught himself and adjusted the infant in his arms. A little awkward, but not as much as most men would be.

Dinah pressed through Sean and Gil, then nearly sprang on Heidi as she wrapped her arms around her. "Oh, it's so wonderful to meet you."

Heidi managed to raise her hands to return the embrace, though it felt like she was experiencing the scene in a dream. When Dinah pulled back, she gripped Heidi's upper arms, her smile as warm as if they'd always been friends. "You must be tired. Did you come from the Salish village? Or have you been traveling much longer?"

She willed her mouth to speak and managed to say, "Virginia City."

Dinah's eyes flared wide. "Oh, you poor dear." She turned and tugged Heidi forward, keeping hold of one arm. "You must be exhausted and cold." Over her shoulder, she spoke to the others. "You boys bring in her things. Lilly, bring the baby inside. Let's help Heidi get settled."

Heidi had no choice but to follow. Honestly, the immediate acceptance eased a load from her shoulders. She sent a quick glance over her shoulder to see Two Stones's reaction to her leaving him.

He was watching her, his expression too hard to read. Not anger. Not pleasure either. It almost looked like…longing? Certainly not for her. But for what?

Dinah stopped them and looked back too. "Two Stones, come in as soon as you can. We'll help your wife settle in, but she'll want you, too, of course."

He dipped his chin, but Dinah tugged Heidi forward before she could send him any kind of message with her gaze.

The truth was, she *did* want him with her. Though she should be more than capable of managing by herself among these friendly people, his presence gave her courage. She wasn't weak. Nor fearful. If a little of those emotions churned inside her, she wouldn't let them hold her back.

But Two Stones felt like a partner. They'd endured so much together this past week. Long days in the saddle, fighting the wind and cold, and even the snow. Meeting those two men from Virginia City, then the aftermath, when he'd been her strength, there in the abandoned cabin.

He'd done so much for her. She'd tried to carry her part of the load, cooking and helping as she could. Did he regret tying himself to her yet? Probably he did, but he was too honorable to ever let her know it.

She heaved out a sigh as Dinah led her into the warm cabin.

She couldn't let herself linger on thoughts like that. She had to stay focused on what lay ahead. On building the life she wanted for herself.

Surely becoming friends and allies with these women would help toward that end. Yet as she turned to answer Lillian's exuberant question about the length of their journey and what adventures they'd met, her gaze caught on the sleeping face of the precious babe nestled against the girl's shoulder.

How could she think so selfishly with such innocence before her?

Then another sensation slipped in, one that tightened her chest as her feet moved toward the babe of their own accord.

If she held to the arrangement she'd made with Two Stones, would she ever have a child of her own?

~

As Two Stones stepped into the cabin and paused to let his eyes adjust to the dim interior, his gaze caught on a sight that made his heart beat faster.

Heidi.

She stood with Dinah on one side and Lillian on the other, staring up at the loft where Dinah pointed as she spoke. Did she intend for him and Heidi to sleep up there? Maybe. That was just what he'd come inside to talk over—sleeping arrangements. He needed to know how much of their agreement Heidi wanted him to tell Jericho.

But seeing her there with the little bundle of babe resting on her shoulder stole every clear thought from his mind. She looked radiant. Happy. Such a sweet smile lighting her face. Her chin rested on little Mary Ellen's head as she spoke with Dinah.

She would be such a good mother. He'd thought of that once or twice as she prepared food or anticipated a need on the trail before he asked. She was thoughtful, and as she'd finally started to trust him these last few days, her kindness had caught him unexpectedly over and over.

But holding the babe... A longing pressed in his chest, something he'd not allowed himself to even think about since Yellow Mouse refused him. He would have loved to have his own son or daughter—or both. Children he could teach and encourage.

He wouldn't have that, and he could be content with his lot. But Heidi... Was he robbing her of that dream by keeping himself from her? Maybe he should give her the choice again.

Later. When she was settled in the village with his parents and they knew each other better.

He inhaled a deep breath and eased it out as he stepped forward.

Dinah was the first to notice his presence, and she turned with a smile. "Two Stones. I was just asking Heidi if she thought the two of you could be comfortable in the loft. If not, Jericho and I can stay there while you have our room."

Heidi turned to him with wide eyes, shaking her head in an unspoken message of concern. "No. I'm sure the loft will be fine." Even as her eyes questioned him, her words were for Dinah.

He gave her an easy smile. "Yes. The loft will be fine." If Heidi wanted a room alone, he could sleep in the barn or the new bunkhouse with the rest of the men.

"Oh, good." Dinah turned to Lillian. "Will you bring down anything you'll need for the next few days? You can room with Naomi."

As if she'd recognized her mother's name, little Mary Ellen came to life on Heidi's chest with a cry. Panic flared in his wife's eyes as the babe squirmed in her arms. He'd seen Mary Ellen do this before. One heartbeat she slept, and the next, awoke with a fierce hunger. The babe was crying too loudly now for him to reassure his wife.

Dinah reached for her niece and took her, bouncing and

speaking softly to Mary Ellen as she hurried her into the room where Naomi must be sleeping.

As the door closed behind her, quiet descended on them like a cloud. Heidi stared after the pair. "What happened? Did I hurt her?"

He stepped closer but stopped himself from pressing a hand to her back. "No. She startles awake when hungry. She does not think she will live another heartbeat without eating, I think." He tried to give a smile that would lighten her concern.

He had to use these moments alone to ask his question. He dropped his voice lower. "I have not told Jericho that we are not..." He scrambled for the best way to say it. "That we have not..."

She nodded quickly, making it clear she knew what he meant.

He breathed out and continued his question. "Do you wish me to speak of it? Or let them think all is as usual with us? I can sleep in the barn if I tell him."

Her eyes showed her indecision, and her bottom lip crept between her teeth—something he shouldn't allow himself to look at for long. His mind had tried to wander that direction far too many times, and the only way he could stop those thoughts was by picturing Callum. Her father had been so excited to see his daughter again. Then so worried about her safety.

That safety had to be foremost in Two Stones's mind also. Nothing else.

"I don't think they need to know. Do you?" Heidi sounded uncertain, like she very much wanted his opinion. "Do you wish to tell him? If it bothers you to hide the truth... I know he's a good friend."

Red had crept up to her ears and made splotches on her cheeks. Her pale coloring made her discomfort show so quickly. Part of him wanted to grin at her innocence, but the other part wanted to take away anything that bothered her, even this conversation.

He shook his head. "If you do not mind me sleeping there too"—he glanced up to the loft where rustling sounded as Lillian moved around—"I can sleep on the floor."

She nodded. But before she could speak, Lillian's skirts appeared at the top of the ladder. At the same moment, the door Dinah had disappeared through opened again, and she stepped out, without the babe this time. "She'll feel better with food in her tummy." Her expression seemed clouded though. Did something about the babe's actions concern her? Or maybe her sister, Naomi.

He didn't have time to ask, for the front door opened, and the rest of the brothers trickled in, those who had been out with the herds when he and Heidi arrived. Jude first, then Jonah, still limping but walking without even a stick for support.

As the men greeted him and met Heidi, the cabin came alive with voices and laughter.

Lillian and Dinah carried plates of food to the table, and Heidi moved to help them.

The talk quickly turned to preparations for Christmas, and Sean jumped in on the topic. "We're going out to cut a tree first thing in the morning. Uncle Jericho said I can pick it out."

"Me too." Lillian sent her brother a glare.

"You can help, but I've already found the perfect one."

Miles nudged his nephew. "Actually, I've already found the perfect tree." His grin showed he was teasing the boy, and Sean responded with a pretend fist to his uncle's gut.

Miles was only five winters older than the lad, so they often scuffled in play.

Dinah stopped the commotion by calling all to the table, pointing Heidi to the seat beside Two Stones's usual chair. Though the table was large, with so many people packed around it, his knees pressed against Heidi's.

Perhaps she would have had more room if he attempted to stay on his side, but it felt good to touch her again, even in this small way. Since that night in the abandoned cabin when she fell asleep leaning against his side, her head on his shoulder, he'd craved the feeling again. Their hands occasionally brushed as she handed him her reins or a plate of food, but not the steady firm contact of her leg against his.

When Jericho bowed his head and everyone at the table joined hands, Heidi fit her palm in his as though they'd done this for years. He wrapped his fingers around hers, closing her hand in his and relishing the warmth of her.

He tried to hear Jericho's prayer, but all he could manage was his own, *Thank You, Lord, for this woman.* He shouldn't let himself be so affected by her, but how could he not when she was so near all the time? What man could resist a woman as beautiful as his wife, both inside and out?

When Jericho spoke the *amen* and Sean released his hand on one side, Two Stones had to force his fingers to unwind from Heidi's hand. She sent him a shy smile before reaching to accept a dish of potatoes from Dinah.

Could it be possible that she craved his touch as much as he did hers? Surely not. But…was there a way he could find out for certain?

CHAPTER 10

Heidi snuggled little Mary Ellen closer the next morning as she gently rocked in the chair by the fire. The babe was so sweet. Heidi had volunteered to hold her any time the opportunity presented.

"I think they're coming with the tree." Dinah turned from the cookstove and sent Heidi a smile.

Dinah's sister, Naomi, moved to the door. "I'll let them in." She was such a quiet woman, it'd been hard to get to know her. Maybe because Naomi had stayed in her room much of last evening and this morning.

Dinah said her sister was still recovering from the birth. But Mary Ellen was more than two months old. Shouldn't Naomi be able to participate more with the family by now? Who was Heidi to judge, though? She'd never given birth. And before meeting little Mary Ellen, she'd not realized the wonderful gift she was missing.

Part of her was thankful not to have a child from Winston.

Two Stones though... He would be such a good father. The thought of what that would require made her middle flip and her chest tighten. She couldn't do it. Not after the way it had been with Winston.

Her eyes burned even as the sound of laughter and happy voices drifted through the open door. She pressed her face into Mary Ellen's hair while she worked to pull herself back together.

"It's beautiful." Dinah spoke to the group from the doorway as Jericho appeared on the stoop, holding one side of a large evergreen. "I'm not sure how you think we'll get it inside the cabin though."

Heidi stood and moved toward them so she could better see the tree. Two Stones held the other side of the wide base, grinning when he saw her.

Something in her belly flipped at that handsome smile. This man could turn heads anywhere he went, even in a Savannah ballroom. She nearly chuckled at that notion. The older matrons would pretend to be scandalized at a black-haired native in their high-brow society. But she knew many a young woman—married or not—who would sigh and swoon every time Two Stones flashed a grin.

How in the world had she landed with such a man? In truth, it was his strength of character that appealed to her even more than his looks, considerable as they were.

His grin deepened as though he could hear her thoughts, but then he was distracted by something Jericho said.

She stepped back with the baby while they sorted how to bring in the tree and where to place it. She could join in the merrymaking by stringing popcorn or placing extra pine boughs and ribbons around the cabin for a festive touch, but having Mary Ellen in her arms gave her an excuse to simply watch. To take in the sweet innocence of it all.

This was nothing like instructing the servants where to place decorations as she'd done her first Christmas with Winston. When he came home that evening and frowned at it all, she'd escaped to her room to avoid his displeasure. By keeping to her chamber, she also managed to be absent when his mother came to rearrange everything the way a *proper* home should be decorated.

For the two Christmases after that, Winston's mother had come to oversee placement of the tree and trimmings before Heidi even began thinking about the holiday. In truth, it had been a relief to hand over the responsibility to someone Winston approved of. Mostly.

Now, she wasn't being censured for her lack of social discernment, so she could join in the decorating if she chose. But the way this family seemed to enjoy being with each other... She could watch this for days.

Sure, the brothers teased each other and sometimes ended up in a play brawl that should concern her. Yet the affection between them all was thick enough to ease any worry.

Two Stones added to banter at times, often being drawn in by one of the brothers or even Dinah. And sometimes he initiated a bit of teasing himself. Watching him made her want to join in, but she didn't dare.

After the tree was secured, he came to settle on the ladder-back chair beside her rocker, his gaze softening as he took in her and Mary Ellen. She wanted to tell him he didn't have to sit just because she was, but the warmth in his eyes and the curve of his mouth kept her from sending him away. In truth, she'd rather shoo everyone else from the room so the two of them could be alone, as they had been this last week.

Too soon though, Mary Ellen squirmed in her arms. At her first hungry cry, Naomi turned with a weary expression. Mary Ellen had already begun wailing by the time her mother took her.

"I suppose that's my cue to start on Christmas dinner." Dinah moved away from the tree. "If I know you men, you'll be hungry long before dark."

Heidi rose from the rocking chair. "I'll help you."

Time with Two Stones would have to wait. There was much to be done to prepare for Christmas.

~

Heidi stood at the edge of the massive wooden table, her hands covered in cookie dough as she laid out stars she'd cut from the flattened batter. The delicious aromas of cinnamon and nutmeg wafted through the air, mingling with the mouthwatering scent of roasting meat and cloves. She and Dinah had been at work for hours, with occasional help from Lillian and Naomi, and the feast was nearly ready.

A fire crackled in the hearth, casting its warm glow on the rest of the room. Everywhere she looked, the spirit of the season seemed to have taken hold—from the sprigs of holly adorning each wall peg and door frame to the massive tree that stretched the length of the wall beside the outer door.

With all the batter cut, she carried the tray of cookies to the cookstove, where Dinah stirred the apple cinnamon drink she was making.

"Those are perfect, Heidi. You have a real talent for them."

She smiled her thanks, the words feeling far better than she cared to admit. A talent for cutting star shapes from cookie dough was hardly a lifesaving ability, but the praise seemed so genuine. Perhaps she was too easily affected.

Dinah shifted to the side so Heidi could place the pan in the oven.

"Doesn't it all smell divine?" Dinah paused her stirring to inhale deeply. "There's something so magical about this time of year."

"Indeed." Heidi's chest tightened. How had she been so lucky as to find herself here, on this day, in time to experience a simple mountain Christmas so full of joy?

As though Heidi had spoken the question aloud, Dinah sighed. "The Lord certainly blessed us all by bringing you and Two Stones in time for today."

"I guess so." Even as she murmured agreement, her mind sorted through the idea. Could God have possibly orchestrated bringing her to the Montana Territory, then meeting and marrying Two Stones? Did that mean He'd intended for her father to die also?

That last thought seemed more in line with the unrelenting rod of the stern God she'd experienced in Savannah, but not the one Dinah spoke of.

Who was right? Was there a way to blend the two into a Deity who made sense? Or perhaps He was a fickle God, commanding events according to his whim and pleasure.

Her middle tightened. If that were the case, it seemed she'd somehow managed to move into His good graces in marrying Two Stones. Maybe, for the first time in her life, she could finally settle into a happy existence.

Dinah paused in the midst of her stirring, studying Heidi with a scrutinizing gaze.

Sweat prickled at her neck. What had she done wrong? Did her thoughts show?

But Dinah nodded toward the door. "Why don't you go outside and cool off? I'll watch the cookies and take them out when they're finished. You've been working all morning and you look overheated."

Heidi shook her head. "I'll stay and stir that while you go outside." She reached for the spoon in Dinah's hand.

But Dinah edged her out of the way. "I'll come out as soon as this is done. You go now." A slight frown gathered at her brow. "You're flushed. The cold air will feel good."

She *was* hot, especially standing by the stove, so she washed her hands in the basin, then headed for the door. "I'll see if anyone needs help out there." She was too warm to wear the fur cape Two Stones had given her, but she reached for the wool coat.

She stepped out into the crisp winter breeze. Relief flowed through her as the cold nipped her cheeks. She drew a deep breath, relishing the sharp clarity of the air as it filled her lungs.

She paused to take in her bearings, her gaze lifting to the distant mountains that rose through a gap in the tree line. There was a majestic beauty in those peaks that crept inside her, weaving its way to her very core. In this place she could be free. No matter the challenges of survival, at least she had the same chance as the next person.

She brought her focus to the clearing around her. The barn seemed quiet now, though there had been plenty of activity around it each time she'd stepped outside for water.

She slipped on her coat and started toward the structure, the snow crunching under her boots. The older section of barn stood weathered and rusty, a testament to the years it had endured and the many, many snowfalls. The new construction had its own walk-thru door. That must be the bunkhouse Dinah had mentioned, where the younger brothers and Sean slept.

When she reached the open barn door, she peered inside, hesitating for a moment as her eyes adjusted to the darkness within.

"Hello?" No voices answered, only the rustle of animals in the stalls. Where had everyone gone? No one had said they were going to check on the herds. Might they have ridden down to the creek for something?

As she walked into the shadowy interior, her footsteps echoed around her, amplifying the quiet. A cow offered a quiet moo as she passed one of the enclosures, and she nearly jumped at the sound. She moved toward the animal. "Hello there."

The cow munched hay and eyed her.

The hairs on the back of Heidi's neck stood on end, and she couldn't help but glance over her shoulder, half-expecting to see someone—or something—coming in from the daylight outside.

But there was nothing, only the light streaming through the open door.

She turned and started back that way. Her gelding and Two Stones's horses had been penned in the corral outside. They would welcome attention, no doubt.

She left the barn and approached the corral, where the three horses grazed on hay. Two Stones's riding horse flicked its short tail slowly, the natural movement easing some of the tension in her chest.

Her own gelding gave a soft snort and wandered toward her. She met him at the fence, reaching through to rub the flat part of his forehead, then his favorite spot on his jaw. "You're such a good boy."

The horse nuzzled her arm affectionately, and she moved to rub his neck.

The crunch of boots on snow sounded behind her, and she turned to see which of the Coulters approached.

Her breath caught at the figure emerging from the shadows of the nearby trees.

The companion of the man she'd shot. Her mind scrambled for his name. Fitz? Walker was the older man, the one she'd killed. Her throat burned as it always did with that though.

"Remember me?" His growl dripped with anger.

Heidi's heart pounded loud in her ears. "Why are you here?" And why hadn't she tucked her pistol in her waistband before leaving the cabin? She'd felt so safe surrounded by the Coulters, but this proved that danger truly lurked everywhere.

He took another menacing step toward her. "You're going to pay for what you did."

Her instincts screamed at her to flee. Could she make a run for it?

No. He would shoot her well before she reached the barn.

So she held her ground. Panic threatened to engulf her, but she fought hard to keep it at bay. Her survival depended on her ability to think clearly.

He halted two strides away from her, close enough that the rifle would kill no matter which part of her his bullet struck.

"What do you want?" Her voice trembled, no matter how much strength she tried to force into it.

His smirk returned. "Justice. For Walker. And probably a nice little reward for taking you back to Virginia City."

Her heart thundered so hard she couldn't breathe. "I'm not going with you. No matter what you do." She would rather die than end up in a brothel.

But maybe...she managed a tiny breath. If she could delay him, perhaps Two Stones or one of the others would come back and help her.

God, if You're up there. If You care at all, help me. Please. Send Two Stones. She lifted the silent prayer even as her attacker edged forward.

"Don't think your injun is gonna save you this time neither." He glared. "He's busy with a little distraction I set up. Plenty long enough for you an' me to get far away from here."

Distraction? What did he mean?

He motioned to the snow beside her. "Git to the ground. On yer belly. Hands behind yer back."

With that rifle pointed at her, she didn't have a choice.

"If you give me even a blink o' trouble, I'll kill you as fast as you killed Walker. No question about it. I'd rather have the reward from Tyson for bringin' you back to Virginia City, but if you make it hard, I'll be done with ya here an' now." The ice in his tone said he meant every word.

She slowly dropped to her knees where he'd pointed. She just needed to buy time. The snow seeped through her skirts in seconds, and when she lay flat on the ground, her legs burned from the cold. Thankfully, her coat slowed the wetness reaching her upper body, but she would feel it soon enough.

"Arms behind you." The man's bark made her jerk.

She obeyed, and when he gripped her wrists with a rough hold, the powerless feeling that swept through her felt far too familiar. The weight of despair nearly suffocated her, bringing back every memory she'd tried to block out. Every time Winston...

She couldn't breathe. She couldn't think. *God, help me! Help me.* Her prayer was nearly smothered beneath the deafening roar of her own fear.

And as the cold darkness closed in around her, her world closed to a single thought. *Send Two Stones. Please.*

CHAPTER 11

Two Stones coughed from the acrid smoke as he scooped another armful of snow and threw it on the billowing flames engulfing the shed. The fire only licked higher into the gray winter sky.

Snow still blanketed the ground all around them. The shed catching fire couldn't be an accident. Was someone trying to get to the crates of sapphires stored inside? But why would they set fire instead of simply stealing the treasure?

His blood turned to ice as realization struck. A distraction.

He spun, staring toward the house, though he couldn't see it for the trees.

The women. Heidi and Dinah and Naomi—and the baby—were alone in the cabin. Vulnerable.

"Jericho!" Two Stones turned once more to find his friend, yelling over the roar and crackle of the blaze. "I'm going to the cabin! The women."

Jericho's face showed question for half a heartbeat, then his eyes widened as the same truth sank in for him. He turned and yelled something to Jude.

Two Stones sprinted toward the house, and as he left the

burning building behind, the sound of Jericho's steps pounded behind him. It usually took a quarter hour to walk the distance from the storage shed to the cabin, and they were traveling uphill this direction. He feared he didn't have fifteen minutes. He had to get to Heidi before someone hurt her.

Who would have gone through so much to distract them all? Immediately, an image of the younger man they'd met on the trail flashed through his mind. Fitz. Would he have traveled all the way out here for vengeance on his friend? He'd seemed to only want them to leave. But when he'd had a chance to think, had he changed his mind?

Could the brothel owner from Virginia City have come all this way for Heidi? He was likely desperate for beautiful young women, and she certainly fit that description. But this far?

He could have sent someone. A hired gun.

Urgency propelled his legs faster. He had to get there before they hurt Heidi. *Creator Father, place Your hands around her to protect. Do not let them harm her.*

The clearing appeared through the branches ahead, and he could just barely make out the outline of the barn. He slowed to stop at the edge of the trees so he could see what was happening before he entered the clearing.

There was no sign of movement except from the horses in the corral. The animals stared toward the trees to his right.

His gaze caught a motion in that direction, and his breath closed off. That was Fitz, heaving something onto a horse.

A body.

Two Stones tucked farther behind the tree, waving to stop Jericho as he reached him.

He did his best to quiet both his breathing and his racing heart as he focused on the bundle Fitz was adjusting on his horse's shoulders. That was the skirt Heidi had been wearing.

Anger surged through him. Had the man killed her? He had to assume she was alive. Had to act quickly to save her.

Using the stealth his father and uncles had taught him as a child, he moved through the trees around the edge of the clearing, closing in on Heidi's attacker.

But the man must have seen him, for he swung onto his horse behind Heidi's body and spun the animal, then dug in hard as they lurched into the woods. Just before the trees hid them, he caught sight of Heidi's legs, kicking furiously.

Relief took away a single layer of fear from his chest, but didn't cool his anger. She was alive but still very much in danger.

He took off toward the horses in the corral.

"Wait. We need rifles," Jericho yelled as he sprinted toward the house.

Yes. He could get the horses while Jericho gathered guns.

It took too long for him to grab bridles from the barn, then slip them on his and Heidi's geldings in the corral. Jericho's pinto was pastured down the hill, so he could ride Heidi's horse for now.

Two Stones leaped onto his mount bareback as Jericho arrived with the weapons.

Dinah stood in the cabin doorway, her worry clear in the outline of her shoulders. "We'll be praying."

He took the rifle and shot bag from Jericho, then plunged his heels into his horse's side. Fitz might have a head start on them, but at least the snow would help them follow his tracks at a run.

Maneuvering downhill in the snow wasn't easy—for them or the horses—but he used every one of his senses to keep his gelding on the trail at a swift canter. The bitter cold stung his face, and branches caught them several times. He ignored it all, focusing on catching up with Heidi and her attacker.

They were gaining ground, they had to be. But the slope became steeper as they followed a route so rocky, the horses kept slipping on ice.

Two Stones eyed the ravine at the bottom. If he remembered

right, there was no way to cross it. The man would have to turn left or right. He would likely go right, toward the Mullan Road with access to Virginia City and all the other mining towns.

They could turn now and cut him off—if he took that route. *Lord, don't let me choose wrong.*

Two Stones glanced back at Jericho and pointed to the shortcut he was thinking of.

Jericho nodded. "Let's try it." They would need to pick their way carefully, but it was their best chance of heading off the man.

Guide our horses' steps. Let us reach her. Protect Heidi.

He kept up his prayers as he reined his horse toward the steeper section. The animal snorted as its hooves slipped on an icy stone, but Two Stones held his reins steady and leaned back to help the horse keep its balance. One misstep could mean disaster, but God had control over their horses' movements.

And the actions of Heidi's captor.

Thank You that You have already won this battle. Your power is greater than the plans of any man.

At last, they reached level ground beside the ravine. He peered down at the frozen creek far below, then turned his gaze back to the narrow path they were on now. Surely the man had gone this direction instead of turning left at the ravine, which would take him deeper onto Coulter land.

"There."

Two Stones turned to look where Jericho pointed. Fresh tracks moved along the base of the slope ahead of them.

He pushed his horse into a trot as they followed the prints. This was as fast as they could maneuver on the narrow ledge.

He had to fight urgency in his chest. God had already won the battle. They simply had to arrive when the Lord planned for them to.

As the ravine grew shallower and its sides not as steep, the tracks moved down to the creek bed. Two Stones slowed and studied the path ahead. Should they stay up on the bank or follow Fitz's trail down?

"We might be able to see him from above if we stay here." Jericho's quiet words stated exactly what Two Stones had been wondering.

He nodded. "Let's try it." They might have to move slower to watch for sign that the man had tried to ride up the far bank. But it would be worth the chance to have the advantage if he'd stayed down in the ravine.

Two Stones pushed his horse forward, ducking beneath snow-laden branches. The cold air burned his lungs, but that was nothing compared to the pain Heidi must be experiencing. *Father, protect her. She's in Your hands.*

They were getting close now—he could feel it. Every fiber of his being strained toward Heidi. If that snake had harmed one hair on her head...

A gunshot rang out, echoing through the silent forest.

Two Stones's heart seized. *No.*

He drove his heels into his horse's sides, racing along the top of the ridge. In the ravine below, a flash of movement made him slow.

A horse bucking. That was Fitz atop the animal, struggling to control it. And Heidi...

A form lay on the ground, a short distance from the flailing horse. That was her skirt.

And she wasn't moving.

He couldn't breathe, couldn't move. His mind knew he had to get to her, but his body wouldn't obey.

The bucking horse reared, then tumbled backward. Man and horse screamed together, and Two Stones's own belly lurched.

The horse landed on its back, squashing Fitz beneath his saddle. Then the animal scrambled onto its side, pausing for a single heartbeat before heaving up to its feet.

Fitz still lay in the snow. A second motionless body.

Two Stones finally shifted into action. He jumped from his horse, keeping hold of his rifle, then scrambled down the side of the ravine. He had to help Heidi. If there was any spark of life left in her, he would coax it back to a flame.

Even as he ran, the realization flicked in his mind. He had no ability to breathe life or death. Only the Creator could do so. *Fan the spark to flame, Lord.*

Jericho reached the bottom of the slope just behind Two Stones, and he headed toward the man, leaving Two Stones to focus on Heidi. His wife.

"Heidi?" He couldn't breathe as he approached her, slowing the final step so he could drop to his knees beside her.

She lay on her side, facing away from him. And she didn't respond. No movement at all.

He laid a hand on her shoulder. "Heidi. Wake up."

Her coat was wet through, and he brushed her hair away from her neck so he could feel for the beat of life.

Yes!

The pulse was light and fast, but blood still pumped through her.

He gave her shoulder a gentle nudge. "Can you wake, Heidi? We need to get you warm."

She gave a small moan, but her eyes stayed closed.

He had to get her back to the cabin. He scanned the length of her, checking for signs of broken bones. Her hands were still tied behind her back, so he sliced the cord quickly, then took more care as he adjusted her arms. Did he dare turn her?

Warmth was what she needed more than anything.

He turned to check on Jericho, and his friend was straightening from the man on the ground. His face wore a grim expression as he shook his head. "He landed on a rock. He's bleeding from his head, but I think it might have snapped his neck. He's gone."

Two Stones's belly twisted. He should feel relief. He did, for

Heidi no longer had to fear the man. But to die in such a way… there was no honor in it. And he'd lost his chance to come to Creator Father.

He needed to focus on Heidi now. "I have to get her back to the cabin. She's cold and not waking."

Jericho surveyed the scene, then started toward the side of the ravine they'd descended. "I'll bring the horses down."

While he waited for his friend to find a place where the animals could descend, Two Stones removed his fur coat and lifted Heidi enough to wrap it around her. Her own coat was soaked through, and her dress beneath too. This would have to do until he could get her back to the warm house and dry clothes.

When Jericho reached them with the horses, Two Stones mounted his gelding and Jericho lifted Heidi up to him. He tucked her close in front of him. Her body had begun to shiver now—a good sign. She was coming back to life, though she still hadn't opened her eyes.

"Ride on." Jericho stepped away. "I'll load the body on his horse if I can. If not, we'll come back for him later. Either way, I won't be far behind."

Two Stones paused long enough to meet his friend's gaze. "Be careful."

Jericho dipped a small nod. "Get your wife home."

Two Stones spun his gelding and urged him as fast as the ground would allow, the words echoing through his thoughts.

Yes. Heidi *was* his wife, and wherever she was would be home for him. From this day forward. What would it be like to have a real marriage with her?

Even as the question seeped in, reality pushed through the picture. He lived on the trail, and he couldn't force that life on her. Not only would she never feel at home, but the dangers he faced would be so much more treacherous for her—a woman in such a wild land full of even wilder men.

She would be safer with his family. Could he stay there with her? Not when he'd promised to leave her alone. His chest clenched. Was there a way to keep his word and still make a life for her?

Only if she changed her mind about their marriage, and only Creator Father could accomplish such a feat. *Lord, if it be Your will…*

CHAPTER 12

Heidi awoke to a throbbing ache in her feet and legs. The soft mattress cradled her weary body, so different from the frozen ground where Two Stones had found her the day before.

That awful day.

She'd bounced and fought with every step the horse took, though she was bound and gagged, laying over the mount's shoulders with all the blood pooling in her head.

Fitz had grown tired of her struggling and dumped her on the ground so he could shoot her. She'd squeezed her eyes shut and waited for the slam of the bullet in her body.

That blast of gunfire echoed through the snowy landscape and through her head.

But she'd not been shot.

Her body had already passed the point of shivering, her hands and legs nearly numb as she lay in the snow. Then strong arms had lifted her, out of the snow and onto another horse.

Two Stones. His warmth had wrapped around her, cradling her in his strength. Not even the miserable cold could steal away her relief at being in his arms.

When he'd carried her into the cabin, Dinah had insisted he bring her into the room she and Jericho shared. Two Stones had laid Heidi on this bed, and Dinah changed her to dry clothes, then piled blankets on her, tucking them around her shivering form.

Again and again, Two Stones had come with heated stones wrapped in cloth, placing them at Heidi's feet and hands. The heat seeped into her skin, burning as it melted away the chill in her bones.

Each time she'd opened her eyes, his dark gaze searched her face, relief flooding his features when she managed a weak smile. At last, he had sat on the bed, holding her close. Finally, she had stopped shivering, and blessed sleep claimed her.

Now, as daylight shone through the window, the warmth under the covers was almost too much, the tingling in her extremities bordering on pain as feeling returned.

Beyond the bedroom door, voices murmured, the clanking of pans and the thump of boots indicating the others must be gathering for the missed Christmas meal. The scents of roasted meat and warm bread wafted in, Heidi's stomach rumbling in anticipation.

A gentle knock sounded before the door creaked open. Two Stones entered, his hair neatly braided, wearing a rich blue shirt.

"Good morning." His warm eyes studied her. "How are you feeling?"

"Much better, thanks to you." Her voice rasped, so she cleared her throat.

A smile touched his gaze. "Let's get you to the table then."

She pushed the blankets aside and started to rise. Thankfully, Dinah had changed her into a dress, not nightclothes. When her stocking feet touched the hard floor, the shooting pain made her wince.

Two Stones stepped forward and lifted her in his arms.

"I can walk." Even as she protested, she curled against his chest.

"I know." He slid her a look. "But allow me this."

She did, relaxing against him and resting her hands on his shoulders. His strength surrounded her, his heat seeping into her weary body. She felt utterly safe.

This man who had vowed to protect her, who asked for nothing in return, embodied everything she so desperately craved, even if she hadn't allowed herself to admit it. And God had brought him to save her, not just that first day, right before her father died, but yesterday too, when he'd lifted her numb body out of the snow.

She could see Almighty's hand, guiding them together. Tears pricked her eyes as she finally allowed herself to believe it—that God had worked all things for her good these past weeks.

And maybe He had before that too, if she thought back. She would have to spend time talking with Him when she was alone. For now, she offered up a silent *Thank You* that she meant from the very depths of her soul.

Two Stones settled her into her chair at the table, then lingered beside her as the Coulters bustled about, carrying heaping plates of roasted deer meat, potatoes, and warm biscuits.

"I hope you're hungry, Heidi." Dinah placed a dried apple pie in front of her. "Lilly and I have been at it again this morning, cooking even more to go with what we made yesterday."

Heidi smiled. "It smells wonderful. Thank you, truly. All of you." She glanced around the table, taking in the circle of welcoming faces. "I don't know how I'll ever repay your kindness."

"No need for that." Jericho shook his head. "We're just thankful you're here." His unspoken *alive* lingered in her mind.

She ducked to hide the threatening tears. She had lost so much, but she'd gained something precious. Not just Two

Stones, but also this family who loved him as one of their own. And they were extending the same to her.

As they began the belated Christmas feast, laughter and light filled the little cabin. The food tasted every bit as good as it smelled, and she relished every bite, though she grew full far too soon.

Even before most of them had finished eating, Sean's voice rose above the rest. "Can we open our gifts now?"

Miles nudged him. "Jericho said we have to clean out the barn first. You get started and we'll be right behind you."

Sean scrunched his nose at him. "You go first. See if I come help you."

She grinned at the pair, and her face kept the smile as the children were handed their first presents. Jericho and Dinah had given Lillian a doll with blonde hair to match her own. Its beautiful red dress also matched the coat they gave her pup, Apple. The next present Lillian opened came from Naomi—a red dress matching the clothing for her doll and pup. This one was definitely Lillian's size though, decorated with beautiful lace that would make her look like a princess.

The girl's eyes shone with pure joy as she thanked the quiet woman. "It's perfect. More than I ever dreamed."

Naomi squeezed her hand across the table. "It was my pleasure. The color will be lovely on you."

The chaos grew as the others shared gifts with each other, occasional squeals and laughter rising over the hum of excited voices.

Heidi glanced over at her husband. If only she could give him something special for Christmas, to show him what he meant to her. She had nothing. Except...

Two Stones met her eyes as he reached into his pocket and pulled out a small leather pouch. "I have something for you." A shy smile touched his lips.

She took the bag, searching his face for any sign of what it held. He revealed nothing, so she reached in with two fingers and pulled out the tiny metal piece.

It was a delicate gold ring was set with a brilliant blue stone.

She blinked back her tears and lifted the ring. It glimmered in the firelight, the blue gem deep and dazzling.

"It's sapphire. Mined from our mountains." He spoke softly. "Like your necklace."

Heidi's vision blurred, joy and gratitude swelling within. "It's beautiful." And it added to the greatest gift he could have given her—him.

She hadn't brought herself to wear the necklace yet. She needed more time to ponder all that Papa meant with that gift. But this one…

"Here." Two Stones took her hand gently, then slid the ring onto her finger. A perfect fit.

Heidi stared at it, emotions swelling in her chest. "Thank you," she whispered.

Two Stones's thumb brushed over her knuckles, the tender touch sending a tremor through her.

He must have thought the shiver came from cold, for he pushed his chair back. "I'll take you to bed. You still need rest."

She allowed him to lift her again, and the others called "Merry Christmas" as Two Stones carried her back to the bed chamber. She would walk the next time she got up, but for now, being cradled in her husband's arms felt too good.

After he eased her down on the edge of the bed, she patted the mattress beside her. "Sit with me?"

He did so, but now she couldn't quite meet his gaze. How to say this?

She inhaled a breath for courage and began. "I can't thank you enough. For coming after me, for saving my life. You've shown me such care and kindness when I least deserved it."

Two Stones brushed a strand of hair from her cheek. "You deserve all of it and more."

Heidi bit her lip. "I know we married because my father begged it of you, but I want our marriage to be real. In every way." She flushed. "When the time is right."

She couldn't stand not seeing his reaction, so she managed a glance up at him.

Joy sparkled in his dark eyes, along with something richer. He reached for her hand and raised it to his lips, as he had at the end of their wedding ceremony.

But this time he kissed her palm, a feeling far more intimate than when he'd kissed the backs of her fingers.

"I will wait as long as needed." His gaze was so earnest. "You are a gift beyond measure."

A gift?

Her?

After all the rejection and abuse she'd endured at the hands of her previous husband, could anyone consider her that?

And yet Two Stones did. Rather than deny the truth of his words, she let herself sink into his eyes, losing herself in the love there. And when he angled toward her, she raised up to meet him partway.

His mouth caressed hers, a touch so gentle, so reverent, her heart overflowed.

God had blessed her to overflowing.

When he pulled away, he scooped her into his arms, settling her on his lap. She curled into his chest with a contented sigh. "Merry Christmas, husband."

"Merry Christmas, wife." His voice rumbled in her ear, soothing all the way through her. His strength surrounded her, his warmth seeping into her bones.

And in the circle of his arms, she'd finally found home.

I pray you loved Two Stones and Heidi's story!

Jude's book is next in the series, and I think you'll love it! Turn the page for a sneak peek of *Protecting the Mountain Man's Treasure,* the next book in the Brothers of Sapphire Ranch series!

CHAPTER ONE

AUGUST 1868
ROCK CREEK, MONTANA TERRITORY

The sun hung low in the sky, casting a golden glow over the bustling streets of New York City as Jude Coulter stepped out of the ornate office building. The marble and opulence felt foreign compared to the rugged mountains of his family ranch in the Montana Territory he knew so well.

"Have an excellent day, Mr. Coulter." The uniformed man who'd opened the door for him gave a half bow before closing it behind him.

Jude nodded his thanks, though the fellow had already disappeared. He tightened his grip on the carpet bags in each hand and started down the cascade of steps to the street.

It now seemed foolish to carry so many gold coins with him instead of having them sent to the train station by delivery wagon—in padded unmarked crates of course, the same way he'd brought the sapphires from their ranch all the way to the city.

He'd been worried about traveling with so much money though. It seemed safer to always have it with him. Especially since it wasn't too much for him to carry himself.

Yet perhaps these two bags made him stand out from others.

The cab he'd ridden in from the train station still waited for him on the street, as he'd instructed. When he reached the rig, he climbed in. Did the driver wonder what was in the bags? Jude hadn't had them when he first hired the man back at the train station, so their presence now would surely raise a question in his mind.

"The station, sir?" The wiry man on the bench looked back at Jude, brows raised.

"Yes. Thank you." He should have thought to give the direction, not expect the fellow to read his mind. He was out of his element here, no question.

The driver called to the horse, and the cab lurched forward, weaving into the flow of traffic.

Flow might be a generous word. More like a swirl.

Hordes of people and vehicles moved in every direction, their sounds melding into a discordant chorus. Shouts. Calls from street vendors. Horses snorting and shod hooves clopping against cement and stone. Wagon wheels, the creaking of so many harnesses. Too many sounds to dissect, and the effort tightened his body until his head pounded.

He closed his eyes and brought up a memory of the creek on their ranch, the peaceful murmur as it flowed over rocks. That's where they'd first found the sapphires. Blue and pink stones lying visible among the many brown and gold-flecked pebbles.

The gold wasn't real, of course. Just pretty mica. Which is why the place wasn't overrun with miners like other parts of the Montana Territory. But Dat had realized the significance of the other colored stones.

Jude had loved working with him back then. Then when Dat and Mum passed on, he'd spent long days by himself at the creek, searching for more sapphires. Digging in the areas where they'd found the most.

Mining the gems that Dat had treasured became Jude's special role. His contribution to the family. His responsibility.

"Here we are." The driver's words sounded just as the cab jolted to a stop. The vehicle rocked as the horse found its footing.

Jude straightened and scanned the busy station. Even more people packed in here than on the street. He gripped his bags and stepped from the cart.

He had to set down one of the satchels to pull out payment for the driver. "Thank you. Will that suffice?" He'd added another dollar to the amount the man had quoted for the round trip.

The cabby's teeth flashed as he nodded. "That'll do."

Jude re-secured his grip on both bags, and turned toward the end of the station where he'd left his other piece of luggage in locked storage.

The porter who'd helped him before was speaking to a dark-haired woman, so Jude waited his turn. As the man gathered her luggage, she was asking about trains heading west, and the porter was explaining the different options available.

Though she didn't say so exactly, her words sounded like she was traveling by herself. That seemed odd, but maybe things were done differently in the city.

She was a pretty thing. Not bigger than a minute, with dark hair pulled back in a tight knot. Though she was asking questions, she seemed to know exactly what answers she needed. As though the man was simply filling in gaps of her knowledge.

"Thank you, sir. Good day." Her final words held a light accent that hadn't showed in her earlier questions. Not strong, but...different.

When she turned to walk past Jude, she offered a polite smile. Her dark eyes held just a hint of a slant, a look that made her beauty even more striking than he'd first thought.

He tipped his chin in greeting. Should he also say hello?

She passed before he could decide, so he turned to the porter.

"How can I help you, sir?" The man looked like he was forcing pleasantness he didn't feel. Dealing with strangers all day couldn't be easy.

"I have a bag in holding." Jude nodded toward his piece. "That one. Coulter is the name."

The porter nodded and pulled the carpet bag out of the fenced area. "May I see your ticket, please?"

Jude set down his load and pulled the stub from his pocket, then handed it over.

The porter nodded. "Very good." He handed over the bag, then pointed to a large number suspended from the metal rafters by the train tracks. "You'll be leaving from platform number three."

After thanking the man, Jude meandered toward the spot. A crowd had already gathered, but he worked his way around the edge until he reached a place to stand and wait on the platform.

It would be a quarter hour before the train arrived, but he'd wait here. The sooner he boarded the train, the sooner he would get to the Montana Territory.

And home.

He'd never realized how important the peace and quiet of the mountain wilderness had become to him.

Angela Larkin watched the man from a distance, doing her best to keep a bored look that showed neither the target of her gaze, nor the way her heart pounded louder than the incoming train. She would likely have a long journey, unless she could learn what she needed during one of the early legs. If she had to travel all the way to the western territories, she was prepared to do so.

She carried a significant responsibility with this assignment, and she would fulfill her part no matter what it required. She took a deep breath and smoothed the folds in her dress. She was more than capable.

Lord, guide me. This would be a delicate dance of deception and trust, and she had every intention of leading.

The arriving passengers had finished disembarking, and the porter began calling for boarding to begin. She followed the surge of people moving toward the cars. One thing she'd learned early on in this city was to go with the flow when possible. You could weave your way through as you needed to, but you'd reach your goal much faster by working with people than trying to outsmart them. That motto generally proved accurate both in traffic, and in accomplishing each mission she was assigned by the central office.

As she boarded and made her way into one of the passenger cars, she did her best to keep the target in view. She stopped in the same car he did, and slid into a seat three rows behind him. His back was to her, but that was fine. He wouldn't see how often she watched him.

When all had been loaded, the train shuddered, then started forward with an unsteady rocking motion. An older man still standing in the aisle stumbled. Her target started to jump up to help the man, but he grunted and sank onto his bench before Coulter could act.

As the train picked up speed and the view through the windows changed from city streets to rolling countryside, the rocking of the car eased into a smoother rhythm.

She reached for the book in her bag, but she'd barely opened to her marker when a movement ahead caught her notice.

Coulter rose to his feet and stepped into the aisle. He paused for a moment, gripping his seat back as he found his balance with the movement of the train.

She kept her focus on the page before her, watching him from the edge of her gaze. Should she look up and smile? Sometimes it was better for the target to be aware of her, seeing her as just another passenger. Especially if she had a convincing backstory. More often though, she succeeded best when she could fade into the background.

So she kept her gaze down, reading the same line over and over as he moved slowly down the aisle toward her. The outside platform was through the door behind her, and he probably wanted air.

As he passed beside her, a violent jerk shook the train.

Gasps filled the air, and Jude grabbed onto her seat back to keep from tumbling. A scraping sounded above her, and she spun to see its source.

"Watch out." Jude lunged behind her, diving for a box that slid off the upper shelf. A woman screamed.

Angela lost sight of him as he pulled the box sideways, away from the elderly woman on the bench behind Angela.

A crash sounded, and she leaped from her seat to make sure Jude hadn't hurt himself.

The woman screamed again, the one he'd just saved with his quick actions.

But Jude himself lay on the floor, his head slumped against the side of the crate. Eyes closed.

"Mr. Coulter!" Angela sprang to his side, dropping to her knees.

Lord, don't let him be dead. His chest rose with a breath, so she called again, daring to touch his shoulder for a gentle shake. "Mr. Coulter."

He didn't blink. No sign of alertness.

His head was pushed forward by the box, his chin pushed into his neck. With one hand under his head, she pulled the crate out and laid him flat on the train floor.

He still didn't open his eyes.

Her mind scrambled for what to do next. She needed help. She was skilled at many things, but her medical knowledge wasn't nearly strong enough for this situation.

She looked up at the worried faces gathered around them. "Is anyone a doctor?"

No matter what, she couldn't let anything happen to Jude Coulter until he led her back to the source of the sapphires he'd just delivered.

A great deal more than her job depended on her succeeding in this mission.

Get PROTECTING THE MOUNTAIN MAN'S TREASURE, the next book in the Brothers of Sapphire Ranch series, at your favorite retailer!

Did you enjoy Jericho and Dinah's story? I hope so!
Would you take a quick minute to leave a review where you purchased the book?
It doesn't have to be long. Just a sentence or two telling what you liked about the story!

To receive a free book and get updates when new Misty M. Beller books release, go to https://mistymbeller.com/freebook

ABOUT THE AUTHOR

Misty M. Beller is a *USA Today* best-selling author of romantic mountain stories, set on the 1800s frontier and woven with the truth of God's love.

Raised on a farm and surrounded by family, Misty developed her love for horses, history, and adventure. These days, her husband and children provide fresh adventure every day, keeping her both grounded and crazy.

Misty's passion is to create inspiring Christian fiction infused with the grandeur of the mountains, writing historical romance that displays God's abundant love through the twists and turns in the lives of her characters.

Sharing her stories with readers is a dream come true for Misty. She writes from her country home in South Carolina and escapes to the mountains any chance she gets.

Connect with Misty at www.MistyMBeller.com

Printed in the USA
CPSIA information can be obtained
at www.ICGtesting.com
LVHW041057270923
759106LV00002B/139